THE GIRL BEHIND THE WALL

THE GIRL BEHIND THE WALL

THE LAST VAMPIRE™ BOOK 1

JUDITH BERENS   MARTHA CARR   MICHAEL ANDERLE

DISRUPTIVE IMAGINATION

Copyright © 2019 Judith Berens, Martha Carr and Michael Anderle
Cover by Fantasy Book Design
Cover copyright © LMBPN Publishing
A Michael Anderle Production

LMBPN Publishing
PMB 196, 2540 South Maryland Pkwy
Las Vegas, NV 89109

First US edition, May 2019
Version 1.01 September 2019
Print ISBN: 978-1-64202-278-0

THE LAST VAMPIRE TEAM

Thanks to our Beta Readers

Kelly O'Donnell, Mary Morris , Larry Omans, and Crystal Wren

Thanks to the JIT Readers

Jeff Eaton
Daniel Weigert
Jeff Goode
Misty Roa
Kelly O'Donnell
Micky Cocker
Paul Westman
Larry Omans

If we've missed anyone, please let us know!

Editor
SkyHunter Editing Team

From Martha

To everyone who still believes in magic
and all the possibilities that holds.
To all the readers who make this
entire ride so much fun.
And to my son, Louie and so many wonderful friends who
remind me all the time of what
really matters and how wonderful
life can be in any given moment.

From Michael

To Family, Friends and
Those Who Love
To Read.
May We All Enjoy Grace
To Live The Life We Are
Called.

CHAPTER ONE

Victoria barely had time to react before her father scooped her up in his arms, threw her over his shoulder, and ran through the village.

His legs itched to go faster, but he had to wait to use his powers and his enhanced speed until they were out of plain view. The last thing he wanted to do was draw any unwanted attention. Villagers and torches were a real danger to their kind. *Something must be on our heels. Maybe I will have an opportunity to disable it myself.*

The girl pushed up on her father's shoulder to scan the area but couldn't identify any pending danger.

On a normal day, the townspeople might have paid attention to the two of them running like this. But that particular day, nervous energy distracted the town and drew its fearful attention elsewhere. The Hohensalzburg Fortress towered in the distance and was in the midst of several upgrades to its defenses. Workmen scurried over the ground like ants as they raced to transfer weapons and other stock into the keep. Teams of peasants worked themselves ragged building new gunpowder stores and additional gatehouses to fortify the castle against the coming attack. The king and his council tried to maintain order, but tensions were building. The threat of war had that effect on people.

Merely seeing the construction in her formerly peaceful view of the Austrian countryside filled Victoria with unease. Still, she identified no reason for her father to move so quickly.

They passed the city limits and she barely had time to clutch onto the back of her father's shirt as he burst into a full sprint. Beyond the line of the village wall, the world became a blur of color and roaring wind. Finally, they stopped at the castle grounds, several miles away from the village.

Her father set her down when they reached the edge of the north wall of the keep and resumed a normal pace.

"Come," he ordered. "Let's go. Inside." His eyes were dark as he looked over her head at the old village.

Victoria looked at the three towers of her home. The castle was as strong as ever, although dwarfed when compared to the sheer mass of the Hohensalzburg Fortress.

If there is a serious threat, shouldn't we update our defenses? But what is the danger? Why are we in such a hurry?

She had never seen her father like this. Sweat dripped from his brow, his eyes darted back and forth with nervous energy, and his mouth hung open to expose the sharp fangs he usually kept carefully hidden. He struggled to keep his breathing under control.

Despite her surprise, she did not openly question him.

She respected his views. If he felt there was a threat, that was good enough for her.

"Daughter!"

The harsh bark snapped her back to reality, and Victoria ran to catch up.

She brushed her raven-black hair behind her ears as they entered through the castle's large wooden back door.

"Father, what is going on?" she asked breathlessly. "You and Mother haven't spoken to me all day. Can you please explain what's troubling you?"

"Victoria, you..." He trailed off at the sound of a familiar tapping on the floor. Victoria's mother always made that noise when she was stressed. He looked in his wife's direction and sighed tiredly. "We need to have a drink."

"Whatever will help you," she acceded. "But tell me why you two are so nervous."

The man didn't reply. Instead, he turned resolutely and walked into the sitting room, where his wife awaited bearing a small golden chalice. The cup was one of Victoria's favorites. She loved the thick crosses that had been carved into its side.

Her mother handed the chalice to her, and the flames of candles danced around the perimeter of the room to cast quivering shadows over the wooden floor.

"Drink, please, darling." Her mother brushed Victoria's cheek with lingering fingertips as she stared into her daughter's face.

Even the fascinating depictions of the chalice couldn't hide such harbingers from Victoria's attention. "Mother, you look like someone is dying. And Father keeps acting strangely. Please, tell me what is so wrong."

"We'll tell you shortly," her father answered. "Please, drink."

Victoria looked at the cup and didn't recognize the liquid. This one was a deep-green and reeked of stale air. Nevertheless, as the dutiful daughter, she knew what had to be done. She obeyed her father without question, lifted the chalice to her lips, and swallowed the drink slowly. The taste was as bad as the smell and she barely suppressed the urge to gag. The concoction tasted of old mushrooms and the bitter herbs some of the herbalists sold in the market-place. It left a slimy texture in her mouth as though a slug had chosen to crawl over her tongue and cheeks like it would a cave wall.

As she swallowed, her mother whispered under her breath. *"Dieser Becher soll meiner geliebten Tochter Ruhe und Schutz vor den bösen Mächten geben, die uns umgeben."*

Victoria's face contorted in disgust as she tried to swallow the residue mixed with the saliva that released in protest against the vile taste. When it reached a tolerable state and she no longer felt like she was about to be sick, she ran her fingers along the family seal carved into the outside of the cup, as she always did. She smacked her lips a few times for extra measure and used the back of her hand to wipe any trace off her lips. She did not want to relive that experience again.

"I did not care for that," she told them honestly. "What was it?"

"A special drink for you, little one," her mother said. She motioned to one of the many cushioned chairs that dotted the room. "You may want to sit down."

Victoria did as she was bid and sank into the

comforting embrace of a red velvet cushion. Her father took the chalice from her and placed it on the mantle above the fireplace. For a moment, she thought she saw something glitter as it fell in front of the flames. She wanted to ask what it was, what her parents were doing, and why they were so afraid. Instead, the room began to spin, and her head lolled on her shoulders. Darkness encroached on the edge of her vision and then, there was nothing.

Both parents ran to the armchair and held the girl's hands. The steady rhythm of her breathing calmed the fear in their eyes as they looked at one another.

Both breathed a sigh of relief and her father nodded. "It worked."

Her mother looked at the sleeping girl. "Where do you want to put her?"

"I moved her coffin to the family crypt. That will likely be the safest place. We can stay at the base of the steps. If they find us, they might assume that we're alone. It's the only way I can think of to ensure she remains undisturbed."

He cradled the lithe form in his arms and kissed her gently on the forehead. "Look how much she's grown," he said as his voice cracked. "What a strong young woman she'll be."

His wife sighed at the sight and brushed the hair out of her little girl's face for the last time. "We sheltered her too much. She's already fourteen, and we never let her see a single eligible suitor."

"I thought there would be more time. It's not easy finding the right match for one of our kind." The tears dropped freely now, and the fire clearly illuminated the streaks they had left. He grunted as he shifted Victoria's limp body in his arms. "I thought there was time…"

She squeezed his hand gently, and the two began the long march to the crypt. Their footsteps echoed hollowly to count every minute down to the second that they would have left to gaze on their child. He nodded to the lantern that hung by the door.

With a lump in his throat, he led his wife down the steps into the dark basement. She illuminated the stairs from behind by holding the lantern high, then stepped in front of him to guide their way. Eventually, they emerged into a small room on the far end of the lower level.

"Here it is." The woman ran her fingers over a dusty wooden box and traced their family coat of arms that had been painted on the lid. With a heavy sigh, she opened the box to reveal a cushioned burgundy interior.

Gently, the father laid his daughter's body in the coffin. He stretched her legs out to make her comfortable and folded her hands over her waist.

"That's it." He wrapped his arm around his wife's shoulders. The glow of the lantern reflected off the tears in their eyes as they took one more look at their daughter's sleeping form.

"Is this really the only way?" she asked. "Can't we keep her with us?"

"No." His voice wavered. "I couldn't forgive myself if I selfishly held onto her and the Circle reached us. They'll stop at nothing to destroy the Brommers. I'll finish building the wall later. It's our best chance."

Each leaned forward and planted a final kiss on the

girl's cheek. Her mother's face twisted in grief while she held the lantern high and her husband closed the box. He lifted a hammer and nails from a burlap sack on the floor and pounded them in place. The grip on the lamp tightened as she grimaced with each blow.

What they were not aware of, however, was the fact that while Victoria could no longer see or move, she could still hear. It was obvious they had done something with that drink to make her like this. She was upset at first, but at least now she understood their motivations. She would have frowned if she could. That annoying racket made it difficult to think.

What is that pounding noise? Why can't I see? What did they mean about keeping me safe? Who is the Circle?

Her confusion persisted, but she had no way to answer it.

The parents placed their hands on the outside of the coffin, bowed their heads, and spoke a prayer together.

"Schützen Sie unsere Tochter in dieser schwierigen Zeit. Bewahre sie in einem ruhigen Schlaf auf, bis wir uns wieder vereinen können."

Peaceful slumber? Safe? What are they talking about? Am I stuck in here? Safe from what, the Circle?

The pounding resumed for a short time and finally stopped, replaced by the shuffling of cloth and the clack of boots and shoes on stone. The sounds faded slowly, followed by the groaning creak of an old door, and silence descended.

What is happening?

Victoria tried to move—to panic because that was what the situation seemed to demand. Yet even that was denied her as the potion she'd drunk did its work. Her heart rate slowed as she took comfort in the familiar folds of fabric. She was no stranger to this coffin and slept in it every night. But something was seriously wrong. Her parents clearly feared a danger. That much was obvious. Normally, any significant threat would cause her to twitch with anxious energy. Like her parents, she always sought to fix a problem and eliminate anything—or anyone—that threatened her.

Instead, an overwhelming sense of peace washed over her. Her body couldn't move, and now, she felt those tendrils seeking out her mind. She breathed deeply. It was all she could do until finally, inevitably, even her awareness faded into the dark.

Present Day

Alexis smirked as she tore off a doughy piece of her large chocolate-covered pretzel. Her cell phone buzzed, and she looked down to giggle at a funny text from one of her friends back home. She took a quick picture of her Chuck Taylor zipper sneakers and sent the photo attached to a group text before she pocketed her phone.

The birds swarmed closer to her feet to peck at the animal print. She leaned back on the bench and waited until her pigeon friends couldn't bear the anticipation anymore and chuckled as she tossed the food over their heads. It bounced off the stone street and rolled a few inches. The flock pushed and shoved their way past each other to reach the prize first.

So much for birds of a feather.

Once they reached it, they lowered their heads and pecked away. Now and then, the morsel of food was tossed up vigorously to land in a different location, thanks to an overeager eater.

That was her favorite part.

Still, Alexis sighed. Feeding the pigeons was the most exciting thing she had done in days. She looked out over the square and watched as vendors on corners hawked t-shirts and sunglasses to tourists.

Salzburg was an amazing city full of history and beautiful views, with its rolling green hills and picturesque countryside. The mountains clustered around the city in a natural wall, as if they wanted to protect the history and magic the city held. After all, the Von Trapp family had once lived there, and their story had become one of the most famous, thanks to Julie Andrews and her role in *The Sound of Music*.

Still, it wasn't Milwaukee, and even watching pigeons dance on cobblestones for chocolate got old after a while.

"I could be home, hanging out with Jess and Jamie at the Trampoline Park," she said to one of her new scavenger friends. It cooed in response—or, perhaps, in an attempt to wangle more of her food. One never could tell with birds. She sighed. "You get me." She picked another fragment off her pretzel and tossed the bird the extra bite.

A stiff gust of wind blew past and teased her long, dark-brown curls into her face. She slipped a ponytail holder off her wrist and gathered her locks into a sloppy bun where they would be out of the way, then tilted her head back to glance at the Hohensalzburg Fortress. The old structure towered on the mountain overlooking the square. A cable car ascended slowly to its entrance, carrying another load of curious visitors to one of the largest castles in Europe.

Alexis and her father had walked through that castle. And while it was beautiful, to her, it was exactly that—another castle.

It's not the same without Mom. Nothing is.

She nudged a cobblestone with the toe of her shoe and bit her bottom lip. The memories of the grave site were still too fresh in her mind, even after two months had passed.

Her mom had been a master at injecting her goofy personality into trips like these. She'd brought history to life and never failed to make her family laugh.

Alexis missed that and so many other little things she couldn't even begin to describe.

The sun had long begun its descent and hovered only a few inches over the horizon.

I'd better start back. I don't need another speech.

Alexis had free rein over her time in Salzburg as long as she returned before sundown. Her father trusted her with some freedom but didn't want her to enjoy too much. She suspected that he didn't actually know what to do with a fourteen-year-old daughter. Half the time, he smothered her, and the other half, he expected her to, "Go out and meet new people." She often wondered whether he might be bipolar or schizophrenic.

But it was unfair to make such accusations. After what had happened to her mother, he struggled to find any kind of balance. The last thing he wanted was to lose her too. And, whether she was willing to admit it or not, she felt much the same way.

The girl took one more bite of the pretzel and tossed the rest to the birds.

"Eat up, fellas. I'm sure I'll see you tomorrow."

She shoved her hands in her pockets to keep them warm and crossed the bridge over the River Salzach. The water burbled and gushed under the walkway with an attractive white froth that could only be produced by nature. Another shiver traced down her spine. On the other side of town, she boarded a bus that conveyed her beyond the outskirts.

Alexis leaned her head against the window of the bus and watched the houses roll past. It was hard to not feel loneliness creeping in. Only a month ago, Salzburg was a welcome distraction.

Her father Craig accompanied her on tours of the city and did his best to help them both heal. They visited famous landmarks and even took a bus tour to the small town of Mondsee to visit various sites where *The Sound of Music* had been filmed.

She'd explained each stop excitedly to her father, who had never seen the movie. How had such a crime against nature been allowed under her mother's watch? She'd never understand it. Her hands had moved around her face and her smile widened as she explained the portion where Liesl sang to Rolf and sighed. "That's romance."

He had managed to look happy and worried at the same time. Of all the new complications in his parenting life, dating was at the top of his "What Do I Do Now?" list.

Alexis had sat on her bed a little later that day and felt guilty. It was the first time she hadn't thought about her mother all day long. She didn't know if it was too soon yet. What did "too soon" even mean?

The longer they stayed in Salzburg, the more she found herself exploring the city alone. It started early on with her dad spending an afternoon here and there in the study, poring through books and recording his voice. A few times, late at night, she caught him staring at her mother's picture.

Soon, she was told to go on without him. And eventually, Alexis simply stopped asking. Everyone had to get over things in their own way. Even at her age, she was catching on to that fast.

Yet, she reminded herself as the bus trundled onward, they still had two weeks left before they would go home. Alexis sensed that would be good and bad news. She was looking forward to seeing her friends again, but there would be so many reminders, so many times and situations where she would want to ask Mom a question or tell her about something...

"No tears, Watson! Not in public." She balled her fists up at her side as she choked down the lump in her throat.

The bus roared to a stop and Alexis stepped off onto the country road that spiraled up the hill. Dusk was setting in, and she couldn't wait any longer to get back or her father would be worried. She really didn't need another lecture—or worse, that fearful disappointed silence.

It hadn't occurred to her that six weeks in Europe could feel so long. After all the casseroles and visits had ended, her father had felt it would be a healthy break. Besides, Salzburg was such an interesting little town. With his obsession with history and Alexis' fascination with other cultures, it seemed like a slam dunk. She was ready to get away for a little while.

Alexis shook her head.

You're in such an amazing city and you'll probably never be back here. How could you possibly be bored?

Her shoulders sagged as she was forced into lonely introspection.

Not bored, lonely. I need a friend, someone to share this with. Mom would have loved all of it. Shopping, eating, making up dumb stories about who must have lived in that castle.

She managed a smile at that thought, knowing her mother would have made it a dashing young man or some queen and a princess starring in their own story.

Mom always had an amazing imagination.

She walked past a row of trees and up the walkway leading to the large castle in front of her. Its cream-colored brick exterior reminded her of the old buildings back home. Three large towers jabbed from the structure to poke the sky. Alexis glanced at the one closest to the front of the castle and sighed. She knew her father was there, burying himself in his work.

Once she reached the massive wooden front door, she pulled the handle and it creaked open. The setting sunlight bathed the foyer in a warm orange glow and reflected off the chandelier dangling above. The door slammed shut behind her, restoring the darkness to the room.

"Hello?" she shouted. "I'm back."

"Hey, honey," her father yelled. "Be down in a few."

She rolled her eyes.

I bet.

It would probably be another hour before he finished

and they could eat dinner. She stepped off to the side and flipped the large light switch. A familiar hum filled the room as the lights on the chandelier illuminated slowly and allowed her to see the room properly. Every time she turned those lights on, she smiled.

For some reason, the foyer was her favorite part of the old structure. The black and white tiles on the floor were arranged in a spiral pattern, centered beneath the huge chandelier. She walked to the middle of the spiral and stretched her arms out at her sides to imagine a ball being held. Her mother's imagination might be gone, but it had still taught her a trick or two.

The giant staircase leading up to the bedrooms reminded her of old movies with fancy dinner parties and glittering gatherings and men in formalwear waltzing with their ladies.

She dropped her arms and sighed again, then walked through the doorway leading to a sitting room. Hundreds of books on the bookshelf greeted her and each begged for her attention. Alexis scanned the spines of the stacks, hoping to find something interesting enough to read. She didn't know any German, but once in a while, she came across a book with cool pictures.

The caretakers of the castle had filled some of the shelves with classic literature and history books in various languages, including English. When she ran out of things to do—which was more and more often, lately—she'd grab a random one and plop into the red velvet chair beside the fireplace.

On a whim, Alexis dragged the ladder attached to the bookcase along the shelves and climbed to the top row, hoping to find a book that hadn't been opened in a long time. She'd browsed the lower shelves long enough. Besides, she needed a distraction, and this would constitute a little adventure in its own right.

The girl settled on a thick book on World War One. She blew the dust off the cover, pulled it off the bookshelf, and cradled it in her right arm while she descended the ladder.

On her way to the chair, she stopped at the fireplace and ran her finger across the old golden chalice sitting on the mantel. At first, she wondered why something that looked so valuable would be left so carelessly in easy access. Maybe it was a replica, she decided after a moment. If so, it was an exceptionally good one.

She liked the way the family crest forged into the side felt beneath her fingers.

CHAPTER TWO

The pictures in the old volume were only mildly interesting. The book itself read like a textbook with little more than a list of facts about each battle—how many troops died, the dates of the battle, weapons used...the kinds of things that provided dry details with no real appeal.

I guess there must be a reason why this one was tucked away on the top shelf.

She turned the page and focused on another photo of a troop in the trenches when a yellowed piece of paper slid out of the book and landed on the floor.

Alexis glanced curiously at it. The page was folded several times but pressed so flat that it looked like someone had ironed it. It had obviously been in the book for a long time.

She picked it up and inspected it more closely. A little mystery would help to alleviate her boredom, and she had to admit that she was at least somewhat intrigued. Even folded, the sheet was larger than the average message but thin enough in places that she could see the traces of hand-written ink through it.

That's weird. Maybe it's something cool, like an old letter from the 1800s or something.

Now, she was really interested. She allowed herself a brief smile as she closed the big book and set it on the arm of the chair. With extreme care, she unfolded the piece of paper and did her best to not accidentally tear it along the clearly defined lines.

It took her a while, but she finally succeeded and studied the elaborate handwriting in faded black ink that detailed intersecting lines. In the dim light of the room, she had a hard time determining the language. "This has to be German."

She stood and walked purposefully to the kitchen. The modern fluorescent bulbs that had been installed there would make it far easier to read the document. She spread the paper out on the granite countertop of the kitchen island. When fully extended, it measured almost the size of four sheets of notebook paper.

"Whatcha got there, hon?"

Craig Watson walked into the room with his hands in the pockets of his jeans and a warm smile on his face. He ran a hand through his wavy brown hair as he leaned down to kiss the top of her head, and she felt the familiar pressure of his glasses brushing against her.

"I don't know," Alexis replied. "I found this in a book on a high shelf in the bookcase. It must be old, though. Look at that handwriting." She ran a finger carefully over the edge of the paper and struggled to sound it out phonetically.

"I wish your Spanish teacher were here to watch you try to read German." He smiled at her and rested a hand on her shoulder.

Her brow creased into a frown as she tried again. "I don't know why I bother. Even if I could read it, I don't know what it means."

He moved to her side for a better view of the paper and pushed his glasses up the bridge of his nose.

Words were scrawled beside arrows that pointed to what looked like a series of connected rooms. The page itself had been separated by three carefully drawn lines that stretched from edge to edge.

Alexis pursed her lips and squinted at the small lettering. "What do you think it is?"

"You know what? I think this is a blueprint of the castle." He pointed carefully to various places on the paper with his ink-smudged fingers. "See, right here is the foyer, and these lines must be the stairs along the side. Each of these would be the towers. And look here. This area has all these separate rooms. That's the upstairs, and there's the basement."

Alexis' eyes widened. "Oh, yeah, and this would be the kitchen over here." She pointed to a large square space and grinned.

"Yep. That's neat, actually."

"I wouldn't think a centuries-old castle would have actual blueprints."

"Well, it's not exactly a 'blueprint.' It's more of a sketch than anything else. Where did you find this? It's hard to believe the owners would leave something this precious folded up in a book."

"I wonder if it's the original."

"It could be. Or it was made more recently. It's hard to say. This castle is old, after all, and the folds of another book don't exactly provide the same methods of preservation as an airtight sealed room." He leaned in for a closer look. "There's no date on it. But hey, this is fun!"

He straightened and fished out a pan from one of the cabinets to start dinner.

"Wait." Alexis put her hand on the paper. "If this is the basement level, what's this?" She pointed to a small area jutting out from the main room of the basement along the south wall. "That's where that one locked closet is, right? But it's not that big, is it? That's more like an entire room."

Her dad squinted at the paper. "Yeah. Maybe their idea of a closet is our idea of a New York City apartment. Besides, they've probably updated this place since this was drawn, given how many years it's been." He winked playfully at his daughter.

She rolled her eyes. "Don't you want to check? Maybe there's something back there. Someone might have hidden treasure down there and they simply drywalled over it or something."

He walked over to the fridge and pulled it open. "We don't actually own this place, remember?" he pointed out. "It's a rental."

"Come on, Dad, this could be a chance to dig up a little history. Who knows what secrets this castle is hiding."

Craig kept his back to his daughter as he opened the fridge and stared blankly at the shelf holding the ground beef he intended to cook that night.

What would Carol have done here? She would have done something. And you haven't shown her a fun time in a while.

Alexis knew her father well and took courage in his hesitation. "Dad, think about it. Even if we find nothing but garbage in there, it could be historical garbage. You could get a week's worth of episodes for your podcast out of this depending what we find. Come on," she wheedled. "You've spent most days on this vacation up in that second tower recording episodes." She took a step toward him. "You know you love digging up dirt on stuff that even Google doesn't know. Come on...one little hole, just enough to see. We could fix that, right?"

"The thought of being able to record an episode about the castle is appealing, but..."

"Recording an episode about a castle while still in the castle? How cool would that be?"

He turned and looked at her. She looked so much like her mother—the same tilt to the chin and the same excitement over a new adventure. It had been so long since he'd seen that. How could he say no?

"Okay, okay." He sighed and closed the fridge. "But I don't expect this to turn into anything. We'll make one small hole. One. It'll probably be empty, and at best, it might have some old German's belongings."

Alexis jumped up and threw her arms around her father's neck. "An adventure, exactly like the old days," she whispered into his neck.

He felt the same familiar ache in his stomach that had haunted him for two months. "Like the old days," he croaked and returned the embrace.

Her father pulled her arms down from his neck and

walked past her to open the basement door. "One small hole," he said again as he flicked the light switch on and descended the stairs. He didn't dare look back as he brushed a tear off his cheek.

Alexis took one last glance at the sketch of the castle, then turned to follow him. After so many days spent wandering around alone, actually doing something together was a refreshing change of pace. "Like the old days," she whispered again.

Mom would have been the first one down there.

Craig turned on the light by the stairs and walked down into what had become the rental's rec room. The brochure had said that the Airbnb host who owned the castle had renovated the basement years before with a pool table, a seventy-two-inch flat-screen TV, and leather theater seating. "I think the owners thought this would be Party Central."

She wasn't interested in parties at the moment and bounded off the stairs to turn and stare excitedly at her father. "Okay, so the drawing puts that extra room over here." She walked across the space and past the TV to stand in front of a small closet door with a locked handle. "Here's where we start."

Craig humored her and tapped on the walls with the palm of his hand, an expression of exaggerated concentration on his face.

"What are you doing?" she asked.

"Listening. If there really is a room behind that wall, knocking on it will sound different than knocking on an exterior wall."

When he reached the wall that contained the locked

door, a distinct echoing *clack* returned. He pressed his ear up against it and knocked again, then looked at Alexis. "Okay, point for you. There's definitely something back there. It's probably only part of the closet, though."

"First, we have to get in said closet to find out," she countered. "How do we do that?" She dreaded the thought of it being nothing more. The adventure would be over before it started, and for the first time in a long time, she didn't want her time with her father to end.

"I don't have any tools, but I can get the door open."

"What will you do, pick the lock?" she teased.

"Do you have any bobby pins in your hair? Throw me one."

Alexis smirked condescendingly as she dragged one from her hair and handed it to him. He knelt in front of the doorknob, spread the pin apart, and proceeded to pick the lock.

"When did you learn to do that? Were you doing a podcast on 1930's gangsters?"

"I was locked out of the house once too often. Your mom wouldn't let me in so it was simple preservation." He smiled, turned to look at her, and immediately regretted what he'd said. She stared at the wall with a blank expression on her face. "I...think I have it," he said gently. He bit his lower lip and concentrated on turning the clip ever so slowly. "Got it!" He grasped the knob and turned it as the lock clicked open.

"Impressive. I bet Jamie's dad can't break and enter."

"Bonus cool dad points. I'll take it." Craig smiled as he opened the door. There was no sign of a secret chamber of any sort. He frowned. "That's odd. Can I see those plans again? Did you bring them with you?"

"I left them upstairs, but it clearly showed this room was bigger. Hang on, I'll get them."

Alexis was gone and back again in less than a minute. She held the drawing up for him to review, and he smiled as he oriented himself on the map. "This is the basement. And yeah, you're right. This has to be bigger." He raised his chin and peered at the corners and behind the door. It seemed to be nothing more than a narrow basement closet surrounded by old brick walls. A handful of tools were scattered on a shelf along the right side.

"It's a utility closet," he said. "I guess the owner doesn't want people walking off with his tools."

"I thought for sure there would be some kind of room here." She couldn't hide the disappointment in her voice. The adventure was turning into a total bust. Her father shifted his attention to the wall on his left. The surface was dry and chalky and cracks spidered from every crevice. He picked at the mortar and it crumbled in his fingers. "That is one sloppy job. Anyone can tell it was rushed." He wrinkled his nose and peered more closely at it. "I'm no expert, but it looks old."

She smiled hopefully. "So, can we get in?"

Craig shook his head. "No, this is in worse shape than I suspected. Even one small hole could bring down half the wall. We'll lose our security deposit for one thing—and only the security deposit if we're lucky."

"Come on, Dad," she whined.

"I said no, Alexis. I didn't come here to do construction work or get arrested for demolition."

"How about we take out only a few bricks? Then we can peek inside." She clasped her hands in front of her and flashed her best smile as she tilted her head in the way he always found impossible to resist. "Then, we'll put them back. Come on, do you think anyone will notice if you do a bad job replacing them?"

Craig groaned inwardly.

Why do you have to take after your mother?

"Well, you're right about that," he conceded slowly. "This was done by an amateur who was in a hurry."

I can't believe I'm doing this.

He looked through the tools in the closet and located an old hammer and chisel.

Within minutes, he cracked the mortar around one of the bricks in the shoddy wall, wiggled it loose, and removed it with care. A warm rush of moist air caught his face and he grimaced. He put his face closer to the opening. "Hello?" His voice echoed off the walls beyond and he did it again. "Hello? Hellooo." The last call was protracted for greatest effect. His eyes narrowed as they adjusted to the darkness beyond. "Wait a minute. There's definitely something back here. It's over to the right." He reached out a hand. "Alexis, hand me your phone."

She pressed the flashlight icon on the device and handed it to him. He aimed the beam through the new opening in the wall and pressed his face as close to the aperture as the laws of physics would allow without dropping the light source.

"What is that?" A long wooden box lay directly ahead. A few dim flashes of color indicated that something had been painted on top of it, but the angle was too small to see it properly.

"Can I see?" Alexis asked breathlessly.

Craig shrugged. "Sure. It's a little weird, though." He stepped back and handed her the phone. "An Austrian medieval chest, perhaps?"

She took her turn to peek through the hole and grinned at the sight. The box was intact and she squealed with excitement and bounced on the balls of her feet. "Treasure chest! Dad, we can open this, pull the box out, and close the hole. Nobody has to know," she said eagerly and her hands shook from the adrenaline that now coursed through her.

A sad smile touched Craig's lips.

Everything about her reminds me of Carol, even the more danger-prone side of her.

"No, Alexis. I've already done enough here. I won't spend the last two weeks of our trip doing bricklaying work."

"What if there's something really valuable back there? Maybe we could sell it for a million dollars. Who knows?" She was talking quickly, her mind spinning different tales. "You'd enjoy doing your podcasts far more if you didn't have bills hanging over your head. I overheard you talking to Aunt Terry. You used some of the insurance money for this trip. She seemed angry about it."

"That's not something for you to worry about."

"Look, Dad, maybe we're only a few minutes away from a completely new lease on life. But that won't happen if we don't keep going. Imagine not having to worry about finding another job—"

Again, her father shook his head.

And there's Carol's button-pushing.

He pressed his lips together pensively.

I always was the practical one who didn't like risks. "Please promise to live a little." Wasn't that one of the last things she said to you?

He groaned and shook his head.

I absolutely know I'll regret this.

"Move out of the way." He sighed, his expression resigned.

Alexis squealed with glee and stepped back as her dad chiseled more bricks out. One by one, they dropped into his hands and he set them carefully aside.

"Maybe the owner doesn't even know this room exists," Alexis said while he worked. "You could be doing him a favor."

"Sure, or he knows it exists and it's hidden for a reason. We could be treading on dangerous territory here."

"Yeah, or great treasure." She clapped with almost child-like enthusiasm.

Craig removed another brick and created a hole large enough for the two of them to duck through and into the small room to investigate the wooden box.

He approached it slowly and blew on the lid. A cloud of dust erupted and revealed the coat of arms that had been painted on the top.

CHAPTER THREE

Alexis charged into the room, heedless of any danger that might have existed. Craig shuffled cautiously across the floor around the box. The dust and grime of ages coated his shoes and dyed them a dead blue-gray.

"Can you slow down, please? We don't know what's in here," he whispered.

"Come on, Dad. This is exciting stuff."

"Just...hang on." He raised a pleading hand. "Just because it's an adventure doesn't mean we can be careless."

She rolled her eyes with perfect teenage drama.

There goes Dad, always trying to keep us from having too much fun.

He shined the phone's flashlight in each corner of the room. Dust motes floated through the beam, but no traps or nasty surprises awaited them. They were apparently alone with the box.

Alexis ran her fingers along the top and felt the bumps of the nail heads that had been hammered into the lid along the edges.

"Bring the flashlight over here. It looks like whoever put this here didn't want anyone to get in."

He leaned forward and illuminated the lid. "Or out."

Alexis looked at her father in horror and took a hasty step back. "That's not even funny."

Craig laughed. "Hey, you wanted excitement. That's a joke your mother would have made." They exchanged knowing smiles.

"I think it's something valuable. Maybe the old care-taker of the castle hid gold or jewels or something in here. We're gonna be rich."

"Yeah, or maybe they buried the family dog down here or something."

"Alone, without its owners?" she challenged. "I don't think so." She stepped forward again and tried to tuck her fingers under the edge of the lid but couldn't get a grip on the wood. Splinters threatened to dig into her skin under the nails. "Ow! Well, we can't open this by hand."

"Hang on." Her father passed her the phone and exited through the hole they'd made in the wall. Moments later, he returned with a long iron crowbar in his hands. "It sure is handy having the tool closet next door."

He pulled Alexis close to him so she could shine the light where he needed it, wedged the flat end of the tool between the lid and the bottom of the box, and wiggled it deeper into the crack. Grunting with effort, he pushed and shoved the tool, hoping to get enough leverage to raise the lid quickly. "These nails have been here a while," he said.

Once he'd forced the crowbar in sufficiently, he yanked up on it a few times. On the third attempt, the wood squealed loudly as it rubbed against the nails that eased out with the leverage.

Alexis peered through the new gap with the light and frowned. "It's only a white cloth. This might only be an old box of clothing or something."

"I did warn you it might be simple valuables," Craig reminded her. "That being said, I didn't come this far to walk away here. Let's keep going. Even if it is merely clothes, it could be worth something if it's in good condition."

It's nice to see you coming alive, Dad. A little field work is always better than being cooped up in some musty study.

How strange it was to see the shoe on the other foot for once.

He wedged the crowbar into the side of the gap and yanked on it. More nails bent and screeched as the wood creaked in protest. When he widened the gap sufficiently on one section, he would move along the edge and repeat the process again.

Alexis coughed and sneezed as the dust of ages entered her nose and lungs and triggered her allergies. Despite how her body trembled, she struggled valiantly to maintain a steady hand for the beam. Craig attacked the box with renewed effort at the sound of his daughter's plight. Finally, he'd moved full circle around the box and let the crowbar drop to the floor with a sigh of relief. He pulled his glasses down and wiped the sweat that had dripped onto the lenses away with his shirt.

"Okay, big reveal time. Any last guesses?" he asked.

"I still think it's nothing but clothes."

"Pessimist," he teased. By now, he had thoroughly

invested himself in the adventure. Strangely enough, it felt almost as if Carol were there with them again. "Here goes nothing." He wedged his fingers under the edge of the lid and flipped it over to drop on the floor with a loud clatter. The ensuing explosion of dust from the impact sent Alexis into a sneezing fit, and she pulled her light hastily away from the box to make use of her sleeve.

He walked over to his daughter's side to help her clear the air. "We need to get you out of here before you pass out."

She shook him off and composed herself by wiping her runny nose briefly with the back of her hand, then turned back to the box and shined her flashlight on its contents.

Alexis gasped. Her father held his breath.

To their horror, they beheld not treasure, but the still body of a teenage girl in a long white dress with dirt along the hem of the skirt. Her hands had been folded over of her waist, and she looked like she had only recently been interred.

"Wh—what?" Alexis stammered.

Craig raised a calming hand. "Now hang on, Alexis. Stay calm. I don't think that's a real girl in there. It can't be. She would have been a skeleton by now. Remember, this room has been walled off for a long time. This girl looks too perfect to be the real deal."

He was right. The body still had all its hair, which wasn't out of the ordinary with most skeletons and bodies. But her skin was intact. He would even have called it healthy. There were no signs of decomposition at all.

Despite this fact, she hung back.

I'm not going anywhere near that thing. Dad can do it.

Unsurprisingly, he didn't disappoint her. Craig approached the edge of the box for a closer look. The more he stared at the body, the more confused he became. "Keep the flashlight on her." She complied, although the beam now shook with the tremors she struggled to control.

He leaned over the casket to see if he could find some sign of artificial craftsmanship. The closer he got, however, the more lifelike she seemed. The way her skin appeared... the still flawless seams of the eyelids, the pristine lips with their minute cracks and crevices. She looked like she might have been someone taking a nap.

"I don't get it. If this were a real person, she would have long decomposed by now. And even if she just got here somehow, her skin wouldn't look this vibrant." He wiped more sweat away from his brow.

The only way he could know for sure was to touch her to see for himself. But, as he examined her with his keen gaze, discomfort set in. This appeared to be the body of a teenage girl, not unlike his daughter. Despite the time that he had spent around death in the previous months, it turned his stomach to think of his daughter lying in that box.

Still, nothing ventured, nothing gained. And if it is a body, we'll need to report it.

He reached for the girl's folded hands. Much to his surprise, the skin was soft and warm. Before he could voice his astonishment or any of the questions that suddenly clamored for answers, the hand jerked away. His breath caught. His eyes widened, and he stumbled backward in shock. Seconds later, he held his daughter against the wall with a protective arm.

"Dad, what is it?"

"Give me the light, Alexis." His voice was eerily calm as he turned his hand expectantly, palm up.

"All right," she stammered.

Craig's knees trembled as he strode slowly back to the casket with the device in hand. He peered over the wooden surface once more and let the light pass over the girl's face.

Her eyes blinked open slowly as if she were waking after a long nap. It seemed to take a few moments for her brain to catch up with her before she gasped and sat up with a panicked expression on her face.

He bounded back and clutched his daughter protectively, who screamed and closed her eyes for a moment.

The girl in the box shrieked in response, and father and daughter almost tripped and fell as they scrambled to exit the room as quickly as their bodies could move. He slammed and locked the door behind them once they stumbled safely out of the closet.

Inside the darkened room, Victoria stood in the box and climbed out, expecting to see the basement she'd once called home. Instead, she saw a poorly-built brick wall with a hole in it. A strange dull light shone through the gap from whatever source existed outside. It certainly didn't look like candlelight.

Her pulse quickened for the first time in centuries and she became lightheaded. When she regained control of herself, she clambered through the opening and hurried to the door. A simple test revealed that it had been locked. As her anxiety rose, she pushed on it with both hands and the latch exploded. She could hear the clink of metal as it struck dully against a padded surface, then skittered away.

The door swung violently open and into the wall so hard that the knob embedded itself.

She rushed into the large room and her breathing quickened as she stared at the unfamiliar objects and the carpeting beneath her feet.

Her short, panicked breaths did little to ease the light-headedness and she squinted as she searched for something she recognized. *Where are my parents? What is this place? Where does that light come from?*

The latter question was answered readily enough as she viewed the fixtures above. The sconces were somehow embedded into the ceiling. How did they manage to keep the flame from spreading? Some form of…glass? Was this magic? Was she a prisoner?

Not for long.

As the questions swirled through her mind, she sprinted up the stairs on the far side of the room. She would find out what happened and where she had been taken, and then, she would return home. Mother and Father would be sick with worry by now.

Alexis and Craig rushed to the front door as fast as their legs could carry them. He yanked his daughter by the wrist to make sure he wouldn't lose her.

Suddenly, she dug her heels in. "Wait."

He barely managed to catch her when his momentum forced her to stumble. She shouted a protest but made no effort to continue their retreat.

"Alexis, there's no time to wait. We have to go."

"But why? It's only a girl. And she sounded as spooked by us as we were by her."

"Whatever that is, it is most certainly not a teenage girl."

He grabbed her wrist again and shook it as if to get her full attention. "You saw the wood, you saw the nails, and you saw how old that wall was. Nobody has seen that chamber in years. That's a body that was buried in a coffin in the basement, and it was somehow still alive. We're not qualified to deal with something like this. Now, let's go."

"Dad, no." Alexis shook her head and barely managed to pry her wrist loose and step back before her father could grab her again. She stepped away a little farther to gain space between them. "She's probably confused. What if she only needs help?"

Her father was speechless. Scant seconds before, his daughter had freaked out as much as he had. Now she was suddenly ready to bond with the undead?

The argument was rendered pointless when the girl in question burst into the room with a very prominent set of fangs bared for the world to see. She would find out what her captors had done, where they had taken her, and then she would go back. Back to...to...

She paused and looked around the room, her chest still heaving with anxious energy. She looked at the tiled floor of the foyer and was greeted by the familiar mosaic. The strange furniture and humming objects had led her to believe she was somewhere else, but a hasty look down the passage to the living room revealed a familiar fireplace and the glint of gold. She closed her mouth.

I'm still home. I haven't gone anywhere.

"*Mutter? Vater?*" Her voice echoed through the cavernous foyer and beyond to the bedrooms overlooking the space. She disappeared up the stairs almost as quickly as she'd arrived.

Father and daughter gaped at the spectacle.

Super-speed, check. Fangs, check.

She shook her head at the ridiculous thoughts that couldn't possibly have any foundation in reality. Craig pulled his daughter closer as the girl called for her parents and dashed from room to room.

Victoria was swamped with more questions than answers as she searched each of the rooms in rising panic.

The furniture is different. The floors are shiny. They've never been shiny before. What are these paintings of? These candles don't have any flames. How do they give off so much light? What is going on?

In a daze, she wandered to the top of the staircase and looked over the foyer again.

This is home but it isn't the home I remember. What has happened?

Alexis and Craig stood together near the bottom of the stairs. Once they saw the confusion on the girl's face, Alexis took a hesitant step forward.

Craig whispered urgently, "Alexis." He shook his head.

"It's okay, Dad," she assured him nervousness, then turned to stare at the undead girl who now cowered in visible fear. "Hello?"

The girl trembled in her place at the top of the stairs, and her hands clutched the banister. Tears welled in her eyes. "Wer bist du? Wo sind meine eltern?"

That was encouraging. She sounded calmer, which meant she might be reasoned with. Alexis' heart pounded in her chest. Reasoning with a vampire wasn't exactly the highlight on her vacation's to-do list, but the girl seemed legitimately frightened. "My name is Alexis. My dad and I are visiting this place. Do you speak English?"

"Eng-lishhhh?" The girl wrinkled her nose in confusion.

Craig sighed and strode forward hesitantly to stand behind his daughter.

In for a penny...

"*Sprechen sie Englisch?*" He'd memorized a few basic phrases to get by in the city. Fortunately, that rudimentary inquiry was among them.

The girl shook her head. The three stood there in awkward silence for a time, unable to communicate. Finally, her gaze drifted to the small library. The wind generated by her passing guided both to the cozy space, where they found her pointing at the bookcase.

"Eng-lishhh?"

Alexis and her father looked at each other and he shook his head warningly. She ignored his concerned look and walked forward.

Her father grimaced, ready to drag her out the door, but something held him back. *She'll get us both killed.*

Slowly, she stepped in front of the girl. She pulled a German book off the shelf and opened it to point at the words. "Do you speak German?"

"*Ja!*" The girl practically shouted excitedly. "*Ich spreche Deutsch!*"

"Okay." Alexis snatched an English book off the shelf and pointed to her father, then herself, then the words on the page. "We speak English. Here."

In the doorway, her father held his palms up.

What will this accomplish?

"Ahh…" The girl took the book and scanned the pages one by one. The paper snapped as she flicked them rapidly to match the supernaturally fast pace at which her gaze scanned the text.

"What's going on?" Craig asked.

Alexis shook her head and shrugged, her attention focused on the odd scene. "I don't know. She's reading, I suppose."

When she reached the end of the book, the girl raised her head and closed her eyes. Her lips moved silently as she mouthed something to herself. After a few moments, she opened her eyes, nodded, and spoke in a slow and clear voice that was clipped by her accent. "My name is Victoria."

Craig's hand trembled as he dragged his fingers through his hair as he gaped at the girl.

This makes no sense. It has to be a dream. I'll wake up any minute now. I know I will.

"So…you now speak English?" he asked incredulously.

"I have learned the language, yes. At least what I could learn from that book."

Alexis shrugged. "That works for me. Do you live here?"

"I think so. This feels like home, but this does not look like my home. How did you…come inside?"

"We rented the place from its owner," Alexis explained.

Victoria squinted in thought. "Rented? I am sorry. I do not know this word. It was not in the book. What is rented?"

"We paid the owner money to let us stay here for a few weeks."

"You gave my father money?" she asked suspiciously.

Father never allowed visitors. Why would he take someone's money?

"Is your father named Phil?" Craig asked as he sidled toward his daughter. He still didn't feel comfortable with the situation, and he wanted every chance to protect her should the need arise. "He's the owner."

Victoria shook her head vehemently. "No, no, no, no. I do not understand. Her eyes widened with alarm and confusion. My father owns this place, not...Phil. What happened to my family? Did you take them somewhere? Are they hurt? I know there was a war coming. Did the invaders drive them out of our home?"

"We don't know any of that," Alexis said. "We've only been here for a month. How long were you in that coffin downstairs?"

Victoria leaned back, closed her eyes, and scanned her thoughts for a moment. She seemed a little panicked at first, but it was rapidly replaced by bewilderment when she looked at them again. "I remember the year I went to sleep. Tell me, what is the date?"

Alexis pulled her phone out and showed Victoria the screen.

The girl gasped and her face turned ashen. "Has it really been so long?"

"What? What is it?" Alexis pressed.

"Four hundred," Victoria said hoarsely and disbelief vied with fear on her face. "It has been nearly four hundred years."

CHAPTER FOUR

The silence weighed heavily on Craig's shoulders after that last comment. Who was this girl? Was this nothing more than a dream? Could it be a prank? Should he call Phil? The questions rampaged with no relief in sight. He honestly didn't know.

"Wait," he asked finally, "how do you know you have been asleep for four hundred years? You were sleeping. Maybe it only feels like you slept for centuries. We all do that sometimes—I often take a nap and wake up forgetting what day it is."

His protest sounded beyond juvenile and even Alexis raised a brow in amusement. Still, his rational brain needed to reject everything he saw and heard—a defense mechanism that could hopefully keep him from accepting the equally impossible truth. It was way preferable to the reminder that the girl, not too long before, had actually manifested fangs.

Victoria shook her head. "No, this was not a normal rest. I could not see, and I could barely hear anything, but I was…aware. I don't know how else to explain it. I sensed the passage of time as it happened but had no way to judge it accurately."

Alexis finally broke through the cloud of confusion and unasked questions that had distracted her and spoke quickly. "Wow. After all that time asleep, what's the first thing you want to do?"

Victoria thought for a moment, her expression blank. After centuries during which she lay paralyzed in that box, it seemed logical that her mind must have wandered to all the different things she could do when she emerged. Her inward search revealed only a very blank mental canvas, however, until finally, her body settled the question for her. "I'm thirsty."

Alexis and her dad looked at each other with slight amusement and a hint of disbelief.

This is definitely a prank.

He glanced at the ceiling and searched surreptitiously for cameras. At some point, he expected a punchline, so he decided he would play along. "Let me make you some tea. Come to the kitchen."

It didn't take them long to return to the kitchen, where he turned the tap and filled the kettle.

Victoria's mouth gaped in amazement. "Where is the pump for the water?"

"It's a faucet," Alexis told her.

"What is a faucet?"

Craig chuckled and shook his head.

She's a good actress but I think she's laying it on a little thick. For now, I'll go with it, though.

"The water feeds into the house through pipes and

comes out there. The pump is electric. It runs on its own. You just lift the handle and the water comes out."

She made no response and simply stared at the faucet with wide eyes.

He moved the kettle to the stove and turned the knob on to ignite the bright blue gas flame with a *click* and a spark.

Victoria marveled at the tiny blaze and a small smile teased at her lips. "Are there pipes for fire, too?"

The man laughed. "In a way, yes." He retrieved a box of tea bags from the cupboard, along with three mugs, which lined up on the counter before he dropped a bag in each.

"Is that how these candles burn?" The girl pointed to the lights hanging from the ceiling.

"Ah, no," Alexis said. "Those are light bulbs. They're powered by electricity."

"E-lec-tri-ci-ty? That is another word I did not find in the book. The glass holds the fire?"

Craig stepped to the light switch and flipped it on and off. "Yeah. Electricity is a form of energy that comes into the house through metal wires. You'll see that most things in the house are powered by it. This switch controls some of them.

The kettle whistled, and he lifted the water off the stove to fill each mug, then distributed two to the girls. "So, Victoria, how did you learn English so quickly?" His tone carried a measure of skepticism. He was still sure this was a prank and conveniently ignored the odd questions that seemed to challenge this—like how the prankster knew they'd break into the basement room, and how she'd got behind a centuries-old wall.

"I read the book." She sniffed the air as the hot water interacted with the aroma from the tea leaves and sighed. "I am able to process information faster than humans."

"Oh, you're not human?" He smirked. "You sure look human."

"We all do," she replied but immediately clamped her mouth shut as she realized exactly what she was saying.

You do not know these people. Father always told you to be quiet about it. Do not say another word.

"Victoria, tell us what you remember," Alexis said. "What is your last memory before going into that coffin?"

At that, Victoria told them the story of her last day with her parents—carried away from town, drinking a strange liquid, falling asleep but still somehow awake, locked into the coffin by her parents, and eventually, falling completely into the silence.

Craig rolled his eyes as he wiped his glasses with a towel to clear them of the dust and grime that had accumulated over the lenses. "Yeah, right. People don't live for four hundred years. The maximum human lifespan is upwards of a hundred at best. Most live on an average of between eighty and ninety years. Just because you were put to sleep doesn't mean you were magically preserved. Tell me, if you really were down there for that long, how did you not age? How did you breathe without air?"

Victoria avoided eye contact and took slow sips from her cup as if the rhythm eased her nervousness.

Sensing that she was uncomfortable with the questions, Alexis tried to change the subject—or, at least, she thought she was changing the subject.

"You have fangs. What's that about?"

Her father shook his head. "No, she doesn't. I thought so too earlier, but I've watched her while we talked. Perfect teeth, yes. Fangs? No. Go on, Victoria. Show her your teeth."

Victoria obeyed readily. There was no sign of the natural weapons they had seen earlier.

Craig nodded in self-congratulation. "See? She has regular teeth."

Alexis shook her head and addressed the other girl again. "No, when you first ran around the house, you came up to us in the foyer and you had fangs. I know you did."

Again, Victoria shifted in her chair and avoided eye contact. "This tea is very good," she said with a blank expression that was obviously feigned.

He leaned forward and stared into his daughter's eyes. "Alexis, she clearly doesn't," he countered. "What we saw was probably the result of stress—and possibly some form of natural gas or hallucinogen that grew in that chamber and mingled with the dust."

"I know what I saw, Dad. And you do, too, but I'm not about to call it a nightmare when she's sitting right here in front of us."

"I'm a...vampire." The statement came so softly, it was almost a whisper.

"Come again?" Craig asked, his voice a little strained.

Victoria frowned. "But I am already here."

He sighed and shook his head. "Sorry. I meant to say, could you please repeat yourself? Louder, preferably."

"I...that is to say, my family and I are *vampir*."

His daughter raised a skeptical brow. "What, like Count Dracula? For real? A vampire?"

"Who is Count Dracula?"

Alexis shook her head and her hair whipped around her face. "Never mind. But seriously, you drink blood and stuff? And can't go out into the sunlight?"

Victoria twisted her face into a grimace. "We can go out into the sunlight. Why wouldn't we? And no, we do not drink blood. I don't, anyway. There are others—or at least there were in my time. The ones you might call bloodsuckers, but I am not one of them."

"Then besides sharp teeth—which I assume you can change at will—what makes you a vampire?"

"Alexis, I can't believe you're actually buying this," Craig objected.

"I can't believe you're not after everything she's shown us," she countered. "Super-speed, super-strength, and the ability to literally process an entire language in seconds— one that she's never spoken and hardly heard before. If you're not willing to accept she's a vampire, think of her as a mutant like the X-Men."

Victoria took a deep breath. Given the number of years that had passed and the fact that her parents hadn't woken her themselves, she could only assume the worst. They were most likely gone, possibly for good. If she was to survive in this new time—and, in many ways, new world— she would need allies, and this Alexis seemed to at least be somewhat sympathetic. She had little to lose by explaining more to the girl, especially since they were of a similar age. "We have certain abilities that regular humans do not have. For one thing, we are very fast and very strong when we need to be."

Alexis snapped her fingers. "Like when you ran up the

staircase earlier. Holy cow, that was fast. I thought maybe my brain had shorted out for a second."

Victoria nodded. "We often seek to hide these abilities for obvious reasons."

Craig laughed in disbelief. "And studying that book. So, you're saying you have certain superhuman abilities."

"Yes. We have what you might call a heightened sense of awareness. When danger is lurking, our skin tingles and we become very reactive to the environment around us."

He raised his fingers to make air quotes. "So being a 'vampire' is more of a defensive thing. You react to what's around you."

"Yes, although there are certain aspects of it that we can turn on as we please. The running, for example. That's something that we can do any time we wish to."

Alexis nodded enthusiastically. "That must come in handy! So, if you have all these great abilities and you're superhuman, why were you stuck in a box in the basement for so long?"

Victoria leaned back in her chair. "I do not know. My parents never explained it to me. They looked worried and they said several prayers over me beforehand."

"Okay, so if the fangs aren't for drinking blood, what are they for?"

"Alexis," he admonished sharply.

"What? I want to know," she responded petulantly.

Craig fixed his daughter with a chilling stare. "That's a very personal question to ask and exceptionally rude."

"Dad, don't pretend you haven't wondered about it, too," she accused.

"Yes, but I know better than to come right out and say it."

"Why? She said she doesn't drink blood so it's a logical question Why would you need them if you don't drink blood?"

Victoria couldn't help but smile at the exchange between the two. In a way, it reminded her of the time she'd spent with her own father. That wound was still fresh, however, and she didn't wish to shed her tears before these people if she could help it. Instead, she blinked them back and shrugged her shoulders as casually as she could manage.

"Why does a cat have fangs? It does not drink blood. As with all such things in nature, they are for my own defense. Nothing more and nothing less. Sometimes, I use them and sometimes, I don't. But they are there in case I need them. I am a small girl, so these defenses are important to me, especially when I am out in public. Father always wanted us to be careful when we went to the village."

Alexis scooped the teabag from her mug and tossed it in a nearby trash can. "I guess so, but how much defense do you really need in public?"

Victoria stared into the murky depths of her cup with a somber expression. "Vampires are hunted when they are discovered. Many of my kind were left to die in the streets when their true nature was made known," she said quietly. "It is far from pleasant."

"Well, assuming this isn't a dream and you really are a vampire who doesn't drink blood, that's probably not something you'll have to worry about in this day and age." Craig sipped his tea casually. He still believed on some level that this was simply a stupid joke and he should play along until it got out of hand. "Vampires are nothing more than old legends or horror stories nowadays. If you walk up to someone and tell them you're a vampire, they'll probably think you're crazy. Most people would simply not believe you, and we certainly wouldn't want to kill you even if you were one. If that's what you are. I still don't quite believe it," he said pointedly and searched the room yet again for any sign of hidden cameras.

"Have things really changed so much?" Victoria removed the bag of tea from her mug as she had seen Alexis do and dropped it in the trash can.

"Is there anything we can do for you?" Craig asked. It seemed like the reasonable adult thing to do until some other course of action presented itself. "We'll be here for a couple more weeks. And assuming we aren't in some form of reality show, I suppose we're actually guests in your home, at least for the time being. How can we help? Do you know of any friend or family member we could contact for you?"

A brief pause ensued while they waited for her response. She knew what she wanted, but she doubted that it could be delivered.

"It is…unlikely that you will be able to assist me with what I want, but I will ask it of you. Can you find my parents? Or failing that, help me find out what happened to them? I want to know. I wish to see them again if I can."

"Of course! We can definitely try if nothing else." Alexis nodded at her father. "We can look your family up online. Maybe there's some info there. And if there isn't, maybe we can find something in the town archives—right, Dad?"

"This kitchen is so bright." Victoria squinted her eyes at the white cabinets, the shiny granite countertops, and the stainless-steel appliances. "Everything in this room seems to reflect light." The unexpected comment intruded into the conversation like a random thought had settled into her brain.

"What did it look like before?" Craig challenged, seeing an opportunity to perhaps catch her out.

"It was darker—much darker. We used dark wood from the forest to make the floors and counters. Small shelves held spices and herbs Father and Mother would buy from the market. Our stove was black metal and very heavy. We call it Gusseisen. I apologize, but I do not know the English variant. Our pots and pans were of a similar color. The bright colors came from salt, sugar, and wooden cooking spoons. We used torches and wax candles for light. We had none of these strange things you have in here. Please, will you show me what they are and how they work?"

For the next few minutes, father and daughter did their best to explain some of the basic comforts of home that existed in the dwelling, from toilets to heaters to computers and furniture design. Victoria found herself more enamored with each demonstration.

Alexis readily embraced the excitement of the adventure. Her father, however, still had serious doubts about the whole thing. The girl seemed harmless, but it was entirely possible that she'd lost her mind. That and the idea of an elaborate prank were the first contenders on his list of what to believe. At the conclusion of the tour, Victoria glanced at her mug of tea, which gave off a light-green color. Thinking back to the last drink she'd had, she grew a little concerned.

"This won't put me back to sleep, will it?"

Alexis waved her hand airily. "Nah, don't worry, it's only green tea. It's good for you and will help you feel better."

"Yeah, we're not up to date on our potions yet," the father joked. "So it's regular tea for now."

"Green tea, Dad," his daughter corrected absently. Then, she smirked. "And you call yourself a researcher. Get your facts straight."

"I'll get you for that, Missy," he shot back playfully.

"Sure you will, Dad. Sure you will."

CHAPTER FIVE

That evening, Craig drew Alexis aside while Victoria made use of the new bathroom.

"You don't seriously believe this story, do you?" he whispered.

"Why not?" She shrugged. "She learned English in about five minutes, and she still doesn't know it all yet, only enough to communicate. And besides that, I already pointed out how she ran through the house. We both saw it. Are you really going to drag this argument up to flog the proverbial dead horse again? It died hours ago when she showed us her fangs. Multiple times. You watched them grow in. It wasn't a Hollywood trick."

"Do you feel safe around her?"

Alexis looked across the room to the library entrance. Victoria had finished in the bathroom and once again flicked the light switch on and off with open curiosity.

"Yeah, I think she's fine. She won't hurt us. Besides, she's too fascinated by everything that's going on, and she knows we know she's a vampire. If she's that nervous about telling people, it means she's willing to trust us. As long as we return that trust, everything will be fine."

He wanted an excuse to get away and do a little more research on the facts Victoria had given them but leaving his daughter alone with a girl who claimed to be an ageless vampire stretched his comfort level a little too far. Still, he also couldn't hang around and hold her hand forever.

"I have more work I have to do tonight, so I'll be upstairs. But the door will be open if something happens. If anything rubs you the wrong way, shout, call, text…do whatever you have to do to get hold of me, okay?" He followed his daughter's gaze to the vampire. "If she really is telling the truth, maybe she needs to settle and get comfortable with today's world. I'm not saying I believe it entirely, but I'm willing to give…a certain amount of leniency."

Alexis smiled and shook her head knowingly. "I've got it, Dad. Go work."

Even in the midst of the craziest adventure ever, he's still going to work. At least I have somebody to talk to now.

He kissed his daughter on the forehead and left the room.

She entered the library and smiled at their guest—or was it the other way around? Technically, they were the visitors. "So, what do you want to do? Is there something you want to know about us? Or about…I don't know, the world?"

Victoria stopped playing with the light switches and looked at her with some surprise. "Are you a very learned person?"

Alexis shrugged. "I don't know, but I can Google stuff if you want answers."

The girl stared blankly at her. "Google. That is the second time you have used that word. I do not know what that means."

"Never mind." Alexis waved her over. "Let's go to my room and grab my computer. We can learn more about you and where you come from. If you want, you can ask me anything. Just…let's go. It's easier if I show you."

The two girls walked out of the library, across the foyer, and up the stairs. Alexis led her to the second bedroom, where she had stayed for the past month. A large queen-sized bed stood on mahogany floorboards. The stone had been covered by a decorative fleur de lis wallpaper on the upper half and a series of smaller wooden slats that bordered the lower. A picture of the fortress watched over the room and its occupants with a grim sturdiness, while a painting of an open field full of golden grains and wild horses helped to brighten the atmosphere.

"This is your room?" Victoria asked.

"Just for the month, yeah. We don't live here. We live in America and are only visiting. What was this room when you lived here? Or…you know what I mean."

Victoria was quiet as she studied every detail from the nightstands to the wash basin and charging cable. "It is… different than before. Much different, but I remember it well. This used to be my parents' room."

"Really? Wow. I wouldn't have guessed that. It's not the biggest bedroom up here."

The girl nodded. "Yes, but it was in the middle. My parents liked to be close to me and keep visitors away, if necessary. It was simply easier to do so this way." She sighed. "They always tried to protect me."

Alexis smiled sympathetically. The loss of a parent was a feeling she could relate to only too well, and this girl must have experienced double with the loss of both. "Well, I have my laptop right here. Let's start digging in."

Distraction had always helped her to work through her grief, so perhaps it would do more than simply keep them occupied.

When in doubt, use distraction to treat sadness.

She sat on her bed, and Victoria sat beside her and stared at the screen with wonder. "What is this?"

"It's called a laptop computer. We call it laptop for short. It basically gives you the ability to access almost all the world's information in one place. We can look up details on the time you lived here or the groups of people you were with, places you've been, that sort of thing. And that's only the boring stuff. There is fun stuff on here, too."

As she said that, her laptop *dinged*.

"What was that noise?"

"Oh, I received a message from my friend Jess. She's in America right now."

"And yet she can communicate with you from this America?" Victoria asked curiously. "You speak of it like it is very far distant. We only could use letters. The idea of instant transport never seemed possible." She seemed to wear a permanent look of astonishment on her face.

"Yeah, I don't really know how it works, but that's right. It essentially transports the message within a few seconds to my friend's computer to read. An Internet search functions equally as quickly. Okay, let's look up the time you lived in. You said about four hundred years ago, right?"

Victoria nodded and pulled her knee up to her chest to rest her chin as she watched in unfeigned fascination.

Alexis opened a Google search bar and typed in the date.

Austria 1619.

The search results immediately brought them information about the Thirty Years' War in Europe. She scanned the wiki page quickly and searched for highlights to explain to Victoria about how bad things were in Austria at the time.

"Holy cow. You were in the middle of some serious stuff. It says here that this war involved most of Europe and was one of the worst conflicts in human history. Eight million people were killed between 1619 and 1649. That is a lot."

Victoria nodded sadly. "Given the atmosphere at the time, I am not terribly surprised. There always seemed to be tension in the air."

"How so?"

She leaned back and propped herself on her hands. "We had to be more careful about who we talked to. The king was fortifying the castles in the area. My parents were much more concerned about where I was going, why, who I was with, that sort of thing."

"Boy, do I understand that." Alexis rolled her eyes and thought of her father's constant worrying about her when they were home. Ever since her mom died, she had to give out every single detail of her activities before leaving the house. "That much hasn't changed in the last four hundred years. Parents will still worry about you. Was it scary knowing all that war and death was going on around you?"

Victoria shook her head. The thought honestly hadn't occurred to her very often. "I was a child—a…kid, I believe you say? I still am, I suppose. Nobody talked to me about it. I believe my parents wished to shield me from the conflict as much as possible. I was expected to go along with what everyone else told me and do the best I could."

Alexis laughed. "We have a lot in common, then." She continued to read. "It looks like it was a time of serious political and religious turmoil. Countries invading others, rebellions going on, that sort of thing. You really don't remember any of this?"

"As I said, I only remember the mood. People were sad, depressed, and afraid. Some were angry and embittered and worked harder on the construction and preparations. I suppose that with so many people dying, it was probably a loss of family members elsewhere or perhaps the fear of attack."

"And if it was religious turmoil," Alexis said, "it wouldn't surprise me if you had to keep your vampire reality quiet. That's the type of thing that could set off a religious group very quickly."

"I don't know. As I said, my parents always tried to protect me. We had to keep our heritage a secret, not because we were ashamed of it but because it put us in danger. I never knew from what, but Father said we were fighting for survival." She tilted her head up at the ceiling and closed her eyes. "I remember something…"

Alexis leaned forward, pushing her laptop aside. "What?"

"When I was asleep and my parents were putting me in the coffin, I heard my father say something about the Circle. I didn't know what he meant by that. The Circle could be a mob, a religious group, or even a secret place." She shook her head sadly and shrugged. "I only remember him talking about it."

Victoria went really quiet as she once again thought of her last memories of her parents. Her companion respectfully sat silently. A lump formed in the vampire's throat, and her lip trembled. Alexis waited patiently as Victoria took a deep breath while her lip trembled and her eyes watered—signs she knew only too well. She'd struggled against the darkness of grief that had threatened to overwhelm her too many times to count.

"You know what? Enough of this for now." She flipped her laptop shut. "You're awake now. It's the year 2019, and we need to get you into modern times, at least enough to blend in."

Victoria opened her eyes and blinked away the tears for the second time that night. "Okay, how do we do that?"

"First, you need a shortened version of your name. Victoria is fine, but I think you'd be better off as Vickie. That's how we shorten Victoria in America. So, sometimes you'd be Victoria, but more often, people will call you Vickie. That will make you sound a little less old-fashioned. We like to call it a nickname."

"A...nickname. Okay, what else?"

"Clothes and bathing. You have gorgeous, long black hair. Let's take care of it. Hair is very important to a teenage girl. And as for clothes, we have to start with the basics. The good news is, we're about the same size. At least, I think we are. That gown you're wearing is a little loose and not very stylish. You can't walk around in that."

Alexis stood and walked over to the dresser, where she kept her clothes. She pulled out a t-shirt and a pair of sweatpants.

"It's nighttime anyway, so you can sleep in these tonight." She tossed the clothes onto the bed. "Tomorrow, you'll wear jeans, and I have an extra jacket for you, too. But before you change your clothes, we need to get you into the shower."

Vickie didn't know what a shower was, but she had grown tired of repeating words. Instead, she followed Alexis down the hall to a bathroom that was very different from the first one. There was more than one kind of this room?

"How did the bathroom look when you lived here?" her companion asked.

"Oh, this wasn't here at all." Her gaze moved from one contraption to the next. The sink was familiar to her, thanks to the coaching she received from Alexis in the lower room, as was the toilet. The rest was a mystery. "It was unheard of to..." She cleared her throat awkwardly. "Uh, to perform certain bodily functions in the house. We had an outhouse in the back, and we bathed in the lake."

"An outhouse?" Alexis balked in real horror with a hint of disgust. "Oh, man. This really is a new world for you."

She pulled the shower curtain back briskly. "So, instead of having to jump in the lake, you have water brought directly to you through the pipes, like this."

"Like down in the kitchen?"

"Exactly. And you can set the temperature to whatever you want. Strip down, step in, and scrub up. I have a bottle of body wash over on that ledge—that blue bottle there. You rub it over your body and it will lather like a bar of soap. The green bottle is shampoo for washing your hair and works the same way.

She turned the water on and wished her luck before she left the girl to enjoy a little privacy.

Vickie looked in the mirror, which had already gathered some of the steam from the running water, and took a deep breath. This was all so overwhelming and she did her best to keep all of it straight.

But this is the new world now. Father wanted you to blend in. It was for your own good. She's showing you how to do that. This is a good thing. One step at a time.

She stepped into the shower and immediately laughed as the warm water sprayed over her. It felt like a warm rainstorm and helped to relax the tension in her muscles from the shock of the day. And it was infinitely better than a plunge in a cold lake after sleeping for four hundred years.

Once she was thoroughly wet, she picked up the blue bottle of body wash and stared at it. When she flipped the cap open, the aroma that rose from the container almost caused her to sag. She couldn't quite put her finger on it, but it smelled much like food, although something unfamiliar to her, she was sure.

Tentatively, she poured a little of the liquid into her palm and rubbed her hands together experimentally. It frothed as Alexis had promised, and the smell intensified.

She stuck a finger into her mouth to see what it tasted like and immediately regretted it. She hissed and spat furiously as she used the water to rinse as much of the bitterness out as possible.

Now that she knew better, she continued with her shower and gave herself the first proper bathing she'd had in centuries.

Once she was done, she used the towel laid out for her to dry off and carefully slipped on the clothes Alexis had loaned her. At first, she rubbed her knees together awkwardly. A lady never wore pants in the old days. Such things were men's clothes. It was unseemly for a woman to even consider wearing them. But she soon adjusted to the sensation, and she did enjoy the comfort and support the cut of the pants provided.

These are the softest clothes I've ever worn in my life.

She took one last look at herself in the mirror. Her image was both familiar and entirely surreal. She now wore a green t-shirt, as bright as a flower, and gray sweat-pants—she thought those were the terms her benefactor had used. She almost didn't recognize herself in what she felt was utterly ridiculous attire.

I hope I'm wearing these right.

Unable to delay the inevitable any longer, she stepped out of the bathroom and returned to the bedroom where Alexis waited for her.

"So? How did you like it? I bet it felt amazing to have a good scrub after hundreds of years in a box."

"It was...an experience. I think I feel okay. The body wash didn't taste at all like it smelled, though."

Alexis laughed. "That's because you're not supposed to

taste it. The smell is like a perfume. It makes your body smell better. But you look good—a little more like this century. It'll help you fit in."

"Do you really think I can?"

"With my help? I guarantee it."

CHAPTER SIX

Vickie didn't sleep much that night. Between her general unease about her current situation and the fact that she had literally rested for four centuries, she had too much energy to drift off.

Instead, she waited for Alexis to fall asleep and walked out of the bedroom. As she closed the door behind her, she traced her fingers along the ornately carved wooden door. It had somehow been preserved over the centuries. She could swear it was the original one except that the wood was shinier, and it had taken on a darker color through some strange means she was certain Alexis could explain. Despite this, it was definitely the same door.

She thought for a moment about the days when she'd stood outside it as a little girl. Her memories swirled through the times her father and mother had let her sleep with them, the days of lessons and coaching on how to behave like a normal young lady, and the hours spent in quiet meditation with her mother. Those days were long gone now.

Vickie shrugged the nostalgia off the same way she would a wet cloak and walked down the stairs to the library. She sat on the red velvet chair and sighed. If it wasn't the same one from before, it certainly looked and felt like it. Perhaps the...owner of the house wished to retain the sense of originality. Or perhaps it really was the original and was now considered a valuable antique. Regardless, it was the perfect place for her to consider her current position and what to do in the future.

Now that she wasn't fiddling with the light switches or trying to learn the English language, she looked around the room and noticed how little had actually changed. The books on the shelf were different, but this room and the foyer bore the closest resemblance to her old home. She intended to read some books and hopefully, educate herself on what she'd missed while she was sleeping. If nothing else, it would help pass the time until morning.

But before she could set that plan in motion, her eyes settled on the mantel over the fireplace.

The chalice. Her mouth hung open.

How did I not see that earlier?

She bounded over to the hearth, seized the cup, and smoothed her fingers over the familiar crest. With it cradled in her arm, she returned to her seat.

Nearly everything about my former life is gone. My family. My home. This is all that's left. This cup and this chair. My entire life is right here.

When the sun rose the next morning, Craig walked down the stairs from his bedroom. Vickie sat reading the same World War I book that Alexis had read the day before.

If this really is a prank, she's playing the long con. But we don't seem to be in danger, at least.

"Well, good morning," he said cheerfully.

"Good morning." She smiled in response.

"Look at you. Boy, you already reminded me of my daughter, and now you're wearing her clothes, too. Now that you look a little more current, it should draw less attention when we head out later. Are you hungry?" He strolled past her on his way to the kitchen.

She closed her book. "Yes, I am. Should I gather eggs from the coop?"

He stopped and smirked. "No, no, that won't be necessary. Come on. I'll show you."

The two of them walked into the kitchen. The sun shone through the windows to illuminate the space naturally. The magic lights wouldn't be needed at this time, obviously.

"This is my favorite part of the day," he said. "It's so peaceful. There's something about a little natural light that always makes me feel energized."

He opened the refrigerator door and waved her over. She looked curiously at the space and inserted her hand into the air, then hastily withdrew it.

"This box is very cold. Is this also…electricity?"

Craig smiled. "Yes. In part. We keep food here because it will stay fresh longer. You don't have to worry about animals getting into it, or bugs. It won't rot as quickly." He withdrew a strange thin box with a series of ovular bulges shaped from the block to curve around whatever lay inside. "So, this is a carton of eggs. We get them at the store or the market and keep them in here." He also removed a package of bacon and a pitcher of orange juice. "I thought we'd have eggs and bacon today. Is that a meal you're familiar with? We can have fresh orange juice with it."

"That's fine. I want to learn about today's world, anyway. Make what you would normally make for breakfast, and I will eat it."

"Boy, I wish more kids were like you." He smiled as he placed the frying pan on the stovetop. "Maybe you could teach my daughter a thing or two."

Alexis walked into the kitchen, rubbed her eyes, and yawned as she greeted the two with a wave.

Craig cracked a few eggs into the pan, and it sizzled in response. "Today, you'll have a little excitement that will hopefully wear you out. We'll go into town."

Alexis immediately became more alert and her eyes widened in anticipation. "We will? Are you coming too and not simply going to work all day?"

"Nah. I'll take the day off so we can show Victoria around a little bit. She needs to have some things of her own, and it'll give her a chance to see how much has changed since her time."

The vampire cleared her throat. "I'm supposed to ask you to call me Vickie."

He raised his eyebrows, looked from one girl to the other as if uncertain how to respond, and focused on his pan of eggs. "Whatever you want."

The teenagers smiled at each other.

After breakfast, Alexis gave Vickie a pair of jeans to wear, along with a spare jacket and a pair of shoes. Craig waited downstairs, and the trio stepped out of the castle and into the fresh morning air.

Vickie took a long deep breath as the sunshine beamed onto her upturned face.

I've never felt so refreshed in my life. To be in nature again is a beautiful thing.

They walked over to a blue four-door sedan Alexis' father had rented for the duration of their stay.

Vickie slowed as they approached and stared at it with confusion at first, then wariness. "Where is the horse? How does it move without one? Is it safe?"

Craig smiled. "Get in. You'll see."

Alexis half shoved Vickie into the back seat and directed her fumbling attempts to secure her seatbelt. The vampire felt a little safer once it was latched but still had her reservations. When Craig revved the engine, she snatched hold of the door handle on her side of the car.

"It's okay." Alexis put a comforting hand on her shoulder. "It's normal. That's the engine. It's what makes the car move without the horses." She smiled reassuringly. "The belt you're wearing will keep you secure until we reach town. There's no need to panic."

Vickie watched through the window in awe as the scenery around flashed past. She still gripped what seemed to be a safety handle near the roof, but more out of excitement than fear.

We're moving so fast! But how can we without an animal to pull this carriage? And where did all these buildings come from? What happened to the open fields and the dirt paths?

Alexis and her dad discussed the things that Vickie needed. He wanted the girl to have the basics for starters, and they would see what they could afford to get her beyond that. While they were fine with her borrowing clothes here and there, she needed at least an outfit or two of her own.

The car lurched to a halt at a stoplight. While they sat waiting for the light to change, Vickie saw someone standing on the street corner waving his hands and talking out loud with nobody around.

"He looks like a Borachio," she scoffed and glanced at her companions in amusement, expecting a laugh. All she received were blank expressions. Clearly, they had no clue what she was talking about.

"What's a Borachio?" Alexis finally asked.

"A drunkard," she replied. "That's what we called them. They don't use that word anymore?"

"Ah, no, we don't," he said. "But why is he a drunk?"

Vickie pointed at the man, who now had his arms folded but continued to talk to no one at all without any apparent evidence that he was aware that he was entirely alone.

"He's talking to himself. That's either a sign that he is possessed by demons or that he is a drunk. Usually, it's a drunk."

Alexis leaned over to get a better look at the man, then laughed. "No, no. If you look in his ear, you'll see a blue thing sticking out? That's an earpiece for his cell phone."

"You just said too many words I don't understand."

Alexis smiled and spent the next several minutes explaining the concept of a telephone, then a cell phone, and finally, a Bluetooth headset. While many girls would be frustrated at not knowing these things and feel alienated in what was once her own home, Vickie soaked this information up like a sponge. She was fascinated by it all. Quite literally, she was living in the future, and every new piece of information she learned was magical.

As they continued toward the center of town, she pointed at strange-looking buildings that she didn't recognize. "What is that large building?" She gestured to a tall structure ten stories high.

"That's a hotel." Craig turned right at a corner. "It's a place where people can pay to sleep for the night. Like what we do with your castle, except we would only hire a room instead of the whole place. You would have called it an inn or a hostel in your time."

Vickie nodded. "That used to be a town square. We had a few of them, places where people could get together and enjoy one another's company. The children would run around and play while the adults would sit and gossip. It was a central gathering place."

"I guess I didn't think about how much the land itself had changed, too," Alexis said. "If you were overwhelmed by the differences in the castle, then the rest of the country will blow your mind." Vickie looked at her with a blank expression. "Uh...truly astonish you?"

The explanation seemed to suffice and a few minutes later, Vickie stared at a smaller building with a pair of bright yellow arches that protruded from the roof. "That building there with the fancy roof. Is that a cathedral?"

They both chuckled. "That's a McDonald's," Craig said. "It's a place people go to buy food. You give them money and they cook the food and give it to you to eat instead of you cooking it at home. What was there back in your day?"

Vickie turned around to make sure she had her sense of orientation right. "I think that was Farmer Mayer's cattle farm. He raised a lot of cows."

"Well, there are still cows there, I guess." Alexis laughed. Vickie sighed inwardly. There was obviously much about this new world she still had to learn because no matter how hard she looked, she saw no signs of cattle at all.

Craig soon joined his daughter's amusement, while Vickie struggled to understand what she assumed was a joke, although it made no sense at all. The minor difficulty was swept aside, however, when a car driving in the right lane cut them off. Craig stamped on the brake pedal, and the tires squealed. The car swerved back and forth as he tried to steady it without running off the road. He gripped the steering wheel with both hands and wrestled for control.

Vickie dragged her heels under her and crouched on the car's cushioned seat as she clung to the door handle like her life depended on it. Her eyes had widened to the size of dinner plates, and her fangs were bared in a snarl as the car screeched to a stop.

"It's okay." Alexis tried to calm her with a gentle touch. "It was only a bad driver. We're okay. You can relax."

The frightened girl's gaze darted around the vehicle and she breathed rapidly. Gray pieces of plastic lay scattered on the floor. Alexis leaned over and picked them up.

That's weird. I didn't see those before.

She put them on the seat between them as her dad continued to drive.

"Is everyone okay back there?" he asked.

Alexis confirmed that they were as the other girl finally calmed enough to return her feet to the floor of the car. Once they parked in the lot in front of a department store, Vickie still appeared anxious, so Craig walked around the car to open the door for her.

"It's all right," he assured her. "I'm sorry about that scare. I had to brake hard to avoid a collision with that guy. It happens on the road sometimes but doesn't mean we're under attack or anything. The car itself also has safety features in case we do have a crash."

Vickie nodded and got out of the car to join Alexis. The girl insisted on holding her arm, but at least she had settled enough not to make too much of a scene. Alexis helped to distract her from the experience by explaining where they were going to buy the clothes and other items.

Craig was about to close the door when he looked at the handle on the inside. The plastic casing had been completely shattered. Tiny slivers of plastic lay on the floor of the car, and a few bigger chunks had been laid on the car seat.

He picked up one of the chunks, sat quickly, and held it up to the steel bar on the inside of the handle. He frowned when he noticed it didn't fit quite right. There was no question that the plastic came from the bar. The color and fracture patterns both matched. Closer inspection yielded the answer. The steel portion of the handle had been bent in several places and the indentations took the shape of four fingers—teenaged-girl-sized fingers.

His eyes widened as he turned to look at the girls. No amount of special effects work could replicate that.

Maybe this isn't a prank, after all. Shaken, he closed the door and locked the car. Shopping suddenly seemed a gloriously boring and ordinary thing to do—something he usually hated but which gained instant appeal when compared with the magnitude of what his poor brain had to try to assimilate.

CHAPTER SEVEN

U pstairs in the bedroom, the girls unpacked several large bags full of everything a teenage girl could need.

"I love this top," Alexis announced as she pulled out a navy-blue shirt with a scoop neck. "This will probably be the first thing I borrow from you."

Vickie laughed in response. "I can't believe how many colors everything comes in. I always wore white or brown, whatever color the cloth was. Dyes were usually saved for the nobility, and we liked to blend in as much as possible with the village." She held a deep-purple shirt against her torso and admired it in the mirror. "With these clothes, I'll feel like a princess every day."

"Really?" Alexis folded the navy shirt and set it on the bed. "Just because you get a purple shirt?"

"You don't understand. Only royalty ever wore colors like these. If you wore purple, it meant you were a person of great wealth. My family owned this castle and it was passed down for several generations, but we were not a people of means. They would be stunned by these clothes." Her smile faded slightly as the reality of her loss set in again. The day's adventure had been a distraction for a while, but it was only a temporary respite from the river of grief that snaked through her soul.

Alexis continued to remove tags and fold clothes for her new friend. Sometimes, she took for granted how lucky she was to be born in this era. She really did have far more benefits than she'd previously considered.

Even basic clothing impresses her while I always wish for more stuff. I don't think I could have survived in her time. I'd have been bored to death.

"I hope you'll help me with these, too." Vickie held up a bag of toiletries.

"Oh yes. I'll help you with all of it." Alexis fumbled in the bag and pulled out several bottles. "Shampoo, conditioner, body wash, hairspray, your own brush, deodorant. There are things you'll borrow of mine, like my blow dryer. That's fine. But it's important to have your own soaps and things like that."

"Why do we need all this? It seems like so much."

"Welcome to a world I like to call Being A Girl," she joked. "We require maintenance. Boys can basically shower with a bar of soap, brush their hair, and get dressed. Girls have to take care of themselves. Our hair needs to be healthy, our skin needs to be healthy, and everything needs to look and feel its very best. You're lucky, too, because your skin looks great already, so at least we don't have damage to fix before we start on the positives."

She smiled at the girl, but anxiety replaced the smile Vickie had worn during their shopping. "Don't worry. I'll help you get it all straight. It'll be like second nature for you in no time. My mom used to help me with this at first. It's not really that much. We could be a lot worse. Some girls take hours in the mirror and spend hundreds of dollars every month on makeup and beauty products. Mom taught me to do this with minimal investment. You'll do great—and you'll feel great, too."

For a moment, she remembered standing in front of the bathroom mirror while she learned all about wearing makeup and doing her hair. Her mom would crack jokes and make her laugh. Everything had been a game to that woman. Alexis missed that.

"So, your father doesn't have to do these things?"

"Goodness, no. He wouldn't even know where to start. That's why I'm down here with you and he's up in his little office working on his show."

At that same moment, Craig settled at his desk in the second tower. He double-clicked on his email and glanced out the window overlooking Salzburg while his messages loaded, and he smiled. He was rarely a fan of working at night, but his time in Austria had really allowed him to explore it. The lights shining from the city gave him a sense of peace and calm, one he hadn't experienced in over a year.

Unfortunately, that calm didn't last when he ran through the day's events in his mind.

A vampire. A real, actual vampire. What am I supposed to do? Do I take her in? This could be the scientific breakthrough of a lifetime. But she's only a girl. And yet...that temper. That strength!

He looked at the framed picture of his wife on his desk and sighed.

What would you do about this, Carol? How would you handle it? I sure wish you were here to help. You were always great at handling difficult decisions.

He had a few new emails, but he scanned them until he found two messages labeled:

RE: The Truth About...Ad Rates.

Both messages were from potential sponsors for his podcast, *The Truth About...* He had built up a small but loyal following of listeners, and sponsors had started to take notice.

To his delight, both messages revealed that the companies would sign on to buy ad time on his broadcast. Craig pumped both fists and let out a little cheer, confident nobody could hear him. "Woo!"

Each was willing to pay him two hundred dollars per episode to have their products mentioned. It wasn't all that much, but it meant four hundred dollars more in the bank per week.

Not too shabby for a rookie. Finally, some good news!

He hastily drafted and sent his replies in the affirmative and informed them he would draw contracts up in the morning. That done, he glanced at his watch.

Shoot. I have ten minutes before that guy's going to call.

He pulled his notes up on his laptop in preparation for his interview. "That guy" happened to be Dr. Richard Thurgood, a Boston hematology expert who claimed to have developed a blood test that could detect most cancers early.

Dr. Thurgood was the perfect interviewee for the second season of *The Truth About...* which was titled *The Truth About Cancer*. His first season, *The Truth About Climate Change*, had gone over very well and snagged many listeners.

This particular podcast would be a tonal shift, especially for him. But cancer had become an obsession for him after what happened to Carol. He wanted the truth about the disease as much as he wanted to share that information with others.

His notepad included a few basic questions in preparation for the discussion to come. He always took very detailed notes to avoid missing anything. That quality had always served him well as an investigative journalist for the Milwaukee Journal Sentinel.

Still, it was hard for him to separate his emotions from the questions he planned to ask.

"How does it work?"

Is it even possible to do something like this?

"Why isn't it available on the market yet?"

You know, like twelve to fifteen months ago, when it could have saved my wife's life.

"How much would it cost?"

Probably ten thousand dollars a test. I'd have taken out three mortgages to get my hands on it back then.

The old notepad reminded him of better times, although he usually kept a small notepad in his pocket back then, right next to his digital voice recorder. Politicians, even

U.S. Presidents, police chiefs, CEOs, and anybody who was worth talking to would meet up with him sooner or later. If they came through Milwaukee, he usually managed to sit down with them and ask at least a few questions.

It had its challenges, but it also came with the perks of getting to meet a seemingly endless line of famous men and women. That thought led him to lean back in his chair and think about the final six months of his job. He grimaced.

The unpreparedness. The distraction. The stress. It still had the power to overwhelm him at times when he thought about it.

He went from a clean-cut professional to an unshaven schlub, at least to those on the outside looking in. He'd taken pride in his appearance and professionalism. That was how he'd risen through the ranks to lead journalist in the first place. But more important things came up. Caring for a dying wife and a teenage girl proved a weight that was too heavy to bear when combined with his newspaper work. Something had to give.

He didn't want to leave his job but being fired removed the necessity to make a decision. In the cutthroat world of journalism, your personal life didn't matter. There was no excuse for bringing your personal problems to the job. If it affected your work, you were out. Never mind that Craig had faced the hardest challenge of his life. He got sloppy and when things were at their worst, his boss asked him to come to his office.

He thought about that day often and the long, slow walk from his desk to the corner office. He knew what would happen long before he arrived, but his mind seemed unable to process it in a meaningful way. There was no way out, and he wouldn't be able to avoid the inevitable. When the reality was confirmed, he had no idea what to do. After everything that had happened, how could he go home to his daughter and tell her that Daddy now had no job?

He still couldn't recall what he did immediately after that fateful meeting. Some details stuck out—he knew he'd packed up his desk and sat on the curb outside the building for a while. They were, however, simply facts. He didn't remember actually doing those things.

A month later, he and Alexis were on a flight to Salzburg.

At the time, it seemed like an irresponsible, crazy risk. He'd spent a lot of money booking this castle for six weeks and even tapped into the insurance money he had received from Carol's policies. His friends thought he was crazy. With no income and no job to come home to, how on earth could he justify the expense?

He knew this wasn't only about having a good time, though. They needed to heal. *We needed to get away from everybody and everything that reminds us of Carol. Just the two of us. Otherwise, we'd never have got out from under this dark cloud that still hangs over our heads. At least it's a little better now.*

The two emails from his new sponsors had given him the injection of confidence he needed. Now, he knew how he would survive, at least professionally. This was exactly what he had hoped would happen. With six weeks to pour everything he had into this podcast, it was finally getting off the ground.

He checked his watch. Only a few more minutes remained before the interview. He slipped his headphones on, plugged in the microphone, and opened a camera app on the computer to double-check his appearance. His deep-green t-shirt was wrinkled and dirty, but that didn't show on-screen, thankfully. It did give him pause, however.

Your clothes are old and scrappy. You look like a pile of laundry, man. Remember all those power suits back home? Those bold, colorful ties with the crisp white button-up shirts? The well-polished shoes?

He wasn't even wearing shoes now, and he was about to speak with a man who could completely change the course of humanity's fight against cancer.

Sometimes, he missed the suits. He wasn't quite sure if jeans and a t-shirt were a real improvement or not. Even though he was now the proud host of what was about to become a profitable podcast, he was less professional than he ever had been in his entire life.

Still, he knew he had work to do. This wasn't the time to analyze aesthetics. No matter what he wore or how he looked, he had to be the professional he had always been.

One last look into the camera left him a little startled. He had never really noticed how the stress had thinned him out. Quite obviously, he'd lost weight in the past year. His cheekbones protruded slightly. Stress had always spiked his metabolism, and that hadn't changed.

He sighed heavily.

Hopefully, this is the start of something new. I can settle into this venture, and maybe my body will relax. I'm withering away to nothing over here. Alexis deserves better than that.

That little girl was his life now. He worked hard on this podcast because he needed to support her, and he wanted to offer her the stability he had lost. It was something they had both missed lately.

Of course, that was before they accidentally unearthed an undead vampire girl and brought her back to life. That was a new wrinkle he wasn't quite sure how to process—and this wasn't the time to do that.

The light flashed on his microphone as he logged into the conference call. He smiled into the camera as Dr. Thurgood's booming voice greeted him from the other side of the globe.

"Good evening, Dr. Thurgood. Thank you for agreeing to this interview…"

CHAPTER EIGHT

The next afternoon, Vickie approached Alexis as she stared at her phone while seated in the red velvet chair of the library.

"What are you doing?"

"Reading."

Vickie glanced at the bookcase. "Don't you need a book to do that?"

The girl laughed and showed her the screen on her phone. "Not always. I'm reading a book in an e-reader. See?"

She walked closer to observe as the girl swiped her finger across the phone to move the pages of text back and forth across the screen. "It's really hard to keep up with all the differences between our times. We were excited when our town got a new book every six months or so. They were always big and heavy, but we were so happy to see them. Now, you have a book that fits in your palm?" She had begun to settle well into this new language. The contractions had been strange at first but grew easier the more she used them. Thankfully, her ability to learn at an accelerated pace gave her a distinct advantage.

"Yeah, I think the Internet is like the printing press of our generation. There are thousands of new books published on here every day. And with a few taps on this screen, I can buy them, open them, and start reading within minutes. I can take notes, highlight stuff, and send quotes to friends. It's totally cool."

Vickie turned away from her and stared at the bookcase again. "You know, we had a decent number of books on these shelves before I went to sleep. My dad loved to read and educate himself. And he always told me that we vampires could learn faster than normal humans. That's why we had so many. I can't imagine what his reaction would be if he saw how many books were on this bookcase now."

Alexis laughed. "Or how about all the books you can store on your phone?"

She shook her head as if the thought was beyond imagining. "It's remarkable. It really is. What else can you show me? I want to learn more."

Alexis locked her phone and slipped it into her pocket. "Well, this is as good a time as any to show you TV."

"TV?"

"Yep. I waited because I thought it might freak you out. But I think you're ready for it. Let's go downstairs."

They descended the stairs and Alexis paused when they reached the ground floor. "Wait, going down there won't cause you to panic or anything, will it? I mean, you were locked down there for hundreds of years. I don't want to cause any problems for you." She was half-afraid of

another emotional outburst that might damage something
—or injure someone.

Vickie waved her hand in dismissal. "Don't worry about
it. I know I won't go back to sleep. I can handle it."

When they reached the basement, they saw Alexis'
father sitting in the closet, mixing a batch of mortar.

"Oh, hey, Dad."

"Hi, girls. What are you up to?"

"I thought I'd show Vickie the TV."

Craig laughed. "Your life is about to change forever,
Vickie. Hey, I forgot to ask you—do you mind if I close this
hole? You don't need to...I don't know, get back into this
coffin or anything, do you?"

Vickie shook her head. "I think I've seen enough of that
box for a lifetime. Go ahead and close it. I won't need to
take it with me. That coffin was more of a connection to
my past than a necessity."

He gave her a thumbs-up as he slopped mortar onto the
existing bricks before pressing the first replacement into
position.

"Okay, have a seat on the couch," Alexis told her. "I'll get
things going. But try not to freak out, okay?"

"Why would I freak out?"

She honestly had no fears about this, but the second the
giant TV screen turned on to display an episode of *Law &
Order* with German dubbing, Vickie fought her instinct to
react physically.

While the detectives onscreen worked their way
through a murder investigation, her mind went into over-
drive in an attempt to make sense of what played out in
front of her eyes.

"How… What…"

Alexis giggled and gestured to the magical screen. "This is TV, Vickie."

"But there are no people here."

"Nope, this is what we call a video transmission. It's a recording of what people actually did at one point. We call these programs TV shows. The people on the screen are actors, like in a play. They pretended to be these characters, and they were recorded on the video. It's, uh… like if you take a group of paintings showing a rabbit running through a field and place them side by side to show its progress, only this one also includes the sound. Then the TV station replays it for us to watch and broadcasts it through the airwaves to reach our TV."

"This is really unbelievable." She gaped at the screen, her expression awed. "So, what else can you see with TV? Can you tell them what to do?"

"No." Alexis laughed. "I guess this is another one of those technologies that I take for granted. This is only a replay of something that has already happened. You can't change it at all. But you can see all kinds of things like cartoons, games, sports. Lots of stuff."

She then pulled up the program guide and found the channel that offered cartoons. The bright colors and vivid imagery were a complete shock to Vickie's system.

"So, these are cartoons. They're not real, only drawings that people made."

"Moving drawings?"

"In a way, yeah. Think of it like that explanation I gave you for the painting with the rabbit. It's the same thing."

Vickie shook her head, mesmerized as the impossible

manifested before her eyes. "If I'd had this when I was younger, I don't think I would have done anything else. I would have sat here at all hours of the day. I would also have been condemned as a witch, but that's beside the point. How do you fight the urge to sit here every waking moment of your life?"

Alexis shrugged. "Honestly? It gets boring after a while. But there are many people who do have that problem, especially in America."

Craig brushed his hands off and stepped out of the closet to take a break and see what the girls were watching. "I used to be one of those people. I grew up watching TV as much as possible. Whenever I was home, that screen was on too. But Alexis' mom didn't grow up that way, and she knew that kids who watched TV all day had a lot of issues later in life. So, we limited the amount of time she was allowed to watch."

Alexis shook her head. She had many friends who watched more than she did. The screen time limits imposed for her were always a little too strict for her tastes. But since her mom had died, her dad had been fairly lax about it, and she took advantage whenever she could. It was perhaps one of the few good things that had emerged from her death, although the only comfort it really offered was mindless distraction.

"This wonderful thing can damage you?" Vickie scrunched her brows together. "Does it burn your eyes?"

"I guess it would if you stopped blinking." Craig chuckled. "No, it causes problems with your brain. Most of these great inventions are double-edged swords. They're great on the surface, but if you use them the wrong way, you can cause damage to yourself and others."

"Ooh, I have an idea!" Alexis snatched the remote and pressed the buttons to bring up an online streaming service. She searched for the word "vampire" in the box at the top of the screen. "You've wondered about how we see vampires in fantasy, and we've wondered what the differences are."

"Good call, Lex. Pull up some vampire movies and see how she reacts."

"They make shows about vampires?" Vickie asked.

Alexis nodded while the service loaded the search results. "Oh, yes. Lots of them and different kinds. Some are darker than others, so I want to show you two of them. The first is a more recent kind of vampire that everyone seemed to love...for some reason."

She clicked on the poster marked *Twilight*.

Over the next two hours, the girls laughed at the acting while Craig finished rebuilding the wall inside the closet. After the movie was over, the girls looked at each other with broad smiles.

"Well? What did you think?"

Vickie wrapped her arms around her knees and pulled them up to her chest. "I don't really know what to think. But the ideas in the movie were...interesting. Not accurate, but interesting."

"So, you don't sparkle?" Alexis could barely get the words out without laughing.

The other girl tucked a strand of her long black hair behind her ear. "You know we don't. I don't even know why someone would ever think that. The other really funny part was the red eyes. Bloodsuckers don't look any different than anyone else. If they did, they wouldn't survive. Everyone would see them coming."

"So, bloodsuckers don't look any different than other vampires?"

"No, they look like everyone else. Exactly like me. Put me in modern clothing, and I blend in, apparently. Bloodsuckers are the same way. If you knew that they had red eyes, you wouldn't go anywhere near them. They wouldn't be able to catch any prey and they'd die off. That was stupid. Almost as stupid as the sparkly skin. It really was incredibly pointless."

"And what about being indestructible?"

That was a vampire feature that Vickie wished she had. "If that were true, you'd see many more vampires running around right now. Our skin is not like granite. We have flesh and bone like anything else. They did get our fast running speed right, but we don't climb trees like that."

Alexis continued to laugh. "I have never sat through that movie in my life. Oh, man, that was worth it. I'm so glad you're here." She meant it, too. Having another female presence around was comforting.

Craig emerged from the closet once again and wiped the sweat and dust from his brow. "Why don't you show her *Dracula*? There has to be at least one version of it on there."

Sure enough, beneath *Twilight* in the search results was a Dracula movie starring Bela Lugosi.

"That's what I wanted to choose next. This is a really old one, but it'll give you a more traditional look at what our world once thought of vampires."

Vickie laughed again at the end of the short film.

"So that's still funny? I guess this one got stuff wrong, too?"

"It sure did. I don't have a problem with garlic. In fact, I think it's delicious. Wooden stakes and holy items don't have an effect on me. The holy items aspect is very interesting, though, because we are actually a very religious people."

"That's right." Alexis pointed at her. "You said your parents prayed over you the night they brought you down here."

Vickie nodded. "We have our own relationship with God, so holy items don't bother us. And you have already seen that I have a reflection in the mirror. And I don't turn into a bat."

"Does sunlight bother you?" Alexis' father asked as he attached the new lock to the closet door. He hadn't noticed any signs of this, but given all the other funnies, he might as well ask.

"No. I love the sun. I don't know why everyone thinks that we vampires can't go out in daylight. It's such a peculiar idea."

Alexis turned the TV off. "Okay, so that's the stuff they got wrong. What about what was missing? What can vampires do that wasn't shown here?"

Vickie thought for a moment. "Those first vampires seemed to show super-strength at times. That is true. But generally, those strength reserves are saved for moments when we are in a heightened state."

"Like when you perceive a threat?"

"Or when a car suddenly stops in the middle of the road?" Craig interjected.

"It's our natural reaction to a threat. It's not something we can really help. We have a built-in need to protect and serve, especially our own kind and particularly our own families. So that's a big one." Her mind drifted back to her father kicking into enhanced speed while sprinting out of town.

"And we do have a strong ability to sense and understand threats as they develop. Our skin tingles when we are threatened by someone or something. Our animal-like instincts take over, and we tap into those powerful senses and abilities almost automatically."

"So you can't control your temper?" Alexis asked.

"I wouldn't say that. But I will say that it is best to keep us from feeling threatened. We have limited control over that, but the threat brings it out of us in a very powerful way."

Craig nodded and thought back to the demolished car handle he'd discovered during their fateful trip to the city.

I'd hate to see what she would do if she lost control.

"There was actually something else in that *Twilight* movie that they seemed to get right—family. There were many tribes in the movie, and everyone watched out for and took care of each other. That describes many vampire families. We live to take care of each other and do whatever we have to do to protect them."

"Well, I'll be honest. I thought that movie would be a giant swing and a miss." Alexis set the remote down. "The concept was so silly that I thought there was no way any of it was accurate."

Vickie nodded. "I understand. But the second one—the black-and-white movie—was far more inconsistent with what vampires really are. We're not mopey teenagers, but we also are not diabolical monsters. Most of us, anyway, are merely normal people trying to coexist in the world."

Alexis' dad stopped repairing the drywall and looked at her.

"Most of us?"

CHAPTER NINE

Craig sat at his desk in the tower that evening and stared out at the city once again. Instead of opening his laptop, however, he flipped the cover of his small black journal open. As he leafed through the book in search of the next empty page, his eyes caught glimpses of previous entries that he had written. He usually tried his best to skip past them but sometimes, he'd see a line that was scribbled so harshly that he couldn't resist re-reading it.

Every time he saw one, he shook his head to try to push those emotions back a little farther. Reliving that pain wouldn't do him any good.

He reached the next blank page and began writing, doing his best to empty his thoughts before he would turn in for bed.

10:09 PM

The Tower

Feeling: Confused

My research for this season of the podcast is going extremely well. I had no idea how many treatments there were for cancer, at least in development, anyway. I sometimes wonder, if I had started this research a year or two ago, is things would have turned out any differently. Maybe I could have found a way to help my wife, I don't know.

I do know that it's dangerous to go down that road. I've done a lot of reading on lost your spouse blog posts, and the first thing they all say is to not blame yourself. It's the hardest thing to put into practice, though. If there was something out there that could have helped and you didn't find it, you can't help but think that maybe you could have made the difference.

But that doesn't change anything now, so I keep moving forward as best I can.

One of the more interesting tidbits that I came across had to do with two doctors in Switzerland. They've spent years developing a method of blocking cancerous cells from multiplying in the body. Last year, they were given the Nobel prize for their discoveries and contributions to the field of health and science.

I looked it up, and the Nobel prize is worth a cool million bucks. Make a significant contribution to the scientific community, and they'll make you a millionaire.

Naturally, my thoughts move constantly to this girl who is now staying with us. Vickie is sweet, but I have my concerns about her.

Mainly the fact that she's a vampire.

Honestly, there are no blogs out there talking about what to do if you live with a teenage vampire. I keep thinking I'll wake up in the morning and this will all turn out to be some kind of weird, hyper-realistic dream. But it continues. I wake up, and she's here.

Not that I'm complaining. She hasn't caused any trouble

outside of a little damage to the car, but I bought the insurance on it. And my repairs to the house have come along fine.

But what if I brought her back to America and let the scientific community know about her? Like, "Hey, I found a vampire. You might want to know about this."

They'd go crazy, right? And it would be a good thing for everybody.

The reason I'd do it in America is because I already know the human rights laws there. Vickie would be treated with respect. It's not like I'd turn her over to the doctors in Nazi Germany or anything.

They'd no doubt make sure she wasn't mistreated. They'd merely want to study her. It would be an earth-shattering development in the study of human existence—the actual confirmed presence of a vampire living among us.

And what would that do for me? I'd get a ton of press. They'd put me on every late-night show, every talk show, and every news report. My face and name would be everywhere. The Journal Sentinel would be forced to put me on the front page of the paper, which would be so delicious, I would probably frame it.

What would that press be worth? They'd probably give me prize money too. If I can't turn "I discovered a vampire" into at least a million bucks, then I have no business trying to run anything on my own. That's a slam dunk.

Shoot, even a nest egg of a few hundred thousand dollars would do the trick. That life insurance money will go toward so many medical bills anyway.

And how would that affect the podcast? With my name everywhere, people would have to look me up online. Every interview I did, I'd mention the podcast and where you can find it.

Oh, man, it would be so sweet. I'd jump up to a million subscribers overnight.

My ad rates would go through the roof. Major brands would pay me thousands to secure place on each episode. I could multiply my income by a factor of ten, and it would be steady income, too.

Seriously, this would be the responsible decision. We could bring her to America and let the government know about her. She doesn't have any family here anymore, anyway. Is that too cold for me to say?

She'd become a celebrity. Isn't that what every teenager wants?

I could pay the house off and simply focus on doing my podcast. I wouldn't have to work so many long hours on it, either, because the listeners would be waiting for me. Not only would it fix our income issue, but it would also provide more time for me to spend with Alexis.

I could focus on raising her properly. That's what she needs, right?

Craig closed the journal and stared out the window into the darkness of the night. The thought of turning in Vickie brought so many mixed emotions. He didn't care so much about the money as he cared about whether or not the money could provide for him and for Alexis. That's what he told himself, anyway.

Reluctantly, he opened his laptop and pulled up their finances. The medical bills were slowly being paid off, but a few were past due already. He was still waiting for the final life insurance check to arrive, which he expected to see by the time they returned home.

Alexis had, no doubt, enjoyed this trip. He had too and

wanted to do more of them. But without a steady source of income, that would be impossible.

Craig sighed once again and shook his head. He decided he would know what to do when the time was right. The answer would somehow be clear to him.

He closed his laptop, descended the tower steps, and crossed the main level to the staircase in the foyer.

The hour was late, and he assumed the girls would be sleeping after a long day. To his surprise, he heard laughter coming from the room and noticed a light shining beneath the door.

Intrigued, he slid over to the door and pressed an ear close to the crack to listen in. He felt mildly guilty but decided—for only this one time, of course—to indulge his curiosity over their hilarity.

"So you never dated?" Alexis asked Vickie.

"No. It's hard to date when you're a vampire. And in our circles, the parents arranged suitors. Mine simply never got around to it, I guess."

"Can't you date humans and keep it quiet? Maybe keep the teeth away and don't smile too big?"

"Back in my day, you didn't really date. You got married. That's it. But we never got to know anybody. I wasn't allowed to move freely through the city. Meeting boys wasn't that important."

"We should bring you home with us to America. You should see some of the boys there. They would love you."

Vickie didn't respond to that idea. The thought of leaving her home with people she had so recently met— and leaving behind what was left of her life—scared her. The thought scared Craig, too.

Bring another teenager home and worry about boys sniffing around her? That sounds like my worst nightmare. I already have one daughter I have to lose sleep over. Then again, I did consider something similar.

"I don't know. Leaving my home..." Vickie trailed off, her tone tense.

"What's keeping you here? We can be your family. It would be great, at least for us."

"What do you mean?" the other girl asked suspiciously.

"My dad and I are alone now. I know he's trying his best, but he's obviously having a hard time with it. He throws himself into his work and thinks it'll make him feel better, but it doesn't. We're in Austria on this once-in-a-lifetime vacation and he spends almost all his time up in the tower."

Craig looked guiltily at his feet.

She's right. I barely spend any time with her now.

"But since you've been here," Alexis continued, "it's been great. My dad has hung out with us, spent time doing fun things, and made sure you're taken care of. I think...I don't know— I know my dad loves me, but it feels like he trusts me too much. I used to feel like he didn't trust me at all. Now, he lets me go around freely and never checks in. He worries about you because you're new and he doesn't know if you can handle yourself. Sometimes, I wish he'd care a little more."

Craig swallowed a lump in his throat. He focused so hard on being strong and trusting his little girl that he forgot, sometimes, that she was still having a hard time of her own too.

"Besides," his daughter continued. "I really like you. It's

great to have another girl around and you still need a lot of help, if you want to be 'normal.'" She laughed awkwardly. "I didn't mean that to sound the way it did."

"No, I understand, and I am so happy that you are the ones who found me. After being hidden for so long, even walking around and living a normal life is what I crave right now. It's wonderful to be able to walk through the city and see what has changed. That's only one of those things that you take for granted when you can do it all the time. I couldn't back in my day. Thanks to you, now I can. The freedom is exhilarating."

Craig nodded to himself, then knocked on the door.

"Come in," Alexis called.

He poked his head in through the doorway. "Hey, girls, I'm heading to bed. Does anyone need anything?"

The two of them looked at each other and shook their heads. "No, I think we're good, Dad. Are you doing okay?"

He nodded. "Yeah, I'm doing fine. Vickie, are you all right?"

She smiled. "Yep," she said somewhat forcefully. Alexis giggled at the attempt at slang. "Things are good here."

He smiled back. "Good. Well, uh…good night. Love you."

"Love you, too, Dad."

Craig pulled the door shut and walked one room over. He flipped the light switch on and shut the door behind him before he dropped his journal onto the bed.

He sat on the edge for a second, then picked up the journal and pen one more time and cradled it in his lap.

10:28 PM

Bedroom

There's no way I can give Vickie up. She's doing too much good for my daughter. And she wants a normal life, not fame or notoriety. I need to find a way to give that to her if I can. It's the least I can do for the help she's giving Alexis. It would be a poor thank you, indeed, to turn her over to the government or science.

What was I thinking with that idea, anyway?

I'll have to sit down with Alexis and talk about what it would take to bring Vickie back with us. At this rate, it looks like I'll head into the next school year with two daughters instead of one.

In moments like these, I sure wish Carol were around to guide me. Any advice would be appreciated.

But I guess, in some ways, I know she's watching—and probably laughing at me, too. And calling me an idiot at the same time. A loveable idiot, but still an idiot.

CHAPTER TEN

For the first time since they'd discovered her, Alexis woke before Vickie did the next morning. But it wasn't because she was more well-rested. It was because of a comment that the vampire had made the previous night.

"I don't know anything about the Circle. But I know that they had something to do with my parents. They sounded terrified. I'd never heard my father so scared in my life."

It wasn't the craziest thing that she ever said, but it had stuck in Alexis' mind for some reason. She slid quietly out of bed, grabbed her laptop, and slipped out of the room so that she didn't disturb her friend.

Alexis tiptoed into the kitchen and opened the blinds to allow in enough sunshine to wake her body up. Then, she poured herself a glass of juice and flipped open her computer to do a little Googling.

There has to be something out there about this group. Maybe I can find some answers for her.

She knew that Vickie was desperate to know more.

Four hundred years lying in a coffin thinking about it had to have eaten away at her, even if it was only on a subconscious level. But she didn't know if she would be able to find anything, and she didn't want to get Vickie's hopes up. By searching for it in private, she could do so without the pressure of delivering any tangible information.

Surprisingly, that didn't prove to be a problem. After about fifteen minutes of searching, she had all the disturbing details in front of her.

Her father chose that moment to stumble into the kitchen with a tired smile on his face.

"Morning, kid," he said and squeezed his eyes shut to wake them up. Reverse logic, but it seemed to work for him.

"Hey, Dad. Vickie's still sleeping."

"Good. That means she's more comfortable. If that girl wants to be normal, she needs to operate on the same schedule as the rest of us, right?"

He retrieved a mug from the cabinet, put it in the coffee maker, and pressed a few buttons to turn it on. While he waited for the mug to fill, he put both his hands on the counter and hung his head.

"Dad, Vickie was talking about something last night that bothered me."

Craig looked up. "Oh?"

"Yeah, she mentioned something called the Circle."

"Right." He rubbed his eyes. "That's something she mentioned to me, too. It sounded like something to do with a group of vampires or whatever from way back." He yawned and stretched while the coffee trickled and the scent of the grounds permeated the room. Finally, he lifted the mug and sniffed the aroma to give himself an extra preview of what was to come.

"I did some searching, Dad. It's…uh, it's bad."

"Lay it on me." Craig pulled up a chair from across the table and sat down.

"So, it looks like the Circle's full name is the Slayer Circle. And it's exactly what it sounds like."

"A circle of slayers, with slayers being a group of people who kill vampires?"

She pulled up one of the pages she'd bookmarked in a tab. "Yep. But they weren't only a people who fought vampires. This was a religious sect. Their goal—their mission—was to eliminate the vampire species from Earth. They believed that vampires were agents of Satan himself, and they were very active during the Renaissance."

"And that would be right around the time Vickie and her family were living here." He sipped the coffee and waited for the caffeine to feed into his bloodstream.

"Exactly." Alexis continued to scan the information on her laptop. "It was founded by a preacher named Elijah Schmidt. His son, Isaac, was a victim of vampires. One night, he went out into the fields and never came back. In the morning, they searched for him and found him lying face-down in the long grass. He had puncture wounds on several parts of his body, and he was as pale as a sheet. They determined that all the blood was drained from his body." She shuddered involuntarily as an icy chill traced her spine.

"Okay, so the bloodsuckers got him. Wow."

"And all they left behind was the shell of his body. Elijah was devastated, even to the point where his marriage failed and his wife left him. She said he lost his mind. He had a dream, allegedly, where God sat him down and told him that the reason his son was sacrificed was because Elijah was to be the leader of a movement against vampires. It was his mission to rid the world of the species by any means necessary."

He leaned forward and rested his elbows on the table. "But what about all the vampires who aren't bloodsuckers?"

She scanned the page quickly. "It doesn't say. I would imagine that they didn't really differentiate between the two. If they were vampires, they were evil. They moved throughout Europe and cut down everyone they could find."

"How much damage did they do?"

"There aren't any real records, but they credit themselves with the slaughter of tens of thousands of vampires. They called it the Sang Crusade."

This information had all but overloaded her father's brain. He wasn't used to thinking this hard this early—not since he'd lost his job, at least. "Why the name?"

"Sang is short for Sanguinarian. Those are the bloodsuckers. They feast on the blood of humans and animals, and that's where they get their energy."

"Okay, so this group of people led by some crackpot who's mad at vampires for killing his son decides that they will simply wipe out the entire race of vampires indiscriminately, based on the assumption that all vampires are bloodthirsty savages?"

Alexis nodded. "And here's where it gets really sick. They purposely did the most of their killing during the

Thirty Years' War. Why? Because during that time period, everybody was getting killed. They were able to waltz through the countryside and murder virtually anyone whom they believed to be a vampire. They used the cover of a bloody conflict to kill whoever they wanted. The wider the war spread, the easier the rampage became."

"That is a seriously devious scheme," Craig agreed. He was slightly uneasy about the fact that he was impressed by it.

"Some of these entries claim that they inflamed the war and other religious conflicts deliberately to maintain their cover. They took advantage of the chaos going on in the world so that they could carry out their bloody plan."

He sipped his coffee in silence for a moment and processed the main points of the conversation again in his head. A thought stood out that seemed worth exploring. "You know, you said something interesting earlier."

"What?"

"You said, 'they credit themselves' with killing tens of thousands of vampires during this crusade. That's present tense. These guys aren't still around, are they?"

"I don't know how active they are, but they have a website where they lay this all out. Seriously, the Slayer Circle at least wants to appear to be a thing. And if vampires know this..."

"Then there could be more out there, but they're keeping their mouths shut out of fear."

"These guys are doing the opposite of hiding." Alexis shook her head in disbelief. "While vampires are staying quiet, the Slayer Circle website details all their teachings—

supposedly backed by the Bible—and where they get together on a regular basis."

"What, like Boy Scouts and mass meetings?"

"I guess so. Supposedly, they operate out of the crypts beneath larger cathedrals throughout Europe—with permission from the various church leaders, of course."

"Which implies that at least some members of those churches may approve of this crusade. Either that or they simply think there's no harm in letting them use the facilities. These guys get sicker by the minute."

Alexis clutched her father's forearm where it rested on the table. "Dad, we can't leave her here. I wanted her to come with us before but now, we have no choice. We need to find a way to bring her home with us."

"Trust me, I want to. But don't tell her what we want to do yet. For one thing, she has to want to come, too. We can't force her if she chooses otherwise. And another problem is that if I can't resolve the logistics behind it, I don't want to get her hopes up only to let her down. It's not as simple as buying an extra plane ticket."

Alexis sighed and released his arm. "I know. I'll try to keep it to myself. But we have to figure something out. She's really anxious to get out and away from all this."

Her dad furrowed his brow. "She isn't interested in staying at home? I thought she said she didn't know."

"When did she say that?" Alexis asked suspiciously.

Craig remembered in time where and when he'd heard that particular comment. He took a casual sip of coffee to buy time and hastily drafted a lie. "Oh, I talked briefly about it to her. I wanted to find out her plans for the future or if she even had any. That's what she said."

Nice save, Craig.

Alexis gestured at the house with her hands. "This isn't her home, Dad. Nothing in here reminds her of home. Okay, maybe a couple of things. But the rest looks nothing like what she grew up with. Her parents aren't here. Her friends are all gone. She wants a fresh start. She needs a fresh start."

He tapped the side of his mug nervously as he shifted his brain into higher gear. "I don't quite know how we can pull it off yet. Like I said, I need to do some research and make plans before we can move forward. Let me work on that before we say anything to her. Maybe we can get her out of here."

He left it at that when Vickie walked into the kitchen, yawned, and stretched her back. "Good morning," she said to them both, and they returned the greeting. "What are you up to today?"

They exchanged a quick glance. "We were trying to decide if we would all go to the market today to get groceries or if only my dad wanted to go so we could stay home and away from any potential threats."

"Threats? Is there something I don't know about?"

Apparently, saying too much was a family trait.

"No, no," Alexis said hastily. "But you sounded nervous last night. That's all. You said the Circle was scary."

That was close.

"If the Circle is still out there, I would be nervous. But I don't think they are around anymore, whoever they were. A group of people organized four centuries ago wouldn't have survived this long, especially given how the world views my kind now. I should be in the clear."

Craig stood from the table with his mug. "To be safe, though, I think you should probably lay low today. You two can hang out here and watch TV or read. Maybe there's something else that Alexis can show you here that you haven't seen before."

Thankfully, she didn't seem to read anything into the feeble attempt to divert her. She had yet to learn the tells of a man grasping at straws and totally out of his depth. "Okay, we can…hang out here, if you want. But only for today, though. I'm eager to get out and live."

Alexis couldn't help but smile. Vickie was still adjusting to modern colloquialisms, but they came more naturally now. She'd talk like a real teenager in no time. "We're trying to figure all that out, Vickie. We want to make sure you have the best experience when you leave this place."

The girl smiled, oblivious to the bigger issues that weighed heavily on her companions.

Such a sweet gesture. These people are very thoughtful.

As per the hastily concocted cover story, Craig went grocery shopping. To kill time, Alexis showed Vickie more grooming tips and how to apply makeup for the first time. While it did distract the vampire for a while, it also provided another opportunity for the two girls to bond.

Meanwhile, Craig drove past a multitude of cathedrals on his way to the store. He'd never really paid them much attention before but now, he couldn't help but wonder how many housed the members of the sinister organization. At a stoplight, he stared at a smaller cathedral as tourists milled about the area. Only days earlier, it would have been an innocent sight, hardly out of the ordinary. Not anymore, though.

To get Vickie out of Europe and safely to America, I have to find a way to keep her in the castle as much as possible for the next week and a half. Either that or we all have to go out together to keep an eye on each other. I won't take any chances.

Of course, the girl had been hidden for four hundred years so it was very possible that she wasn't even on the radar. The stirrings of paranoia might be completely baseless. That said, if the Circle was as prevalent as they claimed, they might have spies anywhere. It wasn't a stretch that locations that had been home to their victims would be watched, or that they might be aware that the couple they'd slaughtered had a daughter who was never found. The sudden appearance of a fourteen-year-old girl might well trigger unwanted attention.

Back at the house, the two girls admired their makeup in the mirror and laughed comfortably together. While Vickie focused on packing everything away, Alexis watched her in the mirror.

Okay, it's official. I'm adopting her as my sister, and nobody hurts my family. Don't worry, Vickie. We'll get you out of here.

CHAPTER ELEVEN

Alexis dragged her fingertips across the granite countertop of the kitchen island. Her eyes were puffy from a lack of sleep and she rubbed them in irritation. The anxiety was killing her, and a relatively sleepless night hadn't helped. How could they save Vickie from a foe they couldn't track? They needed a council of war.

While she didn't expect her father to get up at dawn, she had listened hopefully for signs of stirring and so wasn't that surprised when he shuffled in at five in the morning. They eyed one another with a shared look of understanding but left it at that while he focused on his coffee. Teenage girls generally didn't get up at that ridiculous hour on their own, so his surprise was justified. But then again, most teenage girls didn't have to deal with the need to protect innocents from being murdered either.

"Is something the matter?" he asked her as he prepped the pot to brew.

"Just save some coffee for me," she slurred as she pulled a stool up and sat at the island. "Why are you up so early?"

"I can't sleep. Apparently, we're starting to make this a habit. Maybe by the time we're ready to leave, all three of us will have a good night's sleep at the same time."

She propped her weary head on her fist and groaned. "I hate this."

"Welcome to my life, kiddo. I used to do this all the time. I guess I still do." The kitchen filled with the savory aroma of coffee as it dribbled into the pot. Her dad spun and rested both palms on the island counter in front of her. Then, his eyes narrowed, he leaned forward and lowered his head to get a good look at her.

"So, what is it? Either you're sick or something is wrong and you're worried. Spit it out."

She forced her body to straighten and struggled to push it into full wakefulness. "I want to talk more about Vickie. We both agreed we can't talk about it in front of her."

He drew his eyebrows together in the first stirrings of concern. "Is something wrong with her?" Even if everything seemed okay, like any good father, he still worried. That, and Alexis had mentioned that she wanted him to be a little more protective. He was merely doing his job. "Did she do something to you?"

"Dad, knock it off," she replied, her tone annoyed. "Vickie's fine. We're fine. It's not like that. I want her to come home with us, that's all. And you don't want her to know, so we have to sneak off to discuss it."

Craig nodded as the coffee maker completed the brew. He retrieved the pot and poured the hot liquid into two waiting cups.

"Cream and sugar?"

"Yes, please." Alexis slumped onto the counter once more.

He located the items in question and paused to fix her with a cautious look. "Look, I don't know what additional information I can bring to this conversation yet. I think it would be great. If you feel safe around her and you're not hiding anything, then it could be good for everyone involved. But it won't be that easy." He opened the cream carton and set it on the countertop next to his daughter.

She grabbed it and slid one of the mugs over to her. "Why not? We have enough room at the house. She comes with us, and we call her my long-lost cousin or something." She poured the sweet white substance into the coffee and watched it cloud as she slid the carton away from her.

Craig picked it up and poured. "What we call her isn't really my concern. We can make up whatever story we want. But you can't simply walk into the country with another human being. She has to go through immigration and all that. She's a citizen of Austria, right? And one who never existed, for all history knows. She has no birth certificate and no death certificate."

He added a few scoops of sugar and fumbled for two spoons from the drawer in front of him. His movements were more by rote as he slipped the first into his cup and pushed the other over the counter with the sugar. His brain was already engaged elsewhere.

Alexis seemed as robotic as he did as she added sugar. "But is she a citizen of Austria, then?" She put the sugar down and stirred the coffee with her spoon. "That's exactly my point. The chances are, no one even knows she exists. Not after four hundred years."

"That doesn't mean we don't have to account for her when we travel." He blew gently over the top of his mug to cool the liquid. "That's only one of the obstacles we have to find solutions for." He sipped slowly and sighed as the heat warmed his body as it traveled down his throat.

Alexis followed his example and her sigh was almost an exact replica. "I'm sure there's a way to do it."

"There's more to it than that too. We haven't asked her yet. What if she doesn't want to?"

"What if I don't want to what?"

Alexis nearly fell off her stool when the unmistakable voice challenged them quietly. Neither had expected Vickie to be up this early. But there she was, and she looked about as exhausted as her companions felt.

"What are you drinking?" she croaked.

"Coffee," Craig announced briskly and raised his cup. "Do you want some?"

Vickie shrugged. "Sure. It can't hurt." She shuffled over to the counter and dragged herself onto the stool beside Alexis. "Now, what is this thing you're talking about that I don't want to do?"

He turned away to pour the coffee as he scrambled for a lie that could keep her calm and unsuspicious.

Alexis had other ideas.

"We were talking about you coming home with us to Milwaukee."

Craig almost dropped both the mug and pot and flashed her an annoyed glance. "Really?"

"What? She asked what we were talking about. We had to bring it up eventually, right?"

He sighed and nodded at Vickie. "We wanted to know if

you would want to come to Milwaukee with us. But that's only if you want to and if we can find a way to make it happen."

Vickie rested her head on her folded arms and stared at the sparkles on the granite countertop, deep in thought for a moment.

Craig slid the promised cup toward her. "It's a little bitter," he warned. "If you don't like it, there's cream and sugar here. Both of those will help make it a little sweeter."

Vickie thanked him and returned to the thoughts that had haunted her all night, now stirred back to life with new possibilities and a slew of new questions.

Should I go with them? What about my life here? Do I even have a life here? What am I clinging to? What would happen if I moved to another country with another family?

"Come on," Alexis urged. "You have nothing here. "Come with us and you can be whatever you want."

Craig sighed. If his daughter was so determined to open this can of worms, he might as well finish the job. "It's… more than that. We've done a little research. And if what we've read is correct, you might still be in danger here."

Vickie took a sip of the black coffee and curled her lip in disgust. The bitterness was bitingly unpleasant, exactly as he had warned. She added a small amount of cream and sugar and tried again. A few sips later, she had adapted to the beverage and found she rather enjoyed it. "What kind of danger?"

"I don't know if it's true or not, but Alexis says it's possible that the Circle is still here. Assuming the information is credible, they would target you the second they realized that you're a vampire."

An expression of concern washed over the girl's face. She thought of her parents and realized that the Circle wouldn't hesitate to kill her if they were right and they had murdered her family.

Vickie grimaced and pushed back a shaft of pain. While she didn't want to accept it, common sense told her that her parents had likely been murdered by the Circle. She had to face that and accept it. "I'd hate to wake up after all this time and still be killed anyway. That's not what my parents wanted."

"So, we get you out." Excitement built in Alexis' voice. "Come back with us. We can help you live life as a normal teenager like me. There aren't any circles in America, right, Dad?"

Craig sighed. "You read the information and never mentioned any. But I have to add the caveat—as far as we know. Aside from that, we have any number of steps we need to take before we can get there, and I've only begun to try to find solutions. There's no guarantee that the Circle won't follow us or already be there waiting. We'll still need to be careful."

"So you're coming?" Alexis asked eagerly.

Vickie glanced at the kitchen, her inner conflict intense.

This is my home. But it's also not my home anymore. It's something else entirely. My parents aren't here. There really is nothing to tie me to this place. But should I abandon what's left of my legacy here?

She sighed. "Okay, I'll think about it."

Alexis nearly squealed with excitement. Her dad chuckled.

"But if I do agree, you have to teach me all about the

place where you live," she said as she took another sip of coffee.

"Milwaukee? Oh, you'll love it. It has…" She trailed off. Describing the city she had spent her whole life in was remarkably difficult. She had taken all the special things her hometown had to offer for granted.

"Come on, sweetheart, surely you can think of something," Craig prompted.

"There's beer."

Her dad shook his head. "Not for you, there isn't. Yes, there's beer, Vickie. It's an alcoholic drink that I think your parents might have been familiar with. It'll be a few years before you can enjoy that particular drink, though."

"What, you can't drink at four hundred years old?" his daughter asked.

He laughed. "If we bring her back, she can't be four hundred years old. She'd be a teenager, like you, and teenagers can't drink."

"Still, the brewery tours are fun," Alexis told her. "You get to see how the beer is made and stuff."

Vickie nodded with an empty look in her eyes. She had absolutely no idea what they were talking about.

"Okay," Craig said briskly, "let's find some other reasons why Milwaukee is great besides beer. It's very modern, but it's smaller than Salzburg, so it's not so overwhelming. We have some big buildings, but not as many as the larger cities."

"Oh, the festivals!" Alexis practically cheered when those came to mind. "There are tons of festivals during the summer months. It's practically a tradition. Milwaukee is known for the different festivals."

Vickie sipped her coffee quietly. She knew what a festival was, at least, but the modern ones might be very different from those she'd seen. She waited patiently for someone to provide more details before she commented.

"You'd probably love GermanFest. It's a celebration of Germany and Austria. All the culture that you come from. You'd feel right at home there. They do all kinds of German stuff, play German music, that sort of thing."

"That sounds like it…could be fun," she said as she cracked a wan smile.

"And hey, speaking of music," Craig added enthusiastically, "what about SummerFest?"

Alexis nodded excitedly. "Yeah, SummerFest! That would be perfect for us. It's the world's largest music festival. Seriously, everybody goes. It's two weeks of live music at the lakefront. You go and wander from stage to stage all day, check out the bands, buy food, play games…it's so much fun."

Craig smirked. SummerFest was fun—if you were young. He sighed as he recalled his first SummerFest with Carol. A night of drinks, games, music, and romance. They had made some wonderful memories there through the years. Today, he wouldn't be caught dead going down there and dealing with all the drunks. But for the two girls, he could see why that would be a good time.

"We have museums, too," he said. "You can learn a lot about our country and our culture. We have a beautiful art museum at the lake, and we can take you to all the different ones and teach you about our history.

Alexis crossed her legs. "So, what do you think?"

Vickie shrugged. "I guess it sounds nice. I don't know

too much about everything you described, but it sounds like there's plenty to do."

Craig nodded as he polished off his first cup of coffee and walked to the pot for a refill. "Milwaukee is actually an underrated town. Most of the country doesn't really care about us. But we have our share of history. Did you know we're the birthplace of the typewriter?" He laughed at the foolishness of the question. "No, I guess you wouldn't know that. You probably don't even know what that is. But there are many interesting little tidbits like that."

Vickie gave him a blank stare. "What is a typewriter?"

Craig smiled. "Funny you should ask…"

CHAPTER TWELVE

Craig sighed with real irritation as he reached the bottom of the stairs. He flipped the light switch and lit up the basement rec room, which had transformed from a fun, clean space into a construction site. On the plus side, the doorknob had been fixed. Now he merely had to check how the wall was holding up.

He opened the door, stepped into the darkness, and ran his hands along the wall on his left. He pushed gently on the brick at first, then threw his full weight against it to make sure that it was solid. There was no give, thank goodness.

All right, not too bad for an amateur job. Maybe I could go into masonry. I wonder what the pay is like.

Now that the hidden room was properly bricked up again and the doorknob replaced, it was time to focus on the drywall Vickie's panic attack had broken. He collected a plastic bag full of supplies stashed in a corner and knelt in front of the hole. Anxious to get the job done quickly, he withdrew a package of mesh material, a flat putty knife, and a small jar of spackle.

Home improvement wasn't exactly his strong suit, but he knew enough to get by. And today, it wasn't only about getting by. It was about saving a significant amount of money in damage fees from the Airbnb host.

He held up a small square of mesh so he could gauge how much he needed for the hole, picked up a pair of scissors, and began to cut out the necessary section. The familiar laughter of two girls reached his ears, followed by the thump of feet on wooden stairs.

Craig sighed, There were times when he really enjoyed a little solitude. Working on home projects usually did the trick. But this wasn't his home, and the girls needed to entertain themselves somehow.

"What's up, girls?" he greeted them as they walked into the rec room.

"Hey, Dad. What are you fixing now?"

"The drywall." He finished cutting the mesh and shrugged. "I still have a little more work to do before I can paint and put all this behind us."

Alexis nodded and watched him work with a vaguely interested expression. "Do you think it'll be done in time?"

"Oh, yeah. This will only need to dry for a day or so. Then I can sand it and paint it. I actually found a bucket of paint in the closet here that I can use for touch-up, so it should be smooth sailing from here."

"Awesome." She plopped onto the couch.

"What will you two do? More TV?"

"We're here to watch a movie," Vickie said. Her voice wavered as she looked hesitantly at the screen. These modern activities were still intimidating, despite how well she'd managed to adapt thus far. "Alexis says there's something called 3D that I should see."

Craig looked at his daughter with an uneasy expression. "Are you sure she's ready for something like that?"

Alexis shrugged. "Why not? There's nothing wrong with watching a movie."

He returned to preparing his materials. "I simply think it could be a little overwhelming, that's all. Especially if she doesn't really understand the concept."

"She has to know this stuff, Dad." She found the remote and turned the TV on. "If she wants to be a teenager and not be a total outcast, these basics are essential." Quickly, she clicked around the screen until she reached a 3D movie selection called *The Last Adventure of Robin Hood.*

"This'll be perfect." She stood and grinned at her friend. "There's a lot of action in this movie, so you'll really experience the 3D properly."

She crouched in front of the TV and opened a small cabinet to retrieve two pairs of black-framed glasses. "But don't freak out, okay? Things will look like they're jumping out at you, but they won't really." She turned to the podcaster-turned-construction-worker. "Dad, are you in?" she asked before closing the cabinet.

"No thanks. I'm still a little busy here."

Of course. I can't remember the last time Dad watched a movie with me. That was Mom's thing. Thank goodness Vickie's here.

Craig dipped his putty knife in the spackle and spread a thin layer over the damaged area. His movements careful and precise, he pressed the mesh piece over the hole and used the spackle to hold it in place.

"What are you doing?" Vickie asked.

"I'm fixing this hole in the wall. This mesh piece helps the spackle stay in place as it dries. Once I've filled it properly and it has dried, I can use sandpaper to rub it down and blend it in with the rest of the wall. Then, I'll paint over it to match. Nobody will know the difference." He looked at her with a self-satisfied smirk.

I bet this is really impressive.

Unfortunately, that was not the reaction he received. Her empty expression said it all. She had no clue what he was talking about.

"I'm fixing this hole in the wall," he repeated. She nodded and looked at Alexis, who now held a pair of glasses in front of her.

"Enough construction talk. Put these on," she ordered. "The movie will look ten times better when you do."

Vickie slid the glasses on and looked at the other girl in confusion. "So how does this work? Why do I have to wear these?"

"Because that's how the 3D works. Without these glasses, we can't see the effect. With them on, the movies will look like it's happening right here instead of on the screen. Trust me, you'll love it."

"I don't understand. Why spend all your time down here watching something that looks like the real world instead of going somewhere and experiencing it for yourself?"

Craig smiled as he spread more spackle over the mesh.

She's smarter than she thinks.

"Just trust me. It's cool." Alexis pushed the button on the remote and cued the movie.

Craig tried to spread as much spackle into place as he could without pushing too much through. He kept one ear tuned to the movie and the girls, though, curious as to what Vickie's response might be.

Keep it thin. Too much and you'll be sanding for days.

It was too easy to be distracted by what might be happening behind him.

He heard Vickie gasp and leaned over to get a good look at the screen. The girl waved her hands wildly in the air while Alexis looked on and laughed. Craig could barely make out a large bird flying across the screen.

These dumb things. The only thing a 3D movie is good for is charging people more money. Nobody wants a gimmick.

"Get this thing out of my face!" Vickie swatted wildly at the air in front of her eyes.

Alexis laughed again. "It's not real. Let it happen. It's fun."

The girl took a long, deep breath to calm herself and the bird flew away when the rest of the movie began.

The laughter those two shared put a smile on Craig's face. It also brought a pang to his heart, because it reminded him so much of Carol. He hadn't heard his daughter really laugh for a long time. Vickie was definitely good for her, and he paused now and then in his work to simply soak the sound in. The odd twist their vacation had taken had certainly injected a little joy into her life again. He paused constantly in his work as he listened to her enjoy herself. That was the whole point of the trip—to find a little joy in life again.

After all the drama back at home, Craig had wanted to give Alexis a little fun and healing. He'd wanted her to enjoy herself and take in a little culture to boot. It might not have been as great as a beach vacation, but it was an interesting trip, nonetheless.

Plus, now, she had another female with her. The thought gave Craig pause.

Another female in the house again, and a teenager at that. Boy, I hope I know what I'm getting myself into. With Carol, I knew her quirks and needs. I could handle having her and Alexis. They were my girls. This isn't my girl. This is a stranger. Can I really handle that?

As a man who grew up with only brothers, Craig had a difficult enough time understanding and dealing with girls as they grew up. With a teenage girl, there were many more complications he wasn't used to. With two teenage girls, those complications multiplied.

And with a teenage vampire, there was an entirely new set of problems to contend with.

Still, as he finished his task and closed the spackle jar, their shared exuberant laughter pushed against those concerns and made them seem less challenging.

If it makes her happy again, it's worth it.

He stood with the materials in hand, smiled at the two of them, and packed everything on the closet shelf before he shut the door.

Vickie gasped and Craig spun to see her head bobbing back and forth as her hands clutched the arm of the couch.

"Vickie, loosen your grip. Don't do any damage to that couch. I can afford spackle, but new European furniture isn't in my budget."

"Okay," she shouted back, seemingly unaware that Craig wasn't in the middle of the same experience she was.

He watched as her fingers dug even deeper into the arm. "Vickie," he said more forcefully. "Loosen your grip!"

This time, she complied, but barely.

"It's okay, Vickie. It's only a show," Alexis told her. "You don't have to worry. It won't hurt you."

"I know." The girl clearly didn't believe her own words, though. Her neck stiffened, and she continued to flinch while her gaze remained fixed on the screen.

Craig walked behind the couch to see what they were watching. A hailstorm of arrows pierced enemies to the left and right. "I don't remember Robin Hood having such a brutal scene."

His daughter laughed. "This is a gritty reboot. They've gone for realism."

"It looks like it's working." He watched nervously as Vickie's fangs poked from her mouth.

Just then, a character in the movie cocked an arrow and released it directly at the camera. Before Craig could warn her, Vickie lurched back and scrambled onto her heels.

The arrow flew closer to the camera. She pushed up, backflipped over the couch, and leapt to one side. Unfortunately, she led with her right foot, which impacted with the wall beside her.

The force of the kick punched a softball-sized hole that drew a loud moan from him.

"Vickie!" Alexis shouted.

The girl hissed at the screen. Craig walked calmly to her and put his hand on her shoulder.

"It's fine." He removed the glasses slowly.

Her heavy breathing slowed as her world returned to normal. It had all been on the screen. Everything that had been unleashed by the glasses was bound by pixels again. There was no threat, only the effects. She gasped, then blushed sheepishly. "I'm so sorry," she muttered and slunk to her seat.

Craig sighed and threw her the glasses. "It's okay. But please, if you get too worked up, take the glasses off, okay? Remember that it's all on the screen. Nothing will harm you this way." He spun to examine the new hole and winced.

"Sorry, Dad. I guess this was a little overstimulating for her."

"I did warn you." He sighed. "I'll have to get the supplies." He shoved everything else on his to-do list to the back of his mind as he opened the closet to retrieve what he needed. Some things seemed never-ending.

Maybe having another girl in the house isn't the problem. Having an overpowered vampire girl in the house? That's like having Mike Tyson combined with the stature and temperament of a teenager.

He shuddered at the thought as he knelt in front of the hole and scrabbled for another square of mesh. Behind him, Vickie dodged and flinched against the leather on the couch. He only hoped she wouldn't freak out again while he worked, or he'd have a hole in his skull rather than another one in the wall.

CHAPTER THIRTEEN

The smell of garlic wafted through the main level of the castle. Vickie and Alexis followed their noses into the kitchen to where Craig sported a blue-and-white striped apron as he tended to a pan of sauce on the stovetop.

"That smells delicious," Vickie commented.

Alexis flashed him a knowing smile. "Are you making your famous garlic chicken pasta, Dad?"

Her father twirled a wooden spoon in his hand. "You know it. I decided we should start making some meals around here with simpler ingredients. I want Vickie to get used to eating my food."

That wasn't the only reason. He also realized that he and his daughter needed to be more of a family than ever before—not only for their own sake but for the sake of their new companion. And like he learned growing up, there was never a better place to bond with your family than the dinner table.

Vickie's stomach rumbled. It had been several days

since she woke, and she hadn't eaten all that much. It wasn't that she wasn't hungry. In fact, sleeping for four hundred years really did work up quite an appetite. Her system of taste buds simply hadn't caught up to the wealth of flavors that modern food offered. As a result, she frequently found herself overwhelmed to the point of losing her appetite.

She approached the kitchen warily.

I really hope I like this. I need to eat before I starve to death. And how could I go back with them if I can't even eat their food?

Craig recognized the look only too well. Raising a daughter to the same age helped with that. "Don't worry. This is a simple dish, Vickie. You've had chicken and garlic before, right?" She nodded. "Okay, so this combines those flavors with pasta and a creamy sauce. It's straightforward stuff."

"I hope I like it." She smiled timidly, afraid that her reaction might have seemed rude. "And I appreciate you going out of your way to try to provide food that I can eat."

He smiled as he stirred the sauce that bubbled in the pan. "This isn't going out of my way. Trust me. This is one of my favorite meals to make."

The two girls sat on stools at the island. Vickie stared at the cook, fascinated by the process of cooking in the twenty-first century.

Alexis chuckled at Vickie's interest and raised a curious eyebrow. "I know a lot of things are different nowadays, but I'm sure your family used to cook dinner, too. Are you really that impressed by watching my dad cook?"

Vickie gestured to Craig with her palm up. "Think about where I come from. In my day, women stayed at home to do the cooking. My mother took care of the house. My father worked the fields. In our society, the men either worked in the fields or they worked in town. They didn't cook."

Craig turned his back to the pan for a moment and caught the drops from the wooden spoon in his palm. "So, in the fourteen years you lived with your parents, your father never cooked?"

She stared off into space as she pondered the question, then shook her head firmly. "It simply wasn't something that was done back then."

The man puffed his chest out, oddly satisfied that the young vampire was impressed with his cooking prowess. He nodded a little smugly and returned his attention to the meal.

Alexis rolled her eyes. "It's not impressive if she doesn't like it, Dad. Let her taste it before you congratulate yourself."

Craig stuck his tongue out at her.

"I'm sure I will love it," Vickie assured him. "It smells delicious. Have you always been the cook?"

He stirred the sauce, then carefully slid some already-cooked chicken breasts from a plate into the pan and turned them to ensure an even coating. "I've always cooked. But I wasn't...uh, the cook of the family until recently."

Alexis nodded somberly. "Dad took over the cooking duties after Mom died. She used to make most of the dinners and was a great cook."

"Correction. Your mom was a fantastic cook. I'd give anything to be able to have her meatloaf one more time."

"Meatloaf?" Vickie asked, the blank expression now firmly established as a sign of confusion.

Alexis waved her hand. "It's not that important. It was a meal my mom liked to make. You take ground beef and ground pork, mix it together with other stuff, and cook it in the oven like a loaf of bread."

The vampire's face twisted in disgust. "Why would you do that?"

"Because it's delicious, that's why." Craig pointed at her with the dripping spoon and accidentally spattered the tiles on the floor.

"So why can't you make it now?"

"Well, the thing about Alexis' mother is that she grew up on a farm so her mom did all the cooking. She was one of seven kids. They didn't have a lot of money, and her mom— Alexis' grandmother—would whip meals up based on whatever they had on hand. They couldn't afford a lot of ingredients. This instilled in her an instinct for how to cook, which she passed on to her daughter, my wife."

"So?"

"So, while most mothers would have a recipe book of some kind, my wife didn't. Instead, if you asked her how to make something, she always had the same response." He gestured to Alexis.

"'There's not really a recipe for it.' That was Mom's answer every time. She was the most brilliant cook, but had no idea how anything got made."

Her dad smiled warmly. "She always listened to her instinct. It took her anywhere she wanted to go." He'd loved that about her, and that wasn't limited to her cooking. Whenever a decision needed to be made, he could lean on her instincts. They never led the family astray. Even when they had to choose treatment options after she was diagnosed with cancer, she knew what to do. She stared death in the face and kept the family from being crushed under the weight of the prognosis.

It was this same ability that led Craig to briefly hold a grudge against her for dying when she did. When he lost his job shortly after her death, his first reaction was to get angry at her for not being there when he'd needed her the most. He eventually realized how selfish and stupid that was, and he still held some guilt for thinking that way. Craig knew he had to start developing instincts of his own so that he and Alexis could move forward.

Cooking was an easy place to start.

He brought the sauce to a boil, turned down the heat to a simmer, and covered the pan. "That has to cook for about fifteen minutes. This is the only meal I fix out of instinct. The rest of the time, I pull out a cookbook or search online for recipes." He chuckled. "I need a little more practice."

"Do you like to cook?" Vickie asked. "I can't picture my father enjoying such a chore."

He washed his hands and dabbed them dry with a hand towel. "Sure, I like being able to cook. It's nicer now with the extra time on my hands. There's something about eating a meal that you cooked yourself, I think." He rubbed his chin thoughtfully. "Then again, it's something you still have to discover. We'll teach you to cook, too. How does that sound?"

Vickie wasn't sure about that yet. She was intimidated simply by looking at the various knobs and switches on the modern stovetop. "I used to help gather sticks for the fire. That was how I helped with dinner every night."

Alexis grinned. "Fortunately, that's one step you don't have to worry about anymore. Don't worry, we'll teach you the rest. I can cook breakfast but not really any other meals. Still, I can show you how to use the appliances and keep you from making any mistakes that can't be fixed."

Her father retrieved another pot and filled it with water from the kitchen faucet. "So, Vickie, have you given any thought about coming to America with us? We'd really love to have you if that's what you want to do, especially if you're in danger here." He didn't want to pressure her, but he needed time to plan the next steps, which in turn meant he needed to know if there would be next steps. If she decided to stay, his mental obstacle course would require much less attention.

She folded her arms and rested them on the countertop in front of her as she slouched forward. "Not yet. I have tried to see what I can remember about my former life. I can feel all these memories baked into my mind but pulling them out has proven to be far more difficult than I imagined."

"Trying to get a clearer view of your past, so you can decide on your future?" Alexis asked.

"Exactly. If I want to make a big decision like this, I have to know where I stand—who I am, I suppose, and how my history and heritage plays a part in that."

Craig turned the water off and lifted the pot out of the sink. "Well, have you been able to...I don't know, access more memories? I don't know how any of this works."

Vickie nodded. "It is strange sifting through everything.

I was sealed away during my nap, but I still have my memories of the time before and there are some things that seem to have penetrated—like I still absorbed some information without realizing it or knowing what it was. I just can't always see it clearly."

"That's often how the subconscious works." Alexis stood and walked to the fridge. "We all have that. It's where our brains work when we're not thinking, I guess." She opened the fridge and pulled out a soda, which she gave to Vickie before she took one for herself and sat again.

"Deep in this...subconscious, I've been able to piece together fragments of information about the Circle." Vickie popped the top on her can of soda. "It is a shortened term for a group known as the Slayer Circle. That is the real name you found, correct?"

"You're right." Alexis was astonished because she hadn't given many details to Vickie. She hadn't wanted to scare her. "But you said you weren't sure before—that you only heard something about a Circle. How were you able to put that together?"

Vickie took a sip of her soda. "When your body is shut down physically, all you have left is your mind. What I've realized is that long before all this happened, I'd gleaned snippets of things I overheard without realizing what they meant. My parents never openly discussed any of this around me, but children are curious and often have a sense for things they shouldn't hear. None of it made any sense—and really, it was only a few snatches of whispered words here and there—so I never really thought about any of it. I had four centuries in which my mind could assemble these pieces and fill in some of the gaps. It helps that vampires are able to process information so much more effectively than humans."

Alexis nodded. "The Slayer Circle was a religious group. I looked into them. They're scary, by all accounts."

"Yes, they were. And from the comments I heard, they did not distinguish between vampires. They wanted all of us dead. I think that's what my parents were protecting me from."

"We thought the same thing." Alexis' dad chose a box of fettuccine noodles from the cabinet. "If there was a murderous group out there ruthlessly killing my entire race, I'd hide my daughter too."

Alexis took a sip of soda and pointed at Vickie. "But you said there were other kinds of vampires, right?"

"There were—and possibly still are—two different species of vampire. My kind were the non-biters. We have no specific need to feast on the blood or flesh of others. We do have fangs and we use them for defense, but that's all."

Craig broke a handful of fettuccine noodles and dropped them into the pot of boiling water. "So, then, the other side would be the biters."

"Yes. The biters viewed the human race purely in terms of survival. They merely wanted to use them and their bodies to further their own race. They bit into flesh, they sucked blood for energy and nutrition—all the things you people apparently believe all vampires do."

Alexis shrugged. "It's what we were told."

Vickie looked down with a touch of grief on her face. "My guess that's because none of us survived. The Slayer Circle believed that all vampires were the same. They were all biters, and they all needed to be exterminated. Once they did that, they told tales of how awful we were, even though non-biters had nothing to do with that horror."

"A lot of this happened while you were still alive, then." Craig stirred the noodles. "The Circle must have won. As we say, 'history is written by the winners.' That saying applies to your situation, too. But you at least knew of the Circle back then? Before you were put to sleep, I mean."

Vickie nodded and sipped her of soda. "I assume so. We weren't allowed to show our powers or our fangs in town. While my parents never explained the details, they gave me strict orders to keep our species a secret. The Slayer Circle had obviously spread enough bad information about us to convince the world that we were all biters and threatened their way of life.

"To be fair, that was true of the biters—they were terrible. But what the Circle—and humans in general—failed to understand was that the biters were our enemies, too. We tried to engage the human race in peace and coexist. The biters waged war, both with us and with humanity."

Craig sighed as he tended to the noodles. *This poor girl has been through so much. I thought we had problems, but she's faced the extermination of her entire race.*

"There is one thing I haven't mentioned," Vickie said. "The reason we could shield our species from the public is because we were able to communicate to some degree without speaking to each other."

Alexis leaned back. "Like telepathically? You could talk to each other using your minds?"

The other girl nodded, then shook her head. "Not exactly. We could always sense when there were other vampires around—biters and non-biters alike. There was a collective understanding of who was a vampire and who wasn't. That camaraderie kept us together, even when we lived in secret."

Craig flinched and already knew the answer to the question before he decided to ask it. Once he'd stirred the noodles one more time, he turned to look at the girl.

"Can you sense any more vampires here?"

Vickie sighed and lowered her gaze. "No, I can't. As far as I can tell, they're all gone. I must be the last one."

Saying it out loud pained Vickie. Part of her had kept the small hope alive in her heart that her parents had somehow survived the attacks. Unfortunately, she had to admit to herself that they hadn't. She would have sensed their presence, otherwise.

CHAPTER FOURTEEN

After breakfast the next morning, Vickie walked back to the room she shared with Alexis and noticed her roommate was slipping shoes on her feet.

"Hey, start getting ready to go. My dad wants us downstairs in five minutes."

"Why?"

"He said he wanted to take us into town for a while. I don't know why."

Vickie immediately smiled with real excitement. She had only been in the city once since she woke up, and she loved taking it all in. Getting out of the castle was a liberating experience. But because they were so protective of her, they ran errands without her and kept her inside and away from the public. So, when Craig told his daughter that they were going to town together, she was confused as to why they would take the risk.

What Craig hadn't shared was that Vickie wasn't the only one struggling with the concept of bringing the girl home. He trusted her, yes, but he needed to see how she reacted when they spent time in public before he finally decided. They had already made the offer, of course, but so much of what lay ahead would be affected by how she could cope. It might also determine whether their plan was viable. He wanted to help her interact with the world around her and to learn how to respond as a person in public places. He also wanted opportunities to teach her how to act. If her instincts veered out of control, he could be there to guide her and keep her species a secret. It was a dangerous task, he knew, but he felt up to it.

And he hoped that spending time with her outside the castle would calm his nerves. He needed reassurance that adopting her into his family would be a wise move and not more trouble than it was worth.

The girls met him downstairs. This time, they took a bus into downtown Salzburg.

It was another bustling day in the metropolis. After they walked across the river and down a few blocks, they navigated a narrow, brick-paved road that seemed more like an alley than a street. The close quarters made it a great spot to be able to interact with others and walk through various shops and restaurants that nestled side by side.

The air was crisp and cool without being cold, and the girls enjoyed the fresh air. There was always something about fresh air that filled Craig with energy too, and he needed that after the last few restless nights he'd endured.

The night before, he'd stared at the ceiling until long past midnight, bothered by questions about how he could get Vickie past the security protocols and into the country. He rarely slept well anyway, since he still hadn't adjusted to sleeping without Carol, but the added weight of this responsibility made things so much worse. Now, with a face full of sunshine and fresh air filling his lungs, he almost felt like his old self again, at least temporarily.

At first, they wandered in and out of shops and looked at the fashionable European clothing on offer. Alexis had never really considered herself much of a fashion expert. She cared about how she looked, but she usually dressed for comfort. The girl wore mainly sweatshirts and jeans, so teaching Vickie about "normal" clothing on this road trip was more complicated than she expected. Yet another job that her mom was better at, she accepted ruefully.

Vickie simply took it all in. She relished the opportunity to be in town and surrounded by people. Being stuck in that castle for so long and sequestered from society had taxed her mind greatly. Today's excursion through downtown Salzburg helped to clear some of the fog that clouded all her attempts to find answers and make decisions.

The square had been busy that day as well. Vendors hawked small tchotchkes with **SALZBURG** printed in bold capital letters all over them, carefully lined up across folding tables. Street performers danced and sang around their hats that lay open on the pavement to collect any donations tourists felt generous enough to offer.

Even the pigeons were more active than usual. The mob of birds pushed and shoved their way from one park bench dweller to another in search of tourists gullible enough to reward their persistence. Alexis smiled as she recounted the fun of feeding the birds to her two companions.

As Vickie's gaze drifted upward, it settled on the

Hohensalzburg Fortress. She stopped where she stood and lost herself in the memories.

The fortifications. The construction. The ammunition reserves. I haven't seen the fortress look this peaceful ever in my life. It almost looks inviting.

"Have you ever been in there?" Alexis asked.

Vickie's eyes widened as if the question had been a ridiculous one. "Oh, goodness, no. Only the king and his servants would go there. Besides, they were being fortified for battle the last time I saw it. Who is the king who lives there now?"

Alexis laughed. "It's not anybody's home anymore. It's actually a place you can visit."

"Visit?"

"It's a museum now."

She had no answer to this. It seemed inconceivable given her final memory of the fortification and the frenzied attempts to make it battle-ready before she'd been shut off from the only life she'd ever known. They showed Vickie various pieces of pottery, knick-knacks, and new foods that vendors tried to persuade them to buy. However, before the girls could actually indulge themselves, Craig would lean in and remind them firmly that they weren't interested in buying, so they would have to put the things back.

They eventually reached a man dressed in a long, shiny purple robe who sat stoically before them. His face was painted to match his garment, and he held a staff in his hand. The confusing part was that the staff was the only thing touching the ground. He appeared to float in mid-air, and his robe dangled behind him. His expression fixed and distant, he didn't react to anyone's comments or actions at all.

Vickie watched the man skeptically. She knew of nobody who had these kinds of powers. As far as she knew, vampires were the only supernatural beings in the area, and her senses told her he was no vampire. She leaned over to study the space beneath him but failed to find anything that might explain how he was doing it.

Alexis and her father stood behind her and muffled their laughter. Finally, the young vampire turned to them and whispered, "What is this, witchcraft? How can he float? He's no supernatural being."

Craig pulled Vickie aside and explained to her how it was done. The staff was attached to a platform on the ground. A metal bar extended through the billowy sleeve of the man's robe and down until it met a small metal seat that he sat on to give him the appearance of floating in mid-air.

"Generally speaking, you don't have to worry too much about witchcraft. At least, not out and out witchcraft like this. You might see someone do something interesting or wonderful, but it rarely actually crosses that line. Logical explanations exist for almost everything."

He had to smile at his own contradictory responses, however. *I'm still working on a logical explanation for a four-hundred-year-old vampire living under the same roof as us.*

They ambled down another narrow road until they reached a small storefront selling shoes. Vickie marveled at the sizes, shapes, styles, and colors available. Finally, they reached a point where Craig decided to let them do their own thing. He wasn't interested in shoes and he wanted to test their independence and willpower.

"There's a little pastry shop across the street. I'll go grab a scone or something. Hang out here, stay together, and keep out of trouble. Alexis, shoot me a text if you need anything. I'll be back in a few minutes."

He walked across the street and left the two girls at the shoe store.

Alexis gleefully showed more shoes to Vickie, and they tried on pair after pair, enjoying the fun of dressing up in different shoes. Some things were simply universal, no matter how far the gap in years.

Vickie paused before she tried on a pair of high heels at Alexis' demand and stared into the distance.

"What is it?" her friend asked as she placed a pair of red pumps back on the shelf.

"I...don't know." She wandered to the front of the store and peered out the window as she brushed her black hair aside. Her gaze roved cautiously over the street, driven by the odd sensation that persisted in her gut. Was there a threat of some kind?

She made eye contact with a middle-aged man wearing a long dark-gray overcoat over a black turtleneck and jeans. He looked away quickly when he noticed her fixed attention.

Vickie squinted and murmured quietly, "Something is suspicious about that man."

By that point, Alexis' father had returned with a small pastry in hand. "Does anyone want a bite?"

"Hang on, Dad. Vickie has a weird feeling about something."

"We should walk," the vampire said and turned to exit the doors and head down the street, away from the stranger. Her companions shrugged and followed her without question. Every few steps, she looked over her shoulder to watch the man's responses.

Despite the fact that she'd obviously noticed him, he continued to follow them down the road with blatant disregard for any kind of caution.

Vickie's breath quickened, and she felt her fangs push against the insides of her cheeks.

Keep it together. Don't let anyone see your teeth. You can't live in this world if you don't control your reactions.

She pressed her lips together to keep her teeth hidden, but her senses strained against her control with every step the stranger took in pursuit

Finally, she turned left and ducked into a small alley between two stores.

"What are we doing here?" Craig looked down the empty alley, his frown almost a scowl.

"I think someone is following us. I want to see if he is or not," Vickie said tersely.

He shuffled his feet and kicked a small stone down the alley with his hands in his pockets.

"So, how long do we have to—" He was cut off by the sound of Vickie's gasp.

The man stood before them and stared intently at Vickie, an expression of recognition on his face.

"Stand back," she ordered and placed herself squarely between the stranger and her friends.

He yanked his hands from his pockets, but before he could gesture with them, Vickie grabbed his wrists, twisted them, and broke the bones. He grunted in pain and stumbled backward.

She vaulted to deliver a kick to his face, breaking more bones. With his injured wrists, he was only able to press the backs of his hands limply to his nose to catch the blood that poured freely.

He fell against the brick wall of the building, his eyes wide with shock. With one devastating punch, Vickie crushed his windpipe.

"What are you doing?" Alexis shouted.

"He was a threat. I don't know what he wanted, but he came here to get something from us—or from me. We have to go."

"No kidding!" Craig agreed. "You nearly killed a man, Vickie. I doubt he'll survive before he reaches a hospital." His eyes were hard and his breathing fast as they power-walked out of the area and did their best to not arouse suspicion. The trio continued their journey to the bus station as rapidly as was deemed acceptable. It didn't take long for the screams to start and none of the companions seemed inclined to comment. The damage was done and all they could do was get as far away as they could in the shortest possible time.

Once again, concern filled Craig as they walked. Vickie seemed determined to protect them, which he appreciated. But what exactly had that man done? She had no proof that he was even a threat. All she had was her gut feeling, which would never hold up in a court of law. One woman's instinct used to comfort him. Now, this girl's instinct terrified him. Of course, one had to do with home and hearth. This one had to do with killing and self-preservation in a time where it literally was kill or be killed.

He took a deep breath as they boarded the bus. They found seats and remained silent, locked in their thoughts for the duration of the trip to the castle. Vickie pursed her lips in defiant anger at the man whom she had been absolutely certain was about to attack them. Her senses had never misled her before, and this instance would confirm that.

Alexis side-eyed her friend and tried to process what had happened and how they got to that point.

Craig stared at both girls, his mind wrestling with the new complications the encounter had stirred up. The fact that Vickie could move so quickly at will raised another dangerous point. If she were to enter a rebellious phase, he wouldn't be able to rein her in. She could literally walk all over him and he wouldn't be able to do a thing.

What would she do in America? And if she pulled something like that, how quickly would she be thrown in jail? What if she started a riot and my baby girl was swept up in it? I would never be able to forgive myself.

He was quick to pull his daughter aside when they disembarked at their stop. He whispered, "We need to teach Vickie more about being a human in public. Try to talk to her a little tonight and see if there's a way we can keep some of this under control. But let her calm down first. She's too wound up now to reason with."

Alexis nodded numbly as they caught up with Vickie who pushed ahead at a spanking pace.

"Steady pace, Vickie," he reminded her gently. "We don't want to seem in too much of a hurry."

CHAPTER FIFTEEN

The vampire sat on the edge of the bed and watched curiously as Alexis pulled a small vinyl bag from the top drawer of her dresser.

"This will be a fun one today. A lot of the stuff you learn is kinda boring. But I wanted to do something a little nicer. We'll make you look good tonight."

Vickie tilted her head in a challenge. "I don't look good? I thought you said I looked wonderful. What are all these new clothes for?"

Her friend giggled and shook her head. "No, you look great. Every day, you look more like you're from this century. Your hair looks good and your makeup game is on point. We're on the right track. But the next thing you need to learn to do is your nails."

Vickie's forehead wrinkled in confusion as she looked at her bare feet. "My...nails? Do people today really care so much about such things?"

"Women do. Boys don't need to worry about it, but girls really have to pay attention to their hands and feet. If you have dirty, gross feet with calluses and chipped nails, it simply doesn't look very good. When we get back to America, it'll be warmer out, and you'll want to wear sandals as much as you can." She unzipped the vinyl bag and ferreted inside for a pair of nail clippers. "And if you wear sandals and show your feet off, you need them to look good."

Vickie frowned. "And you think this is fun? It doesn't sound like fun. It sounds like unnecessary work."

"Don't worry. This will be more fun than you think. It's work, but it's worth it."

She lifted her left heel onto the edge of the bed and tucked her knee next to her chin, then demonstrated how the clippers worked by trimming one of her nails. "Don't cut them too short or curved. Do that, and you'll encourage ingrown toenails. That's when the edges of your nails dig into the skin of your toes. It hurts a lot. I got one playing soccer one year, and I wanted to die. The doctors had to do really gross stuff to fix it. So take a little off each one, and you'll be good."

She handed Vickie the clippers, and the vampire followed her example, her expression taut and a little nervous.

Alexis shook her head with jealousy as she watched. "I'm kinda amazed that your nails look as good as they do. I figured they'd be long and yellow or something after four hundred years, but they're not bad. Just…thick."

"I wonder why that is. I never noticed it before."

"Probably because you didn't wear shoes and socks much back in your day. And I know you didn't pumice or moisturize or anything. I would guess your toenails would get really thick over time even from the abuse."

Once she'd finished her first foot, she handed her companion the clippers and they took turns to complete the process.

Alexis had a deeper plan than simply doing their nails, naturally. She wanted to talk about what had happened earlier in the day, and there were few times when a girl opened up more than during a manicure and pedicure session. She hoped that starting off with her nails would put her in a good frame of mind to talk about it.

Mom used to use them all the time when she wanted to talk about important stuff. It must have worked for her because she did it all the time, so I can only hope it helps now.

"So..." she started casually as she clipped away, "one thing my dad wanted me to do was explain some of the unspoken rules of being a human in the year 2019."

"More rules?"

Alexis nodded. "Yeah. There are things that everyone understands about coexisting. If we all try to live in a civil society—and most of us try to do that—we don't do certain things like punch and physically attack each other without provocation."

She handed Vickie the clippers.

"Oh, that?" The vampire pulled her right leg up onto the edge of the mattress. "As I said, the man was a threat. He followed us around deliberately, and I know that he was going to do something. I responded the way I did because I wanted to protect the two of you."

"And we understand that," she assured her. "But he didn't actually do anything. That's where the problem is. There are laws in place that are different from when you were awake before. If he tried to do something, you could have retaliated without objection. We call that self-defense. But to punch someone for looking like he was about to do something isn't cool. It's against the law, and we call it assault."

"So what happens when I do something like that?"

"In this case, hopefully nothing. Technically, we broke the law when we left, but I think we got away before anyone actually saw us or what happened. What it means, though, is that you really have to be careful in the future. Not only will you make people angry, but they can also put you in prison, especially if you do something like this in America. Everyone sues everybody there."

"Sues?"

"They take them to court, a place where people who've been wronged by others can resolve their difference and demand or request compensation of some kind," Alexis explained.

"Well, I'm sorry that I tried to protect you," Vickie said with a touch of sarcasm. "In my world, if someone poses a threat, you step up and handle it directly. You don't simply wait until it's too late."

"And like I said," Alexis said gently. "I understand that. Dad does too, which is why we reacted the way we did. But this is a different time with different rules. We don't want to lose you after we've worked so hard to help you to adapt. You'll need to learn to fight the urge to attack someone without justification simply because they seem like they might do something wrong. And even if you do have justification or evidence, breaking bones and crushing windpipes shouldn't be your first reaction. Those kinds of things can have serious consequences. You might have killed that man. And unless he drew a weapon on you, you probably would be sentenced to jail and possibly even for execution. We call that corporal punishment."

Vickie had lapsed into a somewhat stiff silence as if resentment still lingered, but she at least seemed to listen.

Once they were done clipping their nails, Alexis brandished a small orange stick. "Now that we've finished explaining the law, we'll push our cuticles back." She pressed the stick's flat head gently against the skin that grew over the base of the nail until it pushed back perfectly to expose more of the nail.

"Why are we doing this?" Vickie asked, some of her displeasure fading as curiosity returned.

"Because we want our toenails to look longer."

The vampire squinted as she watched her friend's deft movement. Some of the twenty-first-century rules frustrated her. "We want to make our nails look longer, but we cut them to be short? How does that make any sense?"

"There are two parts to the nail. We only cut off the portion that needs to stay short." Alexis grinned. "Now comes the filing. I have two nail files, so we can do this part together. We have to rub the side of this along the edges of your nails. It helps us to dull the edges, so they don't become too sharp and poke into the skin as they grow. When you have sharp toenails, you also tear holes in your socks. We don't want that."

As they filed away at their toes, Alexis used the opportunity to explain how things had changed. "How close were the townspeople where you grew up?"

"Very. Everyone knew everybody, and most people got along well—provided that there were no clues pointing to vampires, I suppose. But we always looked out for each other and helped one another."

Alexis sighed. "I'd love to tell you that the world still works like that, but it totally doesn't. Today, people aren't interested in helping each other out."

"Why not?"

"Because people want privacy now. When someone knows everything about you, it makes you more vulnerable and that's not what people want anymore. They want to stay protected from people who would use their personal information against them. We call it 'minding your own business.'"

She tucked the two nail files into the bag and removed a small cube. "This is for buffing. If you want to clean your nails up so they don't look so jagged and gross, you use this. It's also helpful to get that last bit of crud off your toenails."

Toe by toe, she rubbed the square along all edges of her toenails. When she pulled it away, they practically glowed in the afternoon light. "See? Because you have a buffer, you can do almost anything short of removing the nail entirely. The buffer is your safety net."

Vickie nodded. At least this step made a little more sense to her. Even if she was discouraged by the arbitrary rules of fashion, she was very grateful to Alexis for taking the time to help her learn.

"Okay, let's talk shopping," Alexis said. "Do you like to go shopping?"

Vickie shrugged her shoulders. "I guess. It's not the most thrilling time we ever had, but it was something to do. The shoes were fun."

"How did you pay for things back then?"

"Livestock, usually. We were a chicken family, mainly, so we always took a couple of chickens into town. We could trade those for goods and services."

Alexis laughed as she buffed her last pinky toenail once again for good measure. "Okay, well, there's another thing that's changed. You probably noticed we paid with paper bills. We call this paper money. You can't bring animals out in public like that. Occasionally, you might see a dog or a few other animals on leashes, but chickens aren't really acceptable. You'll need real money to shop. You can start earning that money when we get back. For now, however, you can use some of ours."

While she talked, she dug around in her bag and pulled out four little white foam pads with protrusions between curved hollows. She stuck her toes in each shaped gap and the spacers kept them all separate so none could touch. "This is a toe separator. You'll need this on both feet for the final stretch. It keeps you from getting colors all over your skin."

Vickie had begun to get over this being like a human thing. Not everything had to make sense to her, but she also accepted that some things would simply feel bizarre for the first few times she tried them. She snaked the separators between her toes as instructed and waited patiently for the next step.

"Now comes the fun part." Alexis brandished three small bottles. "Pick a color."

Vickie took them, examined them, and finally settled on a deep burgundy.

Her companion nodded in approval. "That definitely looks like your color. I'll pick this green."

Carefully, Alexis painted her toenails with a tiny brush that had been attached to the lid of the vials. She maintained a steady hand as she showed how the process worked with broad strokes and the occasional dip back into the container for more polish that would shine when the job was complete.

"Wow," the vampire said once she'd painted her first toe. "It looks like a completely different foot already."

"And we're only getting started. Now, we can talk for a while we take care of the other nails in the same way. So, tell me, what did you do for fun back in your day?"

"Fun?"

"Yeah. How did you entertain yourself? Were there certain activities you liked to do after a long day?"

Vickie shook her head and stared at her toes in concentration. "We didn't really do anything only for fun. We did work and things that seemed like fun, but it always had another purpose. Entertainment wasn't really the point."

"So you didn't ever get together with your friends and go swimming or something like that?"

She screwed her mouth in concentration as her hands stroked the brush rhythmically over her nails. "Yeah, I guess we did. We liked to walk through town and laugh at the young men in the stocks. Or maybe we'd wander around like we did here today."

"By yourself?"

"Sure."

"Okay, let's move on to another rule that most people follow. There are no stocks anymore, so you won't see them anyway. But you can't go out by yourself. Somebody usually has to be with you."

"You don't go out by yourself?" Vickie was astonished by the lack of freedom. "I thought you two didn't want me going out because I am a vampire, not because I'm a teenager."

"Sometimes, you can," Alexis conceded. "And here, that's why. But when we get back to America, you'll have a little less freedom than here. Usually, when you're my age, you're still asked to tell everybody where you are and where you're going. And the place has to be very controlled if we're going to run around there without any supervision. I know in a year or two, it'll get better, but with my dad being in the shape he's in, I sometimes worry if he'll ever get over the pain. He might worry about me so much that he never allows me any solitude."

"Why does he have to know where you are?"

"For safety."

Vickie laughed. "So you didn't see me take care of that attacker?"

"We don't know that he was an attacker. But as we've already established, you can't run around and punch and kick everyone you perceive to be a threat."

Over the next hour or so, the girls painted two coats on their nails and let them dry, then topped them off with a clear coat to protect the paint and make it shine.

When they finished, Vickie stared at her transformed toes, her expression one of pure delight. "This looks wonderful. Who knew my toenails needed color?"

"And now you know how to do it," Alexis reminded her. "Do this every other week, and no one will question your hygiene. If you take care of your feet, people assume you take care of the rest of yourself, too."

Once the clear coat dried, they pulled the toe separators out and wiggled the appendages in victory.

"That wasn't so hard, right?" Alexis asked. "And now you know one more thing about being a girl today."

"Being a girl is complicated. There is so much to remember."

"Oh, man, you have no idea how much maintenance is required of a female. But it's all worth it in the end if it makes you look and feel good. Do these nails do that for you?

Vickie smiled and wiggled her toes again. "I think so. What a fun little way to show off your creativity."

Alexis smirked. She wanted Vickie to really enjoy the advantages of being a teenager in 2019. Their nail session seemed to have set them off to a good start on that, and it would hopefully go a long way toward helping her with the transition. "And we're only getting warmed up. Are you ready for your hands?"

Vickie grinned.

CHAPTER SIXTEEN

C raig descended the long stairway from the second tower to the main level. He assumed the girls were hanging out in their room, but when he heard the familiar crackle of burning wood, he knew they'd built a fire in the library fireplace.

He strolled across the foyer and poked his head in to see what was going on. The overhead light was off, and the orange glow danced around the room as the only source of light.

Vickie sat on the red velvet chair with her feet up and an open book in her lap. She had her back to the flames to allow their light to illuminate the pages.

Craig knocked lightly on the wood of the doorway. She looked up, smiled, and greeted him.

"Hello."

"Hey. Do you mind if I come in?"

She shook her head and he stepped into the room and stuck his hands in his pockets as he approached the fireplace. Since he was a little kid, he'd loved watching the fire for hours. In the weeks they'd spent in the castle, it might have helped both him and his daughter if he'd made more fires.

The heat warmed his clothes and released waves of relaxation through his body. He glanced at the mantel and noticed the chalice was gone, then turned his head to look at Vickie where she cradled the object in her hand while she read. He smiled, sat on the couch on the other side of the hearth, and released a sigh.

"Did you have a long night?" she asked as she peeked over the edges of her book.

"They're all long." He smiled. "How come you don't have the light on? It would be easier to read, wouldn't it?"

"I spent years reading by firelight. It doesn't bother me, and I find it…comforting."

"I suppose that makes sense. Where's Alexis?"

"Up in the room. She's chatting with some of her friends on some video-based call system."

"FaceTime."

"Sure. So anyway, I said 'hi' to everybody and came down here to do a little reading. It is one of my favorite pastimes."

"What's with the cup?" Craig pointed to the chalice.

Vickie held it up and ran her fingers along the seal carved into the side. "This seal is the Brommer family crest, my family's coat of arms. I always loved running my finger over the grooves as a child. You know how you get attached to things for no reason?"

He chuckled and nodded. "Yes, ma'am. Growing up, my family had this hideous little piece of Christmas décor, a straw plate with a Santa and Mrs. Claus made out of little felt balls. It was only their heads on a plate and was totally hideous. I have no idea why I loved it so much. But when it was up, it felt like Christmas. I took it with me when I moved out and put it up every year. My wife hated it. Alexis loved it, but she loves all things Christmas, anyway."

Vickie laughed. She didn't know who this Santa and Mrs. Claus were, but she let it go for now. The sentiment was still there, after all, and she knew the man meant well.

"So, this is like your chance to feel at home, huh?" he asked. Vickie nodded. "I get it. We are so anxious about bringing you into the twenty-first century that we forget this is all still so sudden for you. It's nice to be able to return to a place of comfort, even for a little while. I'm sorry if we forget that."

She closed the book and placed the chalice on top of it in her lap. "Yes, but it's also important for me to know and understand that home is…not here. Yes, this room feels like home. Sitting by the fire and reading also feels like home. But it's not really home unless my father walks in and sits down where you're sitting. It's not home unless my mother walks through on her way to the kitchen and pats me on the head. It's the same, but it's not."

Craig stared wordlessly into the fire.

It sounds like she's describing our house without Carol. It feels like home, but it's not.

"Tell me about your family," he finally said. "My parents taught me that nobody is really gone if you keep their memories alive. It was you and your parents, right?"

"Toward the end, yes." She sighed.

He leaned forward. "Did you have any siblings?"

She broke eye contact with him and stared at the chalice, playing with it in her hands. "I had a brother and a sister."

"What were their names?"

"Jakob and Hannah. Jakob was a couple of years older than me. Hannah was one year younger."

Craig could tell this was a painful subject by the uncomfortable look on her face. He wanted to know more but he also didn't want to offend her or cause her too much pain. It wasn't his place. As such, he trod lightly.

"What were they like?"

Her smile was full of pain. "Jakob was the protective older brother. He took us out into town and watched over us when our parents were too busy taking care of this place. He was fun but serious. Hannah was my best friend. We were close in age, so we liked to do the same things. She followed me wherever I went, which is annoying when you're younger, but now, I would give anything to have that back."

Craig smiled in sympathy. "Yeah. I know that feeling well."

He wanted to ask what happened to them, but she continued talking. "When I was twelve years old, they went into town and didn't come home one evening. My parents were worried about them, but they assured me that everything was fine. By the next day, they knew what had happened. To put it simply, someone had...I believe the term is gotten to them."

"I'm so sorry. No kid should have to go through that."

Vickie drew a deep breath and placed the book on the floor, still clutching the chalice. "Yeah, it wasn't great. My parents told me, and I couldn't believe it. They said it was a random act, but the more I put the pieces together in my head now, the more likely it seems that the Circle was the real culprit. They had to be. They were the only ones who wanted to see us dead and all our neighbors knew we were good people."

She paused and turned in the chair to look at the fire. "They were hidden in a barn, under some hay. I don't know why the murderers tried to keep it a secret. Back then, death was as much a part of life as anything else. We weren't necessarily scared of it. We were sad, of course, but we moved on quickly. We had to."

"I have a feeling your parents didn't move on as much as you think."

She laughed. "No, I know they didn't. When I think about how protective my parents became, I'm sure that had something to do with it. That's why they put me to sleep. They wanted to save the one child they had left."

"I guess...I didn't know that you could kill a vampire. The way you've talked about how our perspective of vampires is so far off, it sounds like everything we knew about them has been wrong."

"You can kill vampires in one specific way."

"And that is?" He didn't even bother to voice any of the myths so often associated with this uncomfortable subject.

Without saying a word, Vickie looked at him and dragged her thumb across her neck. Craig winced and refused to ask any further questions about it. He didn't want to think about that, and he certainly didn't want her thinking about it either.

He changed the subject quickly. "Ah. It looks like Alexis has taught you to make your toes look pretty. Nice work.

It's hard to tell in the dim light, but it seems like you did a good job with them."

"Thanks." Vickie perked up. "You know what I don't understand, though? Making your feet look good. What's the point? Why do people care so much about how their feet look?"

He had no answer for her. As a guy, he never had to worry about that sort of thing. "You know what? The key to being a girl in 2019 is to simply choose what matters to you. If you want to care about your feet, go for it. Don't do your nails because you want to look good. Do them because they make you feel good. And if you don't like it, do something else."

She nodded. "I like that."

Craig smiled gently. He was proud of his little moment of deep reflection there. His wife had been the one who took care of a lot of those types of lessons while he provided the income for the family. Taking on the emotional support demanded by parenthood was something he still was working on, so this one chalked up as a definite win for him.

"I know we sound anxious to bring you home and build you a normal life, but we won't push you. If you want to stay and create a life here, that's your decision. We really do want you to be there with us, though, and we'd be happy to have you as a part of the family. I'd raise you like a daughter of my own. I'm not saying I can replace your parents. There's no way anyone truly can. But if you want some support in your life, we can provide it."

He perhaps lacked a little of the confidence those words

implied, but that's what he intended to do. Even if it scared the pants off of him.

Vickie chose not to answer and continued to stare at the fire.

"But you keep thinking about it," he continued. "You have a little more time before we have to get out of here. And I still have to finish fixing the basement, provided that you didn't put any more holes in the walls."

Vickie laughed. "Not today, anyway."

"Good." He smiled and pushed from the couch. "I'm going to go say goodnight to my daughter. You get some sleep soon, too. Okay?"

"Okay."

He walked past her and patted her on the head before he left.

Vickie returned her gaze to the flames. She realized that sitting in that room and holding that cup couldn't take her back in time. Her family was gone, and she had two people whom she really liked and who were kind enough to want to care for her. That wasn't something to deride or dismiss so easily, even back in the old days. She picked the book up off the floor and cracked it open, hoping to give her mind some small piece of relaxation before she went to bed.

Every few minutes, she'd look up from the pages to stare at the shadows dancing on the wall and think of the simpler life she'd once led. Finally, she looked at her toenails, and the reality of her new life struck a blow. The duel for her choice had begun.

CHAPTER SEVENTEEN

Vickie woke before the others the next morning. She had a plan and she looked forward to it. She stepped quietly out of the bedroom and into the bathroom. The clock on the wall read an early 6:34 AM.

I have about half an hour until the others wake up. She was proud of how quickly she'd picked up the understanding of time and clocks. It had been something of a learning curve initially because she grew up knowing the time of day by the sunshine.

She changed into a pair of jeans, a t-shirt, and a zip-up hoodie before she applied a little makeup—only enough to freshen herself and not enough to draw too much attention. *Do I look like I belong in this century without Alexis' help?*

Today would be her first real test.

The vampire crept down the hall and descended the stairs. She slipped some shoes on and was about to walk out the front door when she paused for a moment.

It occurred to her that she shouldn't make it look like she was running away or sneaking off. That wasn't the point. So, she walked into the kitchen, flipped the light switch, and found a notepad and pen that the Airbnb hosts had left on the kitchen counter. She tore a page off and wrote:

Went into town. Be back later.

~Vickie~

She patted her front pocket to confirm that she had money, then left the castle by way of the front door. The rising sun beamed over the horizon while she walked along the path. A cool breeze gave her a shiver, so she raised the hood over her head and around her ears to help her keep warm.

For a few minutes, she stood at the bus stop, hunched over with her hands in her pockets. She wasn't prepared for it to be this cold, but it was early in the morning and it was usually chilly in general for that time of year. Still, she was in high spirits. Today, she was going alone, and that kind of independence was exciting.

Not only did she feel the need to experience a little personal freedom, but she wanted to see what life in Salzburg was like independently. If she had to decide whether or not she would go with the family to America, she wanted to know how well she managed without them.

She had paid attention over the last few days as she and Alexis rode the bus, noting where the stops were and how everything worked. She needed to know how to get around.

The brakes of the bus squealed, and she jumped slightly.

It's only a noise, not an attack. You have to get used to this, Vickie.

Disembarking in town almost felt overwhelming with

the sense of freedom it brought. People were already milling about, starting their day. Stores were opening. The smell of freshly-baked pastries wafted out into the air.

It was now after seven, and the town had officially come alive.

The first order of business is breakfast. If you want to survive, you need to eat.

The first place she came across that looked like it offered food was a small storefront coffee shop. There was a short line of people inside waiting to be served.

That must mean there is good food there. People would not line up for bad food. She walked in and took her place in line. The menu confused her, however.

What does venti mean? Is cappuccino even a word? Is hot chocolate a drink or a soup, or is it a sandwich? How does one eat it?

She was next in line, and the woman in front of her ordered a hot chocolate and a warm apple strudel.

Good enough for me.

She was curious about the hot chocolate, anyway. When she reached the counter, she ordered the same thing, paid for it, and waited at the pickup counter, following the example of the other customers without staring too hard at them. She needed to learn from them but not in a way that drew attention or made them uncomfortable.

Look how that woman is standing. Notice how people look at each other when they appear to be strangers. How can you blend into this crowd?

Another customer's order came up, and she watched the gentleman step up to the counter, smile, and thank the servers, then drop money into the jar sitting on the side.

He already paid for the meal. Why is he giving them more money? Do I have to give them more money, too?

Another order in front of hers was called, and the next customer did the same thing.

Okay, don't stand out. Follow their lead. Vickie dipped into her pocket and withdrew some money. When her order was called, she walked up, took the tray, thanked the server, and placed money in the jar.

She watched for his reaction. He smiled awkwardly and thanked her, and she turned to find a table, beaming with pride.

You are doing it!

The vampire scanned the small dining area and she spotted an empty chair at a two-person table where a middle-aged woman was seated. She walked over and put her tray down at the small table, then sat across from the woman.

The woman's eyes widened, and she leaned back as if she had told her something horribly offensive. "Excuse me. Do you mind?"

Vickie looked around and noticed people were staring at her. "Oh, um...sorry," she stammered, grabbed her tray, and stood again.

You're not supposed to sit at the same table as other people. Noted.

She turned her attention to a long breakfast bar up against the window that overlooked the street. A young man with headphones sat on one end of the four-stooled counter. He sipped his coffee casually as she took a seat at the other end and watched his reaction closely.

He didn't even look at her.

Okay, I think you can sit here. He won't be offended.

Once she sat, she was able to assess what she'd actually ordered. The apple strudel looked flaky and delicious. The hot chocolate, as it turned out, was a drink in a cup.

Everything was incredible. The beverage was rich and creamy, and the strudel warm and crisp. She was almost bombarded by flavor. The sweetness was almost overpowering but in a good way.

My taste buds must be adjusting. I hope all food is this delicious now.

When she'd finished eating, she saw a pile of trays above the garbage bin near the exit. She placed hers on top and walked out onto the street.

That wasn't too bad. One hiccup, but I'm doing all right so far. I can do this.

She turned and walked down the street, admiring the shops along the way. Every once in a while, she'd stop in front of a storefront window to analyze what was being sold on the inside.

One window sported a series of unique framed paintings. One, in particular, caught her eye as she examined the scene. A man held some kind of instrument and plucked the strings. He wore a white puffy shirt with the sleeves rolled up, a cream-colored vest, and some kind of elaborate cloth tied around his neck.

Most of that made sense to her, although the clothing looked a little bizarre. The confusing part was the man's head. It had been replaced in the painting by the likeness of a dog that seemed to stare directly at her.

Is this a real-life picture? Did the artist do this for fun, or did he really know a musician with a dog's head? Was this the result of some kind of witchcraft? Did the musician want his head to look like this, or was it some sort of punishment?

She didn't know that one picture could cause so many questions.

As she continued her walk down the street, she noticed an alley that looked familiar to her. It didn't take long to piece together exactly why it did. One's first real fight after a four-hundred-year-old nap tended to settle in one's memory. The man she'd pre-empted was gone by now. She thought of the reaction that everyone had, and Alexis' words from the night before echoed through her mind. This was not how one behaved in society.

Vickie shook her head at the memory. She still believed that she'd done the right thing.

I can't stand by and let someone attack me. Besides, we got away, and no other trouble was caused.

Another clothing shop near the alley caught her attention and she stopped to look in the window. To her surprise, all the mannequins on display wore nothing but underwear.

She looked around but nobody seemed fazed by it. Thoroughly startled, she tried her best to not let her mouth hang open in shock.

I didn't notice this place the other day. Do these people have no shame? They're practically naked but nobody else seems to notice this. Is it socially acceptable to show underwear in public?

Vickie still hadn't quite adjusted to the modern idea of underwear, even without this display to confuse her even more. Alexis had given her advice and they'd bought her some basics to wear in the meantime. But what she saw in this window was very different, and it didn't look all that comfortable.

It made her uneasy, so she walked on quickly until she reached another storefront. This time, the luxurious clothing on offer brought no feelings of discomfort. A male mannequin wore a navy-blue suit with white pinstripes, a matching vest, and a pastel orange tie.

Even I can appreciate this. That's a sharp-looking outfit.

The female counterpart showed off a dark-brown pantsuit, which also looked nice, but the large tan fur coat completely threw the style off for her. Vickie laughed at the sight.

It looks like someone skinned a large bear and threw it over the top of her clothing. That's a rug, not a coat.

She marveled at how many clothing stores were on this street alone. In her day, there had been only one place to purchase textiles and nothing else. You had clothing made for you.

Now, when she ducked into the store to look around, she saw rack after rack of pre-made clothing waiting for someone to come in and buy it.

Vickie allowed herself a few minutes to watch how people actually purchased the items. Although she wore her own clothing, she didn't try anything on in the store. Alexis was about the same size as her, and they bought the same clothes. Besides, such fine materials would be more expensive than what she had purchased with her friends, based on the numbers she saw on the tags.

Instead, she watched women step in and out of small booth-like rooms to stand in front of reflective surfaces that showed their bodies from all angles. It was fascinating.

Then, they would disappear into the booths again and step out in their original clothing.

The entire experience seemed utterly peculiar. But, if she wanted to live by herself here or even if she went with the family to America, it seemed that this was a standard practice she would need to get used to.

As she stepped out to the street again, a loud horn honked. She jumped and looked in the direction of the noise to see a small car creeping slowly down the road, trying not to hit anyone.

The crowd slowly dispersed, allowing barely enough space for the vehicle to move through.

It reminded her of the days when horses were ridden around town. Back then, of course, it was easier for a horse to slip through the crowds than these massive moving machines. In a way, they seemed impractical.

But, she assumed, there had to be a valid reason why society made the switch. The smell was better, anyway.

She reached the end of the block and turned to look out over the river for a moment. *Maybe I can pull this off. What if I simply stayed here? I can blend in, and this is my home. There's something comfortable about being at home, no matter how different it might be.*

CHAPTER EIGHTEEN

The sun was higher in the sky now, and the morning turned into a warmer day. Vickie relished the open air. It was a much-needed contrast to centuries closed up in a box.

She decided it would be pleasant to stroll along the river. Since she was in charge of all the decisions on her adventure, that's exactly what she did. The waters rushed and tumbled alongside as she walked with the short buildings of the town on the other side in the shadows of the Hohensalzburg Fortress.

She strolled casually and felt confident in her ability to be independent. The freedom was almost intoxicating. Then, she stopped, although she couldn't explain why. Her instincts merely alerted her, and she knew better than to question them. The hairs on the back of her neck stiffened, and she shivered despite the warmth of the day. Her senses heightened. Now, she could smell the strudel from the coffee shop again, even though it was several blocks away.

She heard conversations from park benches in the distance.

But still, she had no idea why the warning thrummed through her.

Carefully, she resumed her walk. This time, however, she turned away from the river and started toward the town center.

Once again, she halted. Her eyes narrowed and focused to search her surroundings. A man stood across the street from her and made no effort at all to hide his blatant, arrogant stare. And just like that, her morning high crashed. Her stomach twisted into a knot.

What does he want? Why is he looking at me like that?

He wore a brown leather bomber jacket with a fur-lined collar. His salt-and-pepper hair lifted from his collar in the breeze off the water. Vickie pretended to disregard him and wandered on. Rather than remain—or, even better, leave—he walked briskly toward her and maintained his deliberate scrutiny.

Do not make a scene. Do not make a scene. Do not make a scene. Fight your instincts. Don't stand out. He hasn't threatened you.

"You're that girl!" he shouted as he approached, his attitude now aggressive.

"I'm sorry?"

"From yesterday." He lunged toward her. "You attacked that guy."

"I don't know what you're talking about." Vickie's voice wavered. She was absolutely certain that no one had witnessed the altercation the day before, which could only mean one thing. This man, whoever or whatever he was, knew the stranger she'd confronted. It seemed obvious that he had come to finish whatever his comrade had started.

She kept her head down and tried to walk away, but he followed. And now, his cries had alerted others who started to stare at her too.

"Hey," he yelled as he grabbed her by the arm.

"Let go of me." She jerked away.

"You're that girl. You committed a crime. That man's in the hospital now."

"I don't know what you're talking about," she said, again unsure what else she could say to diffuse the situation.

Her breath quickened and she fought to stay calm. Tears filled her eyes and clouded her vision slightly.

I simply wanted to walk through town, not to get into any trouble. I only want to be here by myself.

Instead, trouble followed her. She scanned the area quickly while the man continued to rant behind her. Another alley lay a short way ahead, directly behind the building where Mozart had been born—or so the sign said. It was as good a place as any, and she hoped that perhaps she could lose him and hide in a different store.

Vickie sprinted away and fought every urge to turn on the true speed of which she was capable. She didn't want to draw attention, however. If she gave in, everyone would know something was different about her and she wouldn't be able to return to the castle safely.

"Hey," the man bellowed, even louder now. "Stop that girl. She's a criminal."

She shook her head as she entered the alley, ran up a block, and darted to her left.

Frantic, she scanned her surroundings, looking for any

place where she could hide. The few stores on that street were closed and at the end of the block, two other men pointed at her.

"There she is," They began to race toward her.

Vickie whirled and froze as others swarmed from that direction too. She stood locked in place, trapped and with nowhere to go.

Her chest heaved with unshed tears. She noticed a small gap to the right side of one of the groups. It would be enough to ensure her escape, but she would have to tap into her vampiric abilities to do so.

Her tongue touched her top teeth and she felt her fangs emerge. It seemed that her entire body demanded that she do it.

If you do, you instantly put a target on your back that won't go away. Too many people are watching. You'll never be able to walk around by yourself again.

When she focused on the rage that burned in the eyes of the growing mob that drew ever closer, she realized her options were exceptionally limited.

There is already a target on your back. It's too late, anyway. Just do it.

She took a deep breath and looked around Salzburg one more time. A lump formed in her throat.

This is the last time you will see your hometown.

Vickie exhaled sharply and blurred into motion, raced through the gap, and banked around her pursuers.

Before they could even register her movement, she had vanished. A wind followed her, and all her would-be attackers stood with their eyes wide as they glanced at one another and muttered, "Did you see that?" over and over again.

The mystery criminal had disappeared in front of their very eyes.

In seconds, Vickie reached the outskirts of town and was safely out of harm's way. She stopped running for a moment and turned to look over the city.

For a long moment, she admired the river and the water that gushed casually under the bridges, the small cathedrals that dotted the perimeter of the town, and the low buildings that lined the streets. And, of course, there was the fortress that towered over it all higher up on the mountain.

It looked so different from the Salzburg she remembered. And yet, the bones of the city remained.

It's still your home. But it's a home that doesn't want you. And now, it's a home you can't return to. This day was a mistake, and there's nothing you can do about it.

Vickie hung her head in sadness. This was supposed to be a fun day. Now, it was ruined and even the few pleasant memories she'd forged seemed tainted and bitter. She briefly considered finding a bus stop and waiting for one to arrive. By now, though, she simply wanted to go back to the castle. She had forgotten a very important fact that asserted itself painfully in the aftermath of the morning's impulsive decision. With freedom came risk. And with risk came danger.

The walls of the castle would keep her safe exactly as they had done for centuries.

The energy built in her legs again, and she tapped into it. Dirt and grass kicked into the air as she hurtled forward.

Fifteen seconds later, she stood in front of her castle. She jogged up to the front door and let herself in. Her friends sat in the kitchen, drinking coffee.

"Well, hey there!" Alexis shouted when she heard the door open.

Vickie walked into the kitchen with a somber look on her face.

"Where were you?" Craig asked. "Did you go into town alone?"

She pulled a stool up, flopped onto it, and put her face in her hands. "It was a mistake. I got into trouble."

Alexis looked at her father with concern. "Trouble? What did you do?"

Vickie lifted her head. "Nothing. I simply walked through the town, trying to fit in. But apparently, everyone was waiting for me because I attacked that man yesterday. He must have had friends nearby, and they stirred the others up."

He nodded, knowingly. He'd vaguely expected something like that and feared it would come back to haunt them. "That's okay. Maybe it was too soon. Give it a little more time and maybe it won't be such a big deal."

Vickie shook her head, then stood to fill herself a glass of water from the faucet. "No, things were different there. I was getting around fine, and I was fascinated by it—the artwork, the clothing, even the food. There was nothing recognizable about it. I guess when I go to town with you two, I pay attention to so many other things. Going by myself allowed me to get lost in my head and explore what interested me."

"That sounds great," Alexis said.

"But it wasn't." Vickie took a sip of water as she struggled to rein in her emotions. "It was enjoyable, but it wasn't home. Other than the fortress and the river, nothing really felt the same. It was good to see the old bones still there, but it wasn't what I remember. I realized that it doesn't offer the same comfort I get here." She pointed to the basement door. "Down there is completely different. The bedrooms upstairs are different. There's a bathroom up there now. This kitchen feels like a different world. The only time I find any comfort is from that red chair and the cup in the library. The rest of this merely feels…foreign to me."

Craig nodded and sipped his coffee slowly. He put his hand gently on her shoulder. "It's okay. That's all completely normal. What do you want to do about it? Wait a while and see how you feel?"

"I don't know." Vickie twisted her lips in confusion. "It made me so sad that I felt so unsafe in the place where I grew up."

"You know where we stand on the issue, Vickie," Alexis said. "We want you to come with us to America. We want you to be a part of our family. And if this place doesn't feel like home, why stay?"

Vickie straightened and looked at the ceiling. "It's as though I'm the last one, you know? Of all my people, I'm the last vampire left. I can't feel any others anywhere here. So, if I leave, am I giving up on my heritage, on my family?"

Craig rested his elbows on the kitchen island and smiled. "Vickie, I love my daughter, right?" She nodded. "Now, let's say I pass away and she's left with nobody."

"Great start to a story, Dad."

He put his hand up. "Hang on. I'm going somewhere with this. Now, Vickie, the one thing I want for my daughter is to be happy. If she wanted to get away from everything—the house we live in, the stuff that we shared, all of that—if getting away from that would make her happy, I would be all for it."

"You would?"

"Of course. Heritage and tradition are wonderful things. But you don't honor your family by staying in the same physical place where they lived. You honor them by taking a little piece of them with you. No matter where you are in the world, you are still a vampire. You still represent your family and your race. You can do that as well in America as you do here. And in America, you'll have friends with you to help you keep from getting yourself in trouble." He winked at her. "At least most of the time."

Vickie's lips twitched in response. She glanced around the room again, took a shuddering breath, and finally nodded in resignation. "All right. Let's do it. I want to go to America with you. I want to be a part of your family."

Alexis and her father looked at each other and beamed.

"Well, if you're going to be a part of our family, there's one thing you have to learn about us," her friend said to her.

"What's that?"

The girl stood, walked around the island, and threw her arms around her.

"We're huggers."

Her father laughed as the two girls embraced and tears flowed down Vickie's cheeks.

He sighed quietly. "Two daughters. I sure hope I know what I'm asking for."

CHAPTER NINETEEN

Alexis grunted as she carried the basket of dirty clothes down the basement steps. A confused Vickie followed.

"Hey, Dad," Alexis greeted her father when they reached the bottom. Craig was hard at work sanding the spackled areas on the drywall in the basement, the final step before painting. He grinned at her as he blew off another layer of dust.

"I'm gonna guarantee we don't get charged for this. They won't even be able to tell."

She giggled, then hauled the clothes through the door on her left and into the unfinished portion of the basement.

The girls stepped into the darkness, and Alexis yanked the pull chain on a light bulb hanging in the middle of the room.

"Whoa." Vickie looked around the newly-lit room with awe. The old stone walls were still there. The dirt floors had been covered with concrete, but this was the closest room to the original home she knew. There was no drywall, no drop ceiling, and no carpet. It felt safe and familiar. After what happened that morning, she needed that feeling.

She walked up to the stone wall and rested both her palms on it, then leaned forward, pressed her forehead against it, and closed her eyes for a moment.

It was such a tiny piece of her home, but it filled her with a sense of nostalgia that she yearned to experience. And now that she was trapped in this castle until they were to leave, it was even more important for her to savor it.

"Are you okay?" Alexis asked with a smirk.

"Give me a minute."

The other girl set the basket of clothes onto the dryer. The unfinished portion of the basement had been set up as the laundry room—a necessity for anyone spending more than a week or two in a foreign country.

Typically, European homes kept a laundry area on the main floor. Many even had theirs in the kitchen. Usually, it was a combination washer and dryer.

What drew Alexis' father to choose this place was the separate washer and dryer in the basement. It was a very American setup, and a few comforts of home were pluses in the Airbnb listing.

"Okay." Vickie sighed and spun around to watch Alexis load the clothes into the washer. "I think I'm ready for this."

"There are a heck of a lot more clothes in this basket than I'm used to at this point," Alexis joked. "We should simply make you wear that dingy robe until you learn to do your own laundry."

"Well, I'm here now, aren't I? Teach me already."

Alexis scattered the clothing into the large, energy-efficient washing machine. "You can fill it to this line here. And then you dump the soap in. The machine will do the rest."

Vickie leaned over to check behind the machine but saw only a few water lines and an electric plug. "How does it do that?"

Her companion shrugged. "I don't really know. But it works. And this model even sets the water level automatically for you. You tell it there are clothes in it, and all the sensors or whatever do the rest."

At first, the vampire looked forward to such an easy operation. She had learned so much over the past few days that she had grown almost overwhelmed. It wasn't that her brain couldn't handle it. Her mind was more than capable of learning that much, and more. But from an emotional perspective, it was exhausting. She was learning years' worth of activities in only a couple of days. Her entire way of life had changed, and laundry was simply the latest culprit.

"How did you do laundry back in the day?" Alexis asked as she measured the soap.

"I didn't. My mother took care of all that. She had a bucket of water and a washboard, I believe. Kids weren't expected to do that. The parents did those kinds of activities."

"Well, not today." Her friend dumped the soap into the washer. "Now, you have to learn. And in our house these days, you really have to step up with my mom not being there anymore." She closed the washer lid to reveal the dozens of buttons and settings on the control panel.

Vickie shot her a confused look. "Seriously? How many different ways can this thing wash clothes?"

"You'd be surprised." Alexis shook her head and pushed a few buttons labeled **Normal**. Within seconds, water poured into the drum of the washer. "That's it. Honestly, it doesn't get much easier than that."

Vickie laughed. "My mom would have killed to have a machine like this doing all that work for her."

The two of them walked into the rec room area of the basement, where Alexis' father stood and welcomed them cautiously to the space.

"You're not going to watch a scary movie, are you? Or a 3D movie? Or anything with sudden movements?" He hadn't quite finished sanding, and truly was tired of doing all this extra work on his last days of vacation.

"Don't worry, Dad. We're only talking." They sat on the couch. "You've mentioned your parents a lot, Vickie. Tell me about them."

The vampire leaned back and sighed. "My father was a stern man. He held very strict rules for the house, and you didn't dare cross him or those rules. But he cared deeply for his children. He always looked out for me, especially after my siblings passed."

"In what ways?"

"Well, for example, I was out in the town one day and I felt a strange presence. I couldn't explain what it was, but it grew stronger the closer I got to St. Peter's Abbey. My fangs started to emerge, and everything grew really tense."

"What was it?" Alexis leaned forward in anticipation.

Vickie shrugged. "I still don't know. Men in black robes walked around outside the cathedral. They had worn hoods that covered their faces, so I couldn't get a good look at who—or what—they were. As soon as I realized that they were probably the threat, my dad whisked me up in his arms and ran."

"Do you think it was the Circle?"

"Maybe. The more I think about it, yes, it probably was. I merely wandered past and didn't engage any of them. But he pushed between us and scooped me up. He never said a word about it afterward, though."

Alexis looked at her dad, who had listened as well. "I can't imagine you doing something like that without explaining to me what was going on. That seems weird to me."

He leaned away from the wall and pushed onto his knees. "I get it. If—and I'm saying if—there really was a group of fanatics who wanted all vampires killed, and your father knew that, he most likely was simply trying to protect you from fear. He didn't want you to be afraid, so he rescued you from the threat without explaining what it was. It's a choice you make in these kinds of situations."

"I don't think it helped." Vickie pulled her ankle up onto the couch and tucked it under her leg. "I always felt safe here at home, but then I always felt unsafe when I was out and about in the town. That's why I went into town by myself today."

"You wanted to see how it felt," Alexis said.

"Exactly. I wanted to know that I could survive out there on my own and that there was nothing for me to be afraid of." She paused. "I guess that didn't really work."

"What about your mom? Tell me about her." She was more eager to hear about Vickie's mom, given how much she missed her own mother.

"My mother was a quiet woman. She took care of the home and the family and was very busy, always cooking or cleaning or taking care of the animals on the grounds."

"I bet cooking was a lot more work back then," Craig commented as he rubbed the last section of drywall with a scrap of sandpaper.

"We didn't have microwaves." Vickie laughed. "We didn't have any machines that generated heat. If you had to manage a fire every time you cooked, you'd probably spend half your day cooking, too."

"I love cooking over the fire," he said. "Actually, we call that grilling. And yeah, it takes almost all day if you do it right. So yes, I understand."

"It's so much easier here. I can process the information easily enough and convert it to memory, but I'm overwhelmed by all the emotional and sensual information that I'm processing. It blows my mind how different—and how simple—all these daily activities are."

Alexis smiled. It wasn't something that she had given much thought to. Like most people, especially kids, she took for granted all the things that she was able to do on a daily basis that simply didn't happen fifty or a hundred years ago, much less four hundred.

That gratitude was an important reminder for herself, too. She would carry it with her wherever she went. The events of the past year had really brought her down hard. She struggled emotionally with the troubles she and her family endured. Often, she fell into a woe-is-me attitude.

She always hid it from her father because he was going through enough on his own. While she knew bottling it up wasn't healthy, in her mind, neither was dumping it on the man, especially after he was fired from his job.

But with Vickie reminding her, Alexis suddenly found herself awash in gratitude for dishwashers and ovens, microwaves and music systems, and everything in between. All the things that made life easier these days were not features of Vickie's previous life. They hadn't even been so much as conceived of yet. It was a sobering thought, and especially so once the washing machine bleated to notify them that it had finished its cycle. The two girls returned to the laundry room.

"We'll put these clothes in a big hot box?" Vickie asked. "Won't they catch on fire?"

Alexis laughed. "If I thought this thing would set your clothes on fire, would I actually do this?"

"I guess not. But what about using the fresh air and the sunshine?"

Alexis bent over and tossed another handful of clothes into the dryer. "At home, that's fine. I like hanging clothes on the clothesline. It's great. But here? We're working with a limited number of outfits. If a clothesline takes a little longer at home to dry, I have other clothes that I can use. Here, I don't have that option so I need to go with convenience."

The dryer rumbled to life as she flipped the timer on it.

"I notice the controls here are much less intimidating," Vickie observed.

"There are only so many ways you can complicate the dryer. It spins the clothes around and blasts them with hot air. Look, a good rule of thumb with the laundry is this: when in doubt, look for all the buttons that say **Normal** or something similar. That's all you need."

They walked out of the room and Alexis yanked the pull chain again on her way out.

"So how long will it run in there?" Vickie asked. "A few days?"

Her friend laughed. "Goodness, no. Maybe an hour? An hour and a half? It doesn't take long. This dryer seems to be fairly new, too, so its drying abilities should be fine."

She shook her head in disbelief. "Seriously, my mother wouldn't know what to do with herself. This technology has literally made everything better and easier."

"Yeah, but you still have to fold the clothes when you're done with them. It's not perfect."

CHAPTER TWENTY

After the clothes were dry, the girls loaded them into the laundry basket. This time, Alexis had Vickie carry them up the stairs to the bedroom.

"You're right. This is heavy."

"Come on," the other girl joked as she walked behind her. "You have super-speed. Don't you have super-strength, too? Use some of those vampire muscles or whatever."

They reached the upstairs bedroom, and Vickie dumped the basket of clothes onto her bed.

"Now, we fold them," Alexis said. One by one, she picked up a piece of clothing and instructed Vickie on how to fold them properly, then stacked the clothes at the front of the bed to be put away when they were done. Once the vampire had the technique down, they were able to relax and chat.

"I told you about my parents." Vickie grabbed a sock and looked for its match. "Now tell me about yours."

"What's there to say? You know my dad. My mom passed away."

She located the matching sock and folded them together. "No, come on. I know your dad a little, but I don't know him on a personal level the way you do. I want to hear the daughter's perspective on your father."

Alexis pulled out a pair of jeans and buttoned them up for folding. "My dad is hurting."

"He's in pain?"

"Big time. If you look into his eyes, you can see it."

Vickie thought back to her interactions with the man. While he always tried to keep conversations light and peppered with humor, there was a certain melancholy to his tone of voice and his attitude.

"Why does he carry so much pain? Because of your mother?"

"Yeah." Alexis dropped a pair of newly-folded jeans onto the bed. "But it was worse than that. My dad used to work for the newspaper. Do you know what that is?"

The vampire shook her head while she folded a t-shirt.

"Okay, it's is a printed collection of papers delivered to your front door every day. It has all the latest news. My dad was an investigative reporter for our newspaper, the Milwaukee Journal Sentinel. And he was good at it. He broke all sorts of news and got interviews with almost anybody who was famous who came through the city. He had a great job, and he loved it."

"That sounds nice. What happened?"

Alexis sighed. "The Internet happened." Vickie gave her a blank stare, clearly having no idea what she was talking about. "It made newspapers basically obsolete. The Net connected everyone together, so sharing the news became something that anyone could do, and that's exactly what they do to this day. The newspaper industry never really tried to take on the Internet in the early days. They simply assumed everyone would still read newspapers."

"But they stopped?"

She nodded sadly. "Most people stopped. You could get your news faster and cleaner through a website. Having the news printed on a sheet of paper and then dropped at your door at five in the morning? What was the point anymore?"

"So are newspapers gone now?"

"No, that's the thing. They're still there but they don't hire people anymore. When things get too tight, they lay people off to make room in their budgets."

"And that's what happened to your dad?"

"Yep. The newspaper kept losing money, so they let their top investigative reporter go. My dad was working on some other stuff, like this podcast, but nothing that generated any kind of substantial income."

"What's a podcast?"

"It's like a radio show." Alexis realized that comparison wouldn't help, either. "That's how you heard the music in the car—the radio. He sits down and records himself speaking to people, then posts it for everyone to listen to when they want."

"It sounds interesting."

"It probably is, but I've never listened to an episode. He's really thrown himself into it, and it annoys me a little."

"Because he lost his job and he's become so sad?"

Alexis picked up the pile of jeans on the bed and walked them over to the dresser on the other side of the room. "My mom died right before the job did. It was all very sudden. He didn't know that he was losing his job, and he didn't know he was losing his wife. It was the perfect storm."

"The poor man. That must have been really hard on him."

"It was. And it still is. She died quickly, and while dealing with that, he had to cope with the job loss and raising me alone. That does things to people."

She stepped over to the window and looked out into the night sky. The bright, full moonlight beamed onto her face. To Vickie, it looked like she herself was glowing in the window.

"Sometimes, I wish that all of that hadn't happened at one time. Honestly, how fair is it that he loses his wife and his job within a week? He lost everything except me. That's what this trip is about." She thought for a moment. "He's kinda like you. You lost everything too, Vickie."

"I suppose that's true. But while your dad lost everything, he still has you. And I do too now."

Alexis laughed out loud. "No pressure or anything."

"Is this podcast a bad thing? Is it taking up too much of his time? What else should he be doing?"

"I wouldn't say it's a bad thing. In fact, I do know that it's a good thing in some ways. He told me he has his first advertisers, so he's working on everything and making it as good as he can. It just…takes all his attention."

"How so?"

"He schedules interviews with new guests on his show whenever possible. When you have somebody who lives in another time zone, you have to accommodate for that. And that's great. But it also means he might be up until two or three in the morning working. Or he'll skip dinner. Or both."

"He's not there for you?"

"No, not right now." Alexis returned to sit on the bed and finish folding clothes. "He's great at it, but it takes all his spare attention. By the time he gets to whatever I'm dealing with, the advice he gives is useless."

"Here's a weird idea. Why don't you ask him? Talk to him about your problems to see if there is a solution."

Alexis raised her eyebrows skeptically. "You have to be kidding me. My father has so many emotional problems that he's trying to work through, and you want me to demand more attention from him?" That was why she kept so many feelings to herself. She wanted her dad to think that she was fine—one less thing for him to worry about.

Vickie folded her last sweatshirt and put it on the pile on the bed. "All I know is that a father wants to take care of his daughter. She means the world to him. If he knew that you were struggling this much, he would change his habits."

The girl gritted her teeth. "I really doubt it. He's struggling, too. I don't want to add any more baggage to what he's carrying around right now. I have school. Well, in a few weeks, anyway. My friends are there, and I can count on them to help me work through some stuff. I can get away. He has nothing. He can't go anywhere or do anything. I simply try to be there for him when I can."

Vickie finished stuffing her clothes into the drawers of the dresser and pushed them shut. "Is it a mistake for me to come with you, then? Maybe I should stay here, and you can visit me once in a while. Because I'll add an entirely new set of problems to this man's life, and I don't know if I want to do that when he's been so kind."

"If there's one thing I know about my dad, it's that he's honest." Alexis pulled the laundry basket off the bed and dropped it to the floor. "If he really had a problem with you, I would know about it by now. I mean, I think he's a little concerned about the fact that he'll be raising another teenage girl, but that would happen whether my mom was with him or not. He's not used to raising people like us. He grew up with all boys in his family."

"It seems a little silly to ignore an opportunity to help each other, simply because you don't want to be a bother," Vickie said. "If you need something, ask him for it. He's your father and a kind man. I'm sure he would be happy to offer his support to you and the things that you are struggling with."

On that note, there was a knock at the door. Craig poked his head into the room. "I'm heading to bed. The first coat of paint is on the walls downstairs. I only hope it'll blend in so we don't get charged."

"I'm sure it's fine, Dad. Goodnight!"

He wished them both a fond goodnight and closed the door.

Vickie pointed at the door. "See? Right there. This was the perfect opportunity to ask him. Tell him that you're struggling right now and that you need a little extra support."

"He's spent the last few days doing all that work in the basement. I really don't want to bother him. He needs to rest." She pulled the blanket on the bed back to reveal her pillow. "At this point, I think I simply need some sleep." She crawled under the covers and released a deep sigh once she got comfortable.

Vickie shook her head and climbed into the bed.

It's like everyone is willing to suffer in silence simply because they don't want to be a bother.

As Vickie lay in bed, anxiety crept in. And it wasn't because of any perceived threats to her safety. It was because the castle had become a melting pot of heartbreak and stress. She was exhausted by having to learn more and more things, and the sadness pressed around her chest like a vice, making it difficult to breathe.

All she wanted to do was fix everything. It was in her nature. She got that tendency from her father, who was very good at it. When her siblings died, he had taken charge and tried to protect others from that pain. It was a trait that she always admired in the man, and she smiled as she thought of it.

But how can I fix this? How could I step into this family and repair their relationships? Eliminate pain? That's not so easily done. What does fixing that even look like? I want to help. but I don't know how.

Then, she thought about America. As nervous as she was about leaving the country, she was also thrilled. Salzburg had become a giant reminder that nothing was the same anymore. Alexis and her dad would deal with heartbreak. And now, Vickie was dealing with her own heartbreak caused by the people of her hometown. None of this situation was ideal, and all three of them carried enough baggage to cause a complete and utter disaster.

In the other bed, Alexis held high hopes. In her view, their bond with Vickie was a wonderful thing, and it allowed them to move forward with a new twist to their lives that didn't upset the status quo. She had long since held the belief that happiness was found when you ran toward something instead of running away from it. With a clear path in front of them—getting Vickie to America—the family now had a goal that they could pursue together to bond them in a much stronger way.

The girl had always been closer to her mother. She'd never really bonded with her dad in the way that she wanted to. But now that they had a mutual goal, she hoped it would blossom into a closer and stronger relationship on its own without potential meddling that could mess things up.

Before any of that could happen, though, they had to find a way to get her out of Salzburg, which would be equally as complicated as getting her into America.

CHAPTER TWENTY-ONE

Rain pelted the windows of the kitchen where Craig sat at the kitchen table with his laptop, a notebook, and a pen. He rubbed his temples and glanced at the clock on the wall.

11:48 PM.

The castle was so quiet. It was unsettling, but he didn't want to risk the girls knowing what he was doing, so he waited for them both to be asleep. On the notebook page in front of him, he scrawled out a handful of words, each carrying their own baggage he would have to sift through

SSN. Passport. ID. Citizenship. School admission.

He knew that he couldn't simply bring Vickie into America. It wasn't as easy as buying a plane ticket. She needed to have a real, verifiable history. And if she was from four hundred years ago, they couldn't walk into some government office and have an ID issued.

Craig wanted to get her to America using the shortest possible route. Initially, he'd thought of getting her Austrian citizenship somehow, then having her emigrate to

America. That was entirely impractical. He didn't want to deal with the paperwork and headaches involved with getting one citizenship only to trade it for another. However it could be accomplished, he was determined to skip the middleman and get Vickie American citizenship off the bat.

If he had to fool a nation illegally, it might as well be his own.

The how was the lingering question. The first thing he did was open up an Incognito Tab on his laptop and start searching for the fabled Dark Web.

He had first heard of the Dark Web years ago while he researched story ideas for the paper. Apparently, there was an entire subsection of the Internet devoted to the buying and selling of illegal substances, materials, and information. Of course, he'd never thought much about it after his projects had taken a slightly different direction, and he'd never expected to seriously consider diving into its murky depths either.

One could, it was said, go to this corner of the Internet and purchase illegal identification, counterfeit money, radioactive materials, and illicit drugs—or anything else weird and not so wonderful.

But the searching made him uneasy. For one thing, he had no idea what he was doing. If he purchased a Social Security number from a Dark Web site, he could accidentally hand his information over to the government. Or he could buy fraudulent identification that wouldn't work, which would trigger an investigation the second they tried to use it.

He straightened, folded his hands on top of his head,

and stared out the window at the pouring rain reflecting off of the light coming from the kitchen.

If he had to break the law and do something illicit like this, he had to make sure his tracks were covered.

That's when he thought of Peter Barnsworth.

When he'd first started his podcast, Craig had dabbled in the Dark Web to see if he could build a season-long narrative around it.

This research led him to Peter, who went by the name CarlDeep67 online. He never asked about the significance of the screen name. Peter was a leading vendor in the Dark Web. He sold mostly illegal information and materials but was more brazen about it than most.

To reach Peter on the phone, Craig had to convince him that he would do a respectable, privacy-protected report on him.

His contact had instructed him to get two apps: Vault-Text and VaultTalk.

They used VaultTalk to speak on the phone. The app encrypted the call over the Internet to prevent any spying by third parties. Peter swore by it. Its sister app, VaultText, did the same thing, but for text messages.

Ultimately, Craig couldn't cobble together enough for a coherent narrative on the Dark Web, so he scrapped the idea. But he kept the apps, and Peter had said to send a text any time he needed to contact him.

He snatched his phone from the table, swiped it open, and tapped on the VaultText icon to open the app.

Me: **Hey, I need your help, if you're up for it**

Anxiously, Craig waited for a response. He'd remained on good terms with Peter, and the man liked his interview style and the respect he showed him. Hopefully, he wouldn't mind offering some assistance. It was an emergency, after all.

He felt reasonably confident that he would get the help he needed and so continued to wait. Within minutes, he received his answer.

CarlDeep67: **What's up?**

Me: **I need to get someone into the US, but she needs a background. She has no records with anybody, so I need all the documentation needed to get her in.**

As the typing notification appeared and he waited for Peter to reply, Craig took a deep breath. He was sailing through uncharted waters at this point. One wrong move and he could go to federal prison, even if he was trying to help someone.

His phone dinged.

CarlDeep67: **Send me your address and the name/age of the girl. I can get her an SSN and passport in 3 days. Would that work?**

Me: **YES. Thank you so much, man! Hope you're doing well.**

They exchanged pleasantries for a few minutes, then Craig told him that Vickie was a fourteen-year-old girl and sent him the address to the castle.

CarlDeep67: **Oh, and get me a picture for the passport**

Me: **She's sleeping. Can I do it in the morning?**

CarlDeep56: **Sure. But do it first thing, so we avoid any more delays**

Craig wasn't interested in waiting any longer, so he agreed without hesitation.

That took care of the paperwork. Now, he had to worry about school. Alexis attended Clear Lake High School in Milwaukee, a large private school with nearly a thousand students. In order for Vickie to attend, she would have to provide two things. First, proof of schooling elsewhere, whether that was a school record or evidence of home-schooling. Second, successful completion of a placement test.

Each of these issues provided their own set of hurdles to overcome.

Craig wasn't exactly sure how he would provide proof of schooling, so he went back to VaultText to ask Peter.

Me: **Also, trying to get her into Clear Lake High School in Milwaukee. She needs a school record and to take a placement test. I can get her the test. Can you get her a record?**

CarlDeep67: **You got it. I'll toss in a school record. You're on your own for the test.**

So, that settled it. After spending an hour researching, a five-minute conversation with a friend might have cleared all the hurdles to get admission.

Craig pumped his fist in silent celebration as he closed his laptop.

He still had to decide how to present this information to the girls without telling them how illegal it was. Alexis was no fool, though. She would know something was up. But still, he had to try to keep them out of the dirt.

He'd figure that out in the morning. For now, it was time for bed, and for the first time in a while, he slept soundly, content with the progress he'd made that night.

The next morning, Craig greeted both girls in the

kitchen as Alexis whipped up some oatmeal for them for breakfast.

"Sorry, Dad." She pointed to the two bowls of oats on the island. "We were hungry."

He rubbed his eyes and yawned. "It's no problem. Hey, girls, we have to talk."

The kettle on the stove whistled furiously. Alexis grabbed it off the burner and poured the water into the two bowls of oats. She stirred them a couple of times and brought them to the table for herself and Vickie.

Craig sat across the table from them. Weariness had taken its toll, and although he'd slept well, a quick glance in the mirror had reminded him that he still had some catching up to do. Even the bags under his eyes now had bags of their own.

"Were you up late on the podcast again, Dad? You look terrible."

Craig shook his head. "Thanks. No, I wasn't working on the podcast. I was actually making plans to get Vickie into America."

Alexis' eyes brightened immediately. "That's great! How did you do it?"

"Don't ask. Just trust me. I know a guy who was able to get us in. We should have all the paperwork in a few days. I only need a few photos of Vickie that he can use for documentation."

The vampire watched Alexis blow on her first bite of oatmeal to cool it off. Following her lead, she blew on hers.

"What do we need to do?" Vickie asked.

"After the pictures are taken and we have the documentation, all that's left for you is to take a test."

"Okay," she responded, her tone decidedly unsure. "I can take a test. But what kind of picture do they want?"

Craig tilted his head to stretch the crick in his neck. "A picture of your head. They need it to make a passport for you."

"It's that easy?" Alexis laughed. "That's unbelievable."

He cocked an eyebrow. "I'm not too sure how easy it is, but we're going to do it. The guy who's getting it together is probably jumping through a lot of hoops. We're simply paying him to do the dirty work."

"What does this test entail?" Vickie asked.

"It'll be a long written test where they determine your proper level of schooling. You'll have to show that you have at least as good a comprehension of math and reading as the average high school student. We'll prepare you for that."

"That shouldn't be too hard," she said. "You saw how quickly I learned English."

"That's what I thought. After breakfast, we'll get a few pictures taken in different clothes and send them off to the guy."

"Hang on, Dad." Alexis held her hand up. "We'll have to make sure she looks good. This is a picture she'll carry around for years. I want her makeup and hair done right so she doesn't have to be self-conscious about it."

Craig rolled his eyes. "Whatever. Then eat a little more quickly. I have to send this picture to him as soon as possible so he can get the paperwork rolling."

The two girls wolfed their bowls of oatmeal down and scurried upstairs so Alexis could work whatever magic she had in mind. Ten minutes later, Vickie stood in front of a white wall in the kitchen, and Craig used his phone to take the picture.

"I hope this guy can clean up the kitchen wall," he said to nobody in particular, knowing a passport photo needed a plain white backdrop. The kitchen wall was white enough but still had glaring inconsistencies.

"Okay, that's one thing done. When do I take this test?"

"You'll take it at the high school after we get home. We'll prep you here and there, then take you to a test session. It looks like their next one is the week after we get home."

"Dad? We're really doing this, aren't we?" Alexis demanded, her excitement brimming.

Craig smiled tiredly. "Yes, Lexi, we really are."

CHAPTER TWENTY-TWO

Three days later, the two girls sat in the library surrounded by books and Alexis' laptop. They had spent every waking moment reviewing the major subjects of the average high school student, covering math, history, and science.

For her part, Vickie had proven herself to be every bit the learner that she claimed. All Alexis had to do was find the right resources and put them in front of the girl to read and review. Vickie could do the heavy lifting from there. Once in a while, the vampire would have a question that Alexis would answer for her, but overall, she simply tapped into her steel trap of a brain and filled it with all the knowledge presented to her.

Alexis stood to stretch her legs and get a glass of water. "This is exhausting and I'm not even the one studying. I don't know how you do it." She watched Vickie's eyes read each page of the book in front of her with the same rapid-scan technique she'd displayed when they'd met her.

On the first day of study, Alexis walked Vickie through

the basics of mathematics—addition, subtraction, multiplication, and division. As the hours passed, she learned more advanced geometry and algebra and challenged Alexis to understand the subjects better herself as they reviewed the material.

Soon enough, it was only a matter of pulling the information up for Vickie to stare at and memorize. This not only sped the process up, but it prevented Alexis from burning out her human brain in an attempt to keep up.

Day two mainly covered the scientific world. By the end of the day, Vickie understood the building blocks of science, like the scientific method and the atom. She knew the common species in the animal kingdom and how the environment worked. The vampire was fascinated, and she laughed repeatedly while she consumed more information voraciously.

"It's funny," she said. "I was raised to believe so many different things about the world. The sun was a god and the moon watched over us at night. I never thought of the world being round or traveling through the universe."

Indeed, her parents had believed a more mythological understanding of the world. They had passed that along to their daughter, but modern scientific studies blew many of these beliefs to pieces.

Day Three was all about history. In the morning, they worked their way through the history of the United States. That afternoon, they discussed and reviewed the major events of world history.

Vickie leafed through a book on World War II, and she frowned suddenly. Her expression seemed to suggest that she didn't understand what she was reading.

"Do you have a problem?" Alexis asked as she entered the room carrying a newly filled glass of water.

"This war doesn't make sense to me. The German leader seems to be so transparently evil. Why would his people follow him so closely?"

Her friend nodded. "I don't know how many fourteen-year-olds really understand this, but Hitler did it gradually. My dad taught me all about it. He worked hard to change people's perceptions of the world by blaming particular groups of people. Then he labeled them evil and turned the people against them. He didn't simply come out and say, 'Let's get rid of all these people and put them in concentration camps.' It was more subtle than that."

Vickie shook her head. "People in society seem really susceptible to this sort of thing."

Alexis nodded sadly. "You see it all over the world. Every country has issues like these to some extent. It's something you have to understand and work with. For example, if you walked out into Salzburg right now, I have no doubt that they would arrest you for being a vampire."

She nodded, read on and explored the statistics and major dates of the war. The reading appeared to disturb her, and a shadow seemed to pass over her eyes as her expression set into a grim line. "Aren't you worried about this happening again?" She looked up from the book. "Do you think the entire world would engage in a war like this?"

The other girl closed one eye, stared off into space, and pondered the question. "Probably. That's how the world is. I don't think we're that close to another world war, but at some point, I think it'll happen again."

"Why? Didn't everyone learn from what happened this last time? Millions of people died and suffered. Do people really want to go through that again?"

Alexis smiled. This was why she stuck around to help Vickie. Learning wasn't only limited to memorizing facts, and she wanted to help the girl understand the world a little better. Fortunately, she read a lot herself and discussed history with her dad often.

"They didn't want to go through it then either. It's simply something that happened. And the people who went through that are largely gone now. They've all died. There are a few survivors, but there are less and less every day. The things that people learned back then are also disappearing. There's an old saying we have—'Those who forget their history are doomed to repeat it.' I think that'll happen. I only hope I'm not around when we do."

Vickie turned the page and sighed. "That is really sad."

They continued their studies until they heard a knock at the front door. Both froze and exchanged wary looks. No one had knocked on their door in the six weeks they had stayed there and the threat of the angry townsfolk still lingered in their minds.

Alexis' father's footsteps echoed as he sprinted down the steps of the second tower. "I've got it. I've got it," he shouted as he barreled to the front door.

He yanked the door open and his gaze settled on a tall, bald man with an angry expression and a dark goatee The visitor sported a crisp black suit, white shirt, and black tie.

Craig's stomach sank.

Is this a federal agent? Have I been caught? Oh, man, they'll take me away from my little girl and arrest Vickie. I knew this was a stupid idea.

"Delivery," the man boomed in a deep voice. He handed him a manila envelope and left.

"What is it, Dad?"

He shut the door and stared at the envelope. His hand shook a little, but he ignored that. The item was unmarked.

"I'll go out on a limb and guess that these are Vickie's new documents."

The two girls bounded to their feet and literally sprinted into the foyer, the studying temporarily forgotten.

Craig opened the envelope and drew the papers out slowly. He held his breath as he summoned the courage to look at the document.

The first thing he saw was the blue Social Security card bearing a number, exactly like the ones he and his daughter carried.

"Vickie Hewitt," he read off the card. "I guess your last name is Hewitt now. You'll always be a Brommer, but we need a new identity with no ties to the past. This looks legitimate, so there will hopefully be no problems with it."

The next thing he leafed through was the small, leather-bound passport. Flipping it open, he saw the picture that he'd taken several days before and sent to Peter. The kitchen wall behind Vickie in the picture had been cropped out and replaced with a plain white backdrop instead.

The passport bore her birthday as well. "It looks like you're fourteen years old here. But you have a birthday coming up at the end of summer."

The girls laughed.

"How did you do this, Dad? It can't be this easy."

She was right. It really couldn't be. He honestly couldn't believe his eyes. But he had all the paperwork right there in front of him. It felt legitimate. It looked legitimate. As far as he could tell, Vickie was a valid United States citizen.

He turned the page on the passport to see the stamps. To his delight, the page already had a stamp showing that Vickie traveled to Austria, so even the passport had their tracks covered.

That is impressive detail.

"Honestly, I don't know, honey. I merely talked to a guy I know, and he took care of everything. And that's all I'll say about it. Do me a favor and don't ask anything more."

Alexis understood and shrugged compliance. The message was loud and clear.

This isn't on the up and up, and I don't want you to know about it.

The last document in the folder was Vickie's school records.

This one made him laugh out loud. "Vickie, it looks like you went to a local public high school in the Milwaukee area. You have all the paperwork you need for a transfer. I see you got good grades, too. An A student."

"That means you get most of the answers right on your homework and your tests," Alexis explained.

Vickie giggled. "Well, that's good. So why do I have to take this other test?"

"Because Clear Lake is a private school. It has its own entry-level tests, especially if you're transferring in the middle of your high school education, which is what you'll be doing here. They merely want you to be on the same level as the other students. Speaking of that, how's the studying going?"

The two girls walked back to the library with Craig in tow.

Alexis rubbed her temples. "I feel like my head will explode, but she's hanging tough. She's working on World War II right now."

"One of my favorite time periods," he said with a smile. "I love me a little World War II."

Vickie looked at him, dumbfounded. "Why would you like this? It looks like this was a horrible time period. So many needless deaths."

He shrugged. "I appreciate the place society was in when this happened. During World War II, Hitler had become such a threat that the people of the United States banded together to defeat him. He was the embodiment of evil thinking. It was a time when the American people united to defeat a common enemy. That kind of unity is something that doesn't happen often anymore, especially in the USA."

"But there was war. That isn't good."

"Of course not. And that part of it truly was terrible. But there was a very clear mission. The young men and women of that time stepped up, put on brave faces, and marched into the theater of war. Many of them sacrificed their lives to achieve that common goal. And they did it. There were no protests back at home that we should be sympathetic to Hitler or anything like that. It was simply good guys versus bad guys."

Vickie still seemed confused, but she accepted his answer.

"I guess that's something about history you don't read about in a book," Alexis said. "There are people out there who love to hear and read these stories. They watch videos on the TV showing how the war was fought. Sometimes there are actors pretending to be soldiers and sometimes, there are real videos of combat. But people are fans of history, just like they're fans of sports or certain books. It's another interest that people can have."

Vickie plopped into the red velvet chair. "I feel like there is still so much to learn. My brain is fine, but it takes a lot of energy to consume all this."

"Just get a basic understanding," Craig suggested calmly. "Know the main points. That's what they'll look for. Don't waste time memorizing every date of every event in the war. They want to know that you've actually studied this kind of stuff."

The girls nodded as they returned to their work. He took the documents to his room for safekeeping and hesitated for a moment to marvel at the accuracy of the passport as he ran his fingers along the textured pages.

That Dark Web sure is something else.

CHAPTER TWENTY-THREE

The girls stood in the bathroom, getting themselves ready for bed. Days of studying had worn them out. As Alexis ran a comb through her curly hair, Vickie brushed her teeth. She had really gotten the hang of the evening routine over the last couple of weeks, and from the outside, she appeared to be like any other teenage girl.

"I'm really looking forward to leaving tomorrow," Alexis said. "I miss home. Although I don't really know what home will be like without Mom there."

Vickie spat her toothpaste in the sink and rinsed her mouth out. "Can I ask you a question?"

"Sure."

"What happened to your mom?"

Alexis sighed. In the past few weeks, she had referred to her mother a number of times but for whatever reason, the topic of what actually happened had never come up.

She handed Vickie the hairbrush, and the two of them switched places in front of the mirror.

"My mom hadn't felt well for a while." She squeezed a

bead of toothpaste onto her toothbrush. "For about a year, she would say once in a while that she felt 'off.' We didn't know what that meant. But she'd get tired or whatever and go to bed early here and there. Sometimes, her stomach felt tight. She thought that maybe she ate too much that night. We chalked it up to her getting older and her body changing."

"Do bodies change as you age? Not to change the topic, but I wondered."

"No, it's fine." Alexis waved the question off. "Bodies can change. How you digest food changes, that sort of thing. You slow down. Although I'm not sure how vampires' bodies change. We'll find out, I guess. Hang on."

Alexis took a break from talking to brush her teeth while Vickie took her turn combing her hair. Once she'd rinsed her mouth, she continued. "Anyway, my mom didn't feel the greatest off and on for a long time, but she'd bounce back the next day. We never thought much about it. Then, a little over a year ago, she said the pressure in her abdomen wouldn't go away. She said it felt like something was there, but she didn't know what."

"What did she do?" Vickie grabbed a face cleansing pad and wiped it on her forehead.

"She went to the doctor. That's what you do when you don't feel well. They have ways to scan your body and find out what's wrong with you. You had doctors, right?"

"Not really. We had people in town who treated the sick, but they didn't do much beyond bleeding you."

Alexis stopped what she was doing. "Hang on. Bleeding you? Is that what it sounds like?"

"Yep. They'd cut you or put leeches on you. It was thought that your blood was the source of your problems."

"That wouldn't fly in today's world. And be thankful for that. Wow."

"Anyway…" Vickie said to steer the conversation back on track again.

"Right, anyway…" Alexis scrubbed her face. "My mom went to the doctor and told them about it. He ordered a few scans of her abdomen. They sent her through a machine that sees through your skin and can take pictures of your internal organs."

"What did they find?"

"Tumors." She sighed. "Lots of them. Her whole abdomen and liver were riddled with tumors."

This jogged Vickie's memory of her day spent studying science and biology. "And were they malignant or benign?"

Alexis shot her an impressed look. "You really do learn fast. They were malignant. The tumors were a rare form of cancer that they said they wouldn't be able to cure. It was called Desmoplastic Small Round Cell Tumor, or DSRCT. It's really aggressive and very rare. In other words, this cancer would kill her."

"How did she handle it?"

"My mom was a fighter, through and through. She wanted to have as much time as she could with me and my dad. She kinda knew she didn't have long, but she said she wanted to try anyway. They ordered really aggressive chemotherapy and radiation treatments. She had surgery where they cut out as much of the cancer as they could, then they'd target the leftovers with more radiation."

"That sounds like it would be really hard on her body."

Vickie tossed out the cleansing pad. Alexis followed suit by throwing hers as well, and the two girls walked to the bedroom and shut the door behind them.

"It was awful and really hard on her. My mom wasn't a big woman. And tough as she was, her body couldn't handle it very well. She would spike fevers and we'd have to rush her to the emergency room. Then they'd pump her full of medicines and other stuff to get it under control."

"How much time did she spend in the hospital?" Vickie sat on the bed and crossed her legs.

"Too much." Alexis shook her head. It hurt to relive the painful experience in her mind. "Every time anything would go wrong, it was like she'd have to spend three days there. She went to New York to have surgery done and spent three weeks there recovering. It simply reached a point where it wasn't worth it anymore."

"And it didn't work, right?"

"Right. Fair enough, it bought her time, but at what cost? I sat down with her one day and sobbed. My mom always held it together. She asked me what was wrong, and I was like, 'Mom, this is torturing yourself. I want to keep you here, but I don't want to keep watching you suffer like this.'"

"You wanted her to give up?"

"It wasn't that." Alexis sat on the bed, her shoulders slouched. "I just... I didn't want all my most vivid memories of my mom being ones where she was sick. And she wasn't able to be Mom. She was in the hospital so much. And nothing worked."

"Is it always that way with cancer? Is this how everyone has to deal with it?"

"No, there are some people who get cancer and are able to get it out of the body. It depends on the kind of cancer and how early you detect it, that sort of thing. With my mom's cancer, it was rare and aggressive. We didn't catch it early enough, so that was it."

"Why didn't she have herself checked out when she first felt bad?"

Alexis smiled sadly. "Mom never liked making a fuss. If she was uncomfortable or in pain, she dealt with it. That's how she was. She came from a rigid family that didn't talk about those kinds of things. You kept your head down and worked. By staying quiet and not being a bother, she basically signed her own death warrant."

"That's terrible."

"I assume, anyway. I don't know if they could have done anything if they had gotten to it earlier. But I do know that this is how it usually is with cancer. The earlier, the better. And they didn't catch it earlier."

"How did it…finally happen?" Vickie asked cautiously.

Alexis swallowed the lump in her throat. She hadn't told the story out loud before, but just like her mother, she was determined to keep her emotions in check.

"She told my dad that it was time. She was tired and ready. He hated hearing that and he didn't want to believe it. But he also knew she was right. They both knew but wouldn't say it up to that point. They had what they call hospice care—a place where they give you drugs to make you as comfortable as you can be until you go. We stayed there for about a week."

"And that's where she…"

"Yeah." Alexis took a deep breath to keep her emotions

under control. "My dad and I held her hands. It became really obvious that it was happening. She was getting more and more tired and had a hard time breathing. We sat by her bed and told her we were there for her. She smiled at us and drifted off to sleep. Then, about an hour later, she stopped breathing and that was it. For all the horrible disasters that raged inside her body, when it actually happened, it was really peaceful. She was calm, she was ready, and she just…went."

Vickie thought of her own parents, how much she missed seeing them, and how she never really got to say goodbye. "Do you think you were better off being with her at the time? I think about my parents and sometimes, I wish that I had been with them when they died. But I also would have had to watch them suffer. I don't know if that would have been better or worse."

Alexis thought for a moment. "For me, yes. It was a peaceful, comfortable way to go for my mom, and I was glad to be there with her. That was important to me. I watched her go, and I felt at peace with it, even if it did make me sad. But for you, knowing how your parents probably died? I think it's best that you didn't see it. I know it's harder that way in some respects, but it would have been very painful, and those images would be seared into your memory."

"I suppose so." The last memory Vickie had of her parents was them surrounding her, caring for her while she fell asleep. They were scared, but they were healthy. Alexis was right. There was no good way for a loved one to die or leave your life, but she decided she should be thankful she didn't have to watch them suffer.

"Anyway, after that happened, we had a nice funeral service for her. Family and friends spent a lot of time at our house going through our stuff, helping us deal with and process everything. But it got to a point where we were tired of dealing with all of it."

"What were they doing?"

"They brought meals, and they sat and talked about Mom and told stories. They all meant well, but it kept us from moving on. Dad sat me down one day and said, 'We need to go away to heal, or we'll never get over this.' So, he told me to pack my bags and that we were going to Austria. And here we are."

"You really haven't been home much since your mom died, have you?"

Alexis shook her head. "It all happened so fast. We were home for a couple of weeks, and then we bolted on out of there. It was tough on us to leave, but my dad insisted. He said we needed to get out. And with him losing his job on top of it, we needed to clear our heads."

"And have you?"

"Oh, yeah. I'm ready to go home. I'm looking forward to it, even if my mom won't be waiting for us when we get there."

"Why?" Vickie stood, walked over to her bed, and pulled the covers back.

"Because we need to be normal again. We need to get into the house and figure out what life looks like. No friends and family getting in our way, no special meals. Just...us. We need to work through the next phase of our lives."

"I guess I have to do that, too." Vickie hadn't really

considered that. For all the learning about the twenty-first century she had done and the hard work she had put in to educate herself on fitting in, she still had no clue what normal life would look like. Deep down, that scared her.

"Exactly. And aren't you ready for that?"

She rested her head on the pillow and looked at the ceiling. "I think so. I haven't thought much about it. But you're right. Now that I've done everything I can here, I need to go where I'll be living and make a life for myself. I have no idea what that will be like."

"Well, it's a good thing we'll all go through it together, then." Alexis and smiled as she turned the light off.

Darkness fell over the bedroom and Alexis lay still for a long while. Tears filled her eyes as she thought about her mom, imagining her warm smile waiting for them at the house. She knew that wouldn't be the case, but sometimes, she liked to dream.

She blinked a few times and took a silent breath to regain her composure. Then she rolled over, hoping to get some sleep.

Another big day tomorrow. The start of a new life in so many ways.

CHAPTER TWENTY-FOUR

C raig smiled and zipped his suitcase as the early morning sun streamed in through the window. His luggage was packed and sat on top of his bed. The last twenty-four hours had been a whirlwind, but a successful whirlwind given all the obstacles they'd faced.

After getting the documents from his Dark Web friend, Craig immediately went to work securing plane tickets with them. He called the airline to transfer the tickets they had to another flight so that they could all fly together.

It was brutally expensive but necessary.

If she were to freak out on the plane with nobody there to keep her in check, she'd be exposed instantly. The feds would be waiting for her by the time the plane touched down.

Their flight left that afternoon. He was able to find one with two seats together and one seat in a different row. Vickie and Alexis would sit together, and he would be in the other to keep an eye on them.

Like his daughter, Craig was ready to get home, too. He had to establish the new normal as well, including his new life as a full-time podcaster. There was a lot to get used to, and even though it would be uncomfortable for him, it was something that he would have to face eventually.

He opened the door to his room and heard movement from the girls' bedroom. Satisfied that they were up and getting ready, he jogged down the stairs and through the kitchen to head to the basement one more time.

To his surprise, the light was already on.

Did I forget to turn it off? The girls are upstairs.

He approached the bottom of the stairs cautiously. "Hello?"

"Oh, hey," Vickie's voice answered.

He turned the corner to see the closet door open and Vickie standing with her hands on the wall. Her head was bowed.

"Is everything okay?"

"Yeah. I'm…saying goodbye, I guess."

Craig nodded. "I didn't mean to interrupt. I wanted to double check all the work I did down here. Not that I can do anything about it now." He chuckled weakly. "I'm paranoid, I guess."

She chuckled. "No problem."

He walked over to the spot where she had made the hole in the wall—the last repair he'd done. It looked solid. The touch-up paint he found in the closet matched up nicely, and the replacement doorknob was hardly noticeable.

The big question mark would be where Vickie was standing. It wasn't identical to the masonry work that had been done before by the vampire's father, but he hoped it would be close enough to not be that noticeable.

They'd never think that we took the wall down and rebuilt it, would they?

He put his hand on Vickie's shoulder. "I'll throw together a breakfast snack for all of us, but you take all the time you need. We don't have to head out for a couple more hours."

"Thanks." Vickie nodded, and Craig walked up the stairs to the kitchen.

She lowered her hands from the wall and stepped back to stare at the brick that had confined her for centuries.

After all this time, I'm finally free. Why do I feel like I'll miss being in there? All I wanted to do was get out and be a part of the world again.

She sighed.

Maybe I miss the time when I didn't have all the answers yet. When there were still possibilities.

While she lay in that box, it was still the seventeenth century. Her parents were still on the other side, waiting for her. Her home was exactly the way that she remembered it. Before she woke up, her world was still the same, as far as she knew.

Vickie stepped out of the closet, shut the door behind her, and locked it. The dark, dirt-floor basement that she remembered was gone, and she missed it. Her footsteps slow and measured, she walked through the door to the laundry room and turned the light on.

She leaned against the stone wall one last time and rested her head against it. She imagined her parents hiding in that room, waiting for the Circle to take them. What must that have been like for them? Were they frightened? Were they at peace? She shook her head at the thought. She would likely never know, and it didn't benefit her to focus on the negative things over which she had no control.

At the bottom of the stairs, she paused and whispered a soft goodbye to the room that had held her for so long. Then, without a backward glance, she walked up the steps and to the bedrooms.

She poked her head into her old bedroom, where Craig's luggage sat. She smiled and closed her eyes as if she were bidding her old life farewell before she walked to the next room.

Alexis smiled at her while she shoved a few more pieces of clothing into her luggage. "You're taking up a lot of room in my suitcase." She laughed. "Are you okay?"

"Yeah," Vickie said quietly. "Just…saying goodbye."

"Gotcha. I'll leave you alone. I can finish this later. I smell food, anyway."

The girl left the room. Vickie stood alone in her parents' former bedroom as memories of the past danced across the stage of her mind. She had spent much of her time there as a little girl, playing on the floor or falling asleep between them. She thought of being tucked in at night by her mother, or her father approaching to kiss her on the forehead before she drifted off.

She savored those memories for a time, then nodded and walked downstairs to the library. The red velvet chair called to her as it always did. She placed her hands on its back and looked at the bookcase. Vickie walked around the chair and up to the mantel, where she picked up the old chalice.

She ran her fingers along the crest one more time.

From the kitchen, Alexis could see into the library and

nodded silently to her father. He peeked through the doorway and watched as an emotional Vickie cradled the cup with a kind of desperate longing. He left his meal preparation for a moment to walk into the library.

"I'm sorry to interrupt, but I want you to go ahead and put that cup in your luggage. Let's bring it home with us."

Vickie looked up with surprise. "Are you sure? Isn't that stealing?"

He shook his head and smiled. "It's yours, isn't it? I'll talk to the host about it and pay him whatever he wants."

"That's really kind of you. Thank you. But you don't have to do that."

He walked across the room looked her in the eye, his eyebrow raised. "There isn't much in this castle left from your old life. That cup is a small thing, but it's your only connection to your history. It's important to you, which means it's important to this family. Take the cup. I'll deal with the fallout."

Vickie was touched by the sentiment and for the first time, she gave the man a hug on her own. He laughed and wrapped his arms around her.

"Dad! The eggs are burning."

Craig's eyes widened and he rushed to the kitchen, hounded by Vickie's laughter. She looked at the chalice and nodded.

At least part of my family gets to come with me.

They ate a simple breakfast of eggs and whatever left-over food they could, so it wouldn't go to waste. They would have a more substantial meal after check-in and while they waited to board, and this would fill the gap in the meantime. When they were done, Alexis hand-washed the dishes and put them in the sink to dry, while her father gathered all the remaining garbage and took it out of the house.

They loaded their luggage into the trunk of the rental car. Alexis and her father stood outside, staring at the castle one last time.

"It was a nice place to stay." He put his arm around his daughter.

"Temporarily," she replied. "I'm excited to get home, for a change."

He looked down at her. "Me, too, sweetheart. Me, too."

Inside the front door, Vickie sat in the middle of the spiraling mosaic tile on the floor of the foyer. She cast her gaze up to the ceiling, then closed her eyes.

Mother, Father, if you can hear this, thank you for doing what you could to protect me. You kept me safe in this house for so many years, and you paid the ultimate sacrifice to keep our enemies from me. I will carry you with me wherever I go in this world, and I will never forget our time here. I will never forget you. And I will always, always love you.

She brushed a tear away and stood, circled the foyer, and walked out of the castle and closed the door.

"Ready?" Alexis asked.

Vickie nodded. "I think so."

They got into the car and drove to the rental car return. Their next stop was the airport.

While on the way, Alexis tried to give Vickie a small pep talk.

"Just remember that the airport will be overwhelming. Your senses will probably be overloaded. Don't panic. It'll be tough but try to keep your composure. You won't be in any danger."

Vickie agreed with her and did her best to internalize the advice.

When they reached the airport and loaded their luggage onto a wheeled cart, the roar of airplanes rumbled through the sky. Vickie held her breath and Alexis touched her shoulder.

"Remember, no danger."

Craig wheeled their luggage into the terminal and checked it in while they went to the kiosk to check into their flights.

"What will happen to our bags?" Vickie asked Craig when he returned empty-handed. The look of confusion she'd worn so often in the early days seemed to have reappeared.

"They'll load them into the bottom of the plane. It'll go with us but not right next to us. When we get to the airport in Milwaukee, they'll give it back to us."

He held his breath as they scanned their tickets, half-expecting the words **FRAUDULENT IDENTIFICATION** to scroll across the screen. Thankfully, that didn't happen. Everything scanned perfectly, and they walked across the terminal to move through security.

The agent checked their IDs and tickets and moved them along, and a wave of relief crashed over him.

We made it. We're through. This is actually happening.

After passing through security, they all agreed to have their meal a little earlier rather than risk a rush before the flight. They walked into a burger restaurant and found a seat next to the window overlooking the tarmac.

Alexis and her father exchanged conversation about going home, what they wanted to do first, and all the things one normally talks about. Vickie did not participate in any of it. Instead, she stared breathlessly out the window at the planes lifting off the ground and soaring into the sky.

"Pretty cool, huh?" Alexis said. "That's what we'll be riding."

"And it stays up in the sky? With all the people on it?"

"Yeah. And there will be plenty of people. It's a full flight. Right, Dad?" He nodded. "We'll all be in it together."

"What if it falls?"

Craig smiled. "Don't worry about that. I've been on dozens of flights. It's safe, and it's fast. We'll be in Milwaukee in no time at all."

The food arrived, and they indulged in burgers and fries. Vickie enjoyed the taste, and Alexis grinned at her.

"This is American-style food," she said. "Once we reach the States, you'll get to eat all kinds of different things."

Craig chimed in. "That's one of the unique things about our country. There are different foods and cultures everywhere you go. You'll have a lot of fun getting to know them all." He patted his belly. "I certainly do."

Once they'd eaten, they milled around a few shops. Alexis bought a few magazines to help pass the time on the plane while Vickie worked to educate herself on US culture.

"Think of it like a form of homework," she said with a wicked giggle. She bought a few candy bars and a bag of Skittles, her favorite candy. She would never fly without a bag of Skittles.

Vickie grew ever more silent while they waited at the gate for their plane to be ready for boarding. When the time came to embark, Craig held out a restraining arm and fixed them both with a level gaze. "I'll be three rows behind you both. If you need anything, wave at me, come get me, or whatever. Just get me. Otherwise, stay calm, behave, and enjoy the flight."

He boarded the plane, leaving the two girls behind to wait for their ticket group to be called.

"It'll be easy," Alexis said. "All you have to do is stay calm. The pilot and the flight attendants will take care of everything else. Get comfortable and entertain yourself. We'll be home before you know it."

They paused at the gate to scan their tickets before boarding. As the fresh air between the tunnel and the plane's door hit Vickie in the face, she realized this was the last time she would breathe Austrian air. She took one more deep breath in and out of her nose, then ducked her head and boarded the plane.

CHAPTER TWENTY-FIVE

Vickie's heart beat hard against her chest as she walked down the aisle of the airplane behind Alexis.

Row after row of passengers stared at her and watched her walk past.

Do they know? Can they tell? Why are they looking at me? Am I in trouble?

Never in her life had she been in such close proximity to so many different people and in such a confined space. While many of them had their heads down, reading books or playing on their phones for a few more minutes, others simply kept their eyes up to watch their fellow passengers.

Vickie grabbed Alexis by the shoulder and squeezed it gently, the signal that she felt anxious.

"Already?" Her friend turned her head. "We haven't even sat down yet. Hang on. Let's get to our seats quickly. It'll be okay."

They pushed down the narrow aisle until they reached their row. Alexis pointed to the window. "Do you want the view?"

"Oh…uh…yeah…sure, fine." Vickie stumbled, then stepped forward and sat in the window seat. Alexis followed and claimed the middle seat.

"All right, what's your deal? Talk to me. Why are you freaking out already?"

"It's just…there are so many people here," she whispered.

"Yeah, I know. It's an overseas flight. These are usually big planes and they carry a good number of people. It's okay. They're here for the same reason we are. Nobody is paying attention to you."

"They're watching me."

"No, they're not. Look around, nobody is paying attention to you anymore. They're only watching people walk past. See?"

Vickie craned her neck and saw everyone on the plane facing forward and not looking at her. The pressure in her chest eased.

Maybe she's right. Of course she's right. She wouldn't lie to you. Listen to her. Don't panic.

"And while you're at it, look behind you."

Vickie turned and saw Craig waving at her from three rows back. She smiled slightly and returned the gesture. He gave her a thumbs-up and she settled quickly into her seat.

"See?" Alexis said. "Everything's great. Now we need to put our seat belts on—like we did in the car."

She showed Vickie how to secure it, then helped her loosen it so that it would rest comfortably on her lap.

"What's that?" The vampire pointed to the back of the headrest in front of her.

"That's your TV. I'll show you how to use it when we get up in the air."

"What's taking so long?" She tapped her feet anxiously.

"You need to relax. Don't worry. They're finishing up the loading process. Once they close the door, the flight attendant will show you how everything works, and then we can take off."

Her gaze darted back and forth, driven by some strange compulsion to stay in motion. Alexis caught her squeezing the armrest and held her arm gently. "Easy. No damage to this one. We don't have the kind of insurance for flights like we did with the rental car."

The plane's engines roared to life and soon, the aircraft taxied over to the runway. As it did so, a team of flight attendants scattered throughout the cabin to demonstrate how to deal with emergencies, use the seat belts, and where the barf bags were located.

This triggered a thought in Alexis' mind. She leaned over and whispered, "Hey, do vampires barf?"

Vickie looked confused. "What does that mean?"

"Throw up, regurgitate. You know, when food comes back up?" She mimed the action in case her words didn't make sense.

"Oh. I don't really know. I never have."

"Maybe we'll find out," Alexis joked.

Once the demonstration was over, the plane lumbered forward. The flight attendants took their places in their seats and the engine noise increased.

Vickie's breath caught. To her, it was like riding a car on steroids. Every noise made her jump. Alexis held her arm steadily as a constant reminder to calm down and avoid damaging anything. The plane accelerated and hurtled down the runway.

"Here we go," Alexis said. "Watch out the window. This is my favorite part."

The nose of the plane tilted up, and the wheels left the ground. Within seconds, they soared over Vickie's homeland. She watched with astonishment and terror while she held her breath.

"Goodbye, Austria!" Alexis smiled and waved.

Vickie covered her ears with both hands and leaned forward, gritting her teeth.

"Oh, the pressure! I knew we forgot to tell you something. It's okay." Her friend rubbed her back. "It won't get any worse. It's only the pressure of the cabin. You'll feel better in a little while."

Alexis remembered that she had gum in her purse. She fumbled under the seat in front of her to retrieve her purse, unwrapped a piece of gum, and handed it to Vickie. "Put this in your mouth and start chewing but don't swallow it. It'll help relieve the pressure."

The vampire chewed obediently and twisted her face as the strong flavor of peppermint overwhelmed her taste buds. She gradually became accustomed to the sharp taste, though, after the initial rush slowed. And the gum did help relieve some of the pressure, so she could live with the fact that she didn't particularly enjoy it.

She sat straighter and stared out the window, watching the ground disappear behind the clouds. "This doesn't feel real. I feel like I'm dreaming."

"Wild, huh?" Alexis grinned back at her.

Vickie put her head back and took a few deep breaths.

The plane stabilized and leveled off as it reached full altitude. "Wait, what if I have to go to the bathroom? We'll be up here for more than eight hours."

"There are bathrooms on the plane." Alexis pointed to the restroom sign near the front of the plane. "Several of them."

"Are they like the bathrooms at home?"

"More or less. They're much smaller, but they're easy to use. You'll be fine. Don't worry. They think of everything."

The plane cruised through the sky and Alexis squealed with excitement. "Next stop, Milwaukee!"

"What happens now?" Vickie asked anxiously.

"What happens now is that you get comfortable. We have long hours ahead of us. That's most of the excitement right there until we land. Someone will be by to get you a drink in a few minutes, and you just hang out. Stay in your seat and relax."

Alexis grabbed one of the magazines she'd bought and leafed through it until she found the latest Hollywood gossip column. Soon, the flight attendant arrived with a cart of drinks. Both girls ordered water and sipped them as the flight continued.

"I want to watch TV," Vickie told her.

"Oh, right. Here, let me show you."

Her friend pulled the wired remote from Vickie's seat and showed her all the options for games and TV shows that she could watch on the screen. She also pointed out a long list of movies that were available.

A flight attendant passed headphones out and Alexis grabbed a pair for her and plugged them into the armrest. She turned on one of the *Twilight* sequels for her to watch, thinking she would get a kick out of watching another one. Vickie wasn't particularly excited about a second bad vampire movie, but it was something to do to get her mind off of the flight. And the first one had helped the pair bond in the first place, so it wasn't all bad.

Soon, the lights in the cabin dimmed. Many of the passengers turned their overhead lights off to get some sleep. Alexis followed suit and reclined her seat a little, so she could get comfortable.

"You can sleep like that?" Vickie asked as she watched her get situated.

"Sure." Alexis closed her eyes and folded her hands in her lap. "It's not the most comfortable thing in the world, but it gets the job done."

She soon fell asleep and snored softly now and then while Vickie watched the movie. Out of the corner of her eye, she saw Craig walking down the aisle on his way to the bathroom. He made eye contact with her on the return trip and mouthed, "Are you doing okay?"

She nodded. He gave her another thumbs-up and a smile and returned to his seat.

After the movie was over, Vickie turned the overhead light off, removed her headphones, and leaned against the wall of the plane.

If Alexis is comfortable enough to sleep, then maybe I can take a nap, too. Many people are. Do what they're doing.

Much to her surprise, it worked. A couple of hours passed, and she woke up beside a wide-awake Alexis, who munched on some Skittles while reading one of her magazines.

"Hey," she slurred.

"Oh, hey. You're awake. How did you sleep?"

Vickie blinked a few times. "Not badly, surprisingly."

"Told ya." She patted her on the arm.

Just then, the plane dropped a few feet. Her stomach seemed to leap into her throat. The aircraft bounced back up again, then dipped a second time.

"What's going on?" Vickie asked.

"It must be turbulence. It simply means the ride will be a little bouncy. We'll be okay."

Sure enough, the pilot's voice came through the speakers: "This is your captain speaking. Right now, we're flying through a small thunderstorm, so that's causing some turbulence. Please stay seated with your seat belt securely fastened, and we'll be out of it soon."

Vickie closed her eyes and tried to keep her sense of calm.

Alexis glanced at her. "Turbulence is very common. It doesn't mean a thing. Everything is fine."

The vampire's stomach, however, remained twisted in knots.

This might be the time we learn if vampires barf. But don't freak out. Fight every instinct you have.

She steadied herself with deep breaths and fought the crazy thoughts that seemed determined to imagine the worst. Alexis suggested she turn the TV on to keep her mind off things, but she wanted to sit with her eyes closed and ride it out.

As Alexis finished one of her magazines, she looked at her friend who was gradually and very obviously losing her grip.

"Stay with me. Hang tight. It's almost over."

Vickie nodded but didn't respond.

"Let me see your teeth," Alexis said. Vickie shook her head. "Come on, show them to me. No one's looking."

The vampire turned her head slightly and spread her lips to reveal her fangs pointing down to poke her bottom lip. They were ample evidence of how threatened she really felt.

Alexis tutted sympathetically. "That's what I thought but stay calm. Nothing bad will happen here. Everything about this is normal."

A few minutes later, the plane leveled off and the rest of the flight went smoothly. By the end of it, Vickie had felt very comfortable, and even grew to enjoy the experience. Of course, the extra TV time didn't hurt either.

Once they announced that the crew should prepare for landing, Alexis warned her friend that it would get bumpy again. She simply had to let it happen and she should relax. This was the home stretch.

Vickie held on to the armrests, but the other girl quickly handed her one of the magazines that she had purchased.

"Squeeze this."

Vickie grabbed the magazine and twisted it into a tube. She did surprisingly well during the landing, although she jumped when she heard the wheels hit the ground. As the plane slowed on the tarmac, the vampire dragged in a few loud, deep breaths to calm herself again. The magazine was destroyed in her hands.

Alexis smiled. "Welcome to the United States, my friend! You made it. And you didn't break anything."

Vickie smiled with relief. "Sorry about the magazine," she said sheepishly.

"Nice work, girls," Craig congratulated them from three rows back. They'd reached the final hurdle. Now, they only had to disembark and get home. The family had reached Milwaukee.

CHAPTER TWENTY-SIX

A blast of humid air hit Vickie in the face as she stepped off the plane and into the tunnel. She entered the terminal with a hint of disorientation that left her a little breathless.

Alexis followed close behind her. "Are you okay?"

"It's hard to believe that we were just in Austria and now, we're on the other side of the world."

Her friend laughed. "That's my favorite part of flying, too. Welcome to Milwaukee, your new home!"

They found a visible place to the side to wait for Alexis' dad to emerge from the tunnel. While they stood there, Vickie looked around the terminal.

Five gates were crowded into this one end of the airport, surrounded by walls of floor-to-ceiling windows. A handful of travelers stood in line at a small coffee stand, and others slumped in their chairs, waiting for their flights to depart.

Craig stepped out with a broad smile on his face and

put his arm around his daughter. "Home sweet home. How was the flight, Vickie?"

"It was fine." She didn't look at him, though. Her attention seemed to be fixed on their surroundings. "This airport looks a lot different than the one in Austria."

"Oh, yeah," Alexis said, "every airport is different. Here in Milwaukee, it isn't huge. It's big enough, but it's not like one of the major hubs of the world. There's a city south of here called Chicago, and they have a sprawling airport. This one is good, though."

"Let's go get our bags," Craig suggested.

Alexis pulled out her phone, switched it on, and sighed with relief as it connected to the local towers. "It's nice to have four bars again." It pinged with notifications. "Oh! The girls and Eric will be at baggage claim. Yay." She did a little dance as they walked.

"I guess you're hitting the ground running," Craig said to Vickie.

"What does that mean?" she asked, her expression a little shell-shocked.

"Oh, I mean we're not going to waste any time. Alexis' friends are here to see her, so you'll meet new people already."

Vickie nodded cautiously. She was a little nervous about meeting them in person, but she had already met the girls on FaceTime with Alexis. Besides, she was too distracted by everything going on around her to be that concerned about it.

They walked down a long corridor where several gates surrounded them on each side, broken up only by the occasional store or restaurant. At another major intersection of gates, a coffee stand served a long line of customers.

"That's coffee, right?" Vickie asked.

"Oh yeah," Craig replied. "Coffee's a big deal here in America, especially at airports, where people try to keep their energy levels up and such."

Alexis walked in front of them. Her head was all but buried in her phone as she texted away. They veered off to the right of the security line and took a hallway to the escalators. "These are moving stairs, so step on one and let it take you down a level."

Vickie hesitated but watched Alexis ride the escalator down. She took her time and eventually worked up the courage to put her foot on the step. It pulled her forward, and she wobbled briefly before she regained her sense of balance. She jumped off at the bottom rather than wait for her feet to scrape against the final edge and possibly make her fall.

They stood now at a long room at the end of the building. On one side were exits to the parking lot and pickup zone accompanied by line after line of baggage claim conveyor belts scattered in both directions.

The group found their gate and they stood at the silent belt, waiting for it to come to life and bring their bags. Craig jogged away to find a cart and pulled it over to the girls.

Someone yelled, "Alexis!"

The teenager spun to see her friends jumping up and down, screaming at her. The girls all embraced in a huge hug, while a young man stood awkwardly off to the side and smiled gently.

Vickie watched from her spot beside the baggage claim. "And there's the gang." Craig winked.

Alexis brought the group over, and they greeted the party.

"Vickie, this is Jessica, Jamie, and Eric. These are my best friends. You met Jess and Jamie on FaceTime."

"Hi," Vickie said politely but nervously. Both girls greeted her warmly and welcomed her to America.

Eric stepped forward. He was a typical teenage boy— skinny with lanky limbs and a shy smile. His brown curly hair covered his head and ears, and he wore thin-framed glasses that were only visible upon closer inspection.

"Hi." His smile was friendly but a little nervous.

Vickie shook his hand and looked deep into his bluish-green eyes.

Wow. What is it that is drawing me in? He is beautiful. Is it only that I haven't seen too many boys my age in a few centuries or could there be something else?

She chastised herself quickly.

Come on, Vickie. You can't fall for the first American boy you meet.

The girls continued to hug each other exuberantly. "I'm so glad you're home," Jessica squealed as she clutched Alexis around the waist. Her curly blonde hair tickled her friend's face when she rested her head on her shoulder.

Alexis pushed her off and spat the hair from her mouth. Jessica laughed, revealing a line of metal in her mouth that Vickie did not recognize. She didn't want to be rude, however, so she stayed quiet. Alexis would later explain what they might be.

Jamie walked up to the vampire. "So, Alexis said you

were coming back with them, but she didn't say why or how they know you."

"Oh, um…" Vickie froze. She hadn't expected to answer any questions like that.

"She's family." Alexis' father put his arm around Vickie's shoulders. "A long-lost cousin. We met up with her while we were in Austria for a visit, and she decided she wanted to move to the States. We opened our home to her. She and Alexis are practically sisters at this point."

Before Vickie could react to that statement, the conveyor belt began to move. The machine's parts squealed as it picked up speed.

"Oh, finally," Alexis said. "Dad, have you got the bags?"

"Yep." Her father stepped up to the conveyor belt. One by one, suitcases were unloaded from the plane and sent down the ramp. After a few minutes of waiting, he secured both large suitcases and heaved them onto the cart.

"Well, we have to go," Eric said. "I only paid for twenty minutes of parking."

"Dang," Alexis said. "Thank you so much for coming to see us, you guys!"

Jessica smiled and the metal in her mouth reflected the overhead lights. "Of course. We're so happy you're back. Text me when you're settled in and we'll all get together. You too, Vickie!"

Hugs were exchanged and the friends waved as they stepped through the doors that led to the parking lot.

"Is that where we have to go, too?" Vickie pointed in the direction they had taken.

"No, no," Craig said. "We'll go up a level. We have to

walk across a little walkway to the covered parking lot. That's where my car is. Then we can drive home."

Vickie looked out the window one more time to watch Alexis' friends walk away until Eric disappeared from view.

"Let's do it!" Craig waved them back to the escalators. He balanced the cart on the moving steps, and the three of them returned to the main terminal. Vickie hadn't gotten a good look at that section of the airport yet. It sprawled out in all directions, with several more restaurants and shops. An old airplane dangled from the rafters.

A foosball table stood in one corner of the main terminal, and leather couches held weary travelers watching screens of local news, daytime game shows, and the arrivals and departures of various flights.

They walked down a hallway and over to a walkway past a small sign that said **Chapel**.

"There's a church in there?" Vickie asked with confusion.

"Oh yeah," Alexis answered. "It's a small prayer room, like a mini-church for those who need it."

The vampire was only familiar with the larger gothic structures that had been used for worship in her time. To see something so tiny and simple seemed oddly incongruous.

They walked through two double doors. The air conditioning ended, and the warm, thick air of the Wisconsin summer swept in like a wave.

"And I'm already sweating," Alexis' father joked, which prompted a laugh from his daughter. After a few more steps, they were out in the parking lot. "We're in 2A. That's where I paid to park the car for two months."

"I still don't know why you didn't get a ride, Dad. You spent so much money."

He waved his hand. "Nah, I'd rather be able to come and go as I please."

Vickie followed in silence, a little numb after the barrage of experiences she'd gone through. The bite of exhaust fumes burned her nose, and she coughed.

"Yeah, that's pollution," Alexis explained. "You'll breathe plenty of that here. Or more, at least, than you would have in Austria."

"Hello, old friend," Alexis' father shouted at his waiting car. The mid-size SUV beeped in recognition when he pressed the button on his key fob to unlock the doors. He pulled the hatch in the back open and loaded the luggage into the vehicle.

"Okay, everybody in. And Vickie, please don't break my car. We own this one."

She smiled politely. While she'd stayed fairly quiet during the majority of the exchanges, she wasn't trying to be rude. The experience had simply left her feeling completely overwhelmed.

Before I woke up, I had never even been out of town. Salzburg was all I knew. Now, I'm in a completely different part of the world. I didn't expect it to be so jarring.

Fortunately, the car wasn't too different. It was basically the same. She buckled her seat belt and held onto the door handle.

"I hope I remember how to drive." Craig laughed as he

backed his car out of the space. He paid for his parking and they swung out onto the road leading to the expressway.

Vickie marveled at how many cars hurtled up and down the freeway.

They're driving so fast.

Her jaw dropped while she observed car after car weaving in and out of lanes. Soon, their vehicle had reached the same speed, and they careened down the road past a sign that said, **Welcome to Milwaukee!** with a picture of a hunk of cheese on it.

"Why is there cheese on the sign?"

Alexis laughed. "Because Wisconsin is the Dairy State. We're known for our cows, milk, and cheese. It's a huge stereotype. Almost everyone in the country makes fun of us for it, but we're proud of it. You won't find better cheese in the world than right here. You'll learn a lot about Milwaukee as we go on."

They cruised down the freeway, and Craig sighed with relief. He shuddered a few minutes later, though, when reality crept in.

Back where everything is familiar again. I don't know if that's a good thing or a bad thing yet.

They drove north of the airport, and downtown Milwaukee loomed in the distance outside their right windows.

"That's the city." Alexis pointed to the skyline.

"Wow," Vickie gasped. "It's so big." Skyscrapers peppered the skyline, surrounded by clusters of buildings dozens of stories high. Along the coast of the city, Lake Michigan spread out as far as the eye could see.

"Well, it's big compared to Salzburg. We have a few big buildings, but we're one of the smaller cities in America."

"And is that the ocean?" Vickie pointed to the coast outside her window.

"No, that's Lake Michigan. It's really big, though, so it feels like an ocean—one of those unique little things about this part of the country. It's like oceanside living without having to live on the ocean itself."

"It's the Midwest charm," Craig announced with a smile.

The downtown area disappeared as they drove, and they pulled off the freeway onto a side street to cruise until they reached a small brown-and-white ranch house on the north side of the city.

"Welcome home, girls."

CHAPTER TWENTY-SEVEN

"I don't know that I've ever been so happy to see this house," Alexis said as they pulled into the driveway.

"I know," her father agreed. "It looks like Wendell did a great job keeping up with the grass." The garage door lifted open and he pulled the SUV in. He killed the engine and the three of them stepped out of the car.

"Leave the luggage for a few minutes, girls. Let's enjoy being home." He walked up the driveway and unlocked the side door.

"Come on, Vickie. I'll show you around," Alexis said.

The vampire complied and followed her into the house. A door leading to the basement stood immediately in front of them, so they turned right and walked into the kitchen.

The room was simple and not nearly as large as the one at the castle, but it still seemed to have all the same convenient appliances. In the corner, a sink stood under a pair of windows looking out over the driveway.

Farther into the kitchen was a large sliding glass door

leading out to the back yard and patio. A table and chairs sat under a large shaded area.

"What's that?" Vickie pointed to the large round contraption beyond the patio.

"That's our swimming pool," Alexis said. "It's like a lake back where you're from, except we control it. There aren't any animals in it, and the water is always clean. Instead of bathing, we use it to swim and have fun."

Her father flinched when he noticed how green the water was. "Well, it's supposed to always be clean. I have to dump some shock in there and get all that green stuff out."

They turned and walked around the kitchen table to the living room, which held two reclining chairs, a nice-sized couch, and a sixty-inch flat-panel TV. Craig walked ahead and opened the front door to let some air into the stuffy living room.

The girls walked down the hall to the bedrooms, but he stayed in the living room for a minute to stare at a pair of recliners. On the left, his Green Bay Packer blanket hung over the back of his chair, waiting for him to perch again. He looked forward to crawling into that chair and putting his feet up. His smile fell when he looked to his right at the other chair. A blue-and-white knitted afghan hung from the back of his wife's chair. It was the same blanket he'd brought to her in the hospice. He sighed.

Everything is familiar, all right.

Down the hall, the girls visited the various bedrooms. The first was mostly empty with only a simple queen-sized spare bed, a closet, and a window with a view into the yard. Alexis had already decided this would be the ideal place for Vickie. The vampire liked it. The space was small but had a nice-sized window and a closet with two folding doors. At the moment, it was a spare bedroom, but Alexis explained that they would clean it out for her and her stuff. The bed looked roomy and attractive to her.

The next stop down the hall was Alexis' room on the left. She had a waterbed, which Vickie had never seen before.

"They're great." Alexis flopped onto it and let the waves rock her back and forth. "Oh, how I've missed this."

"Are these common?"

"Not at all. Actually, they're really old-fashioned. This one is probably thirty years old or something like that. I love it, though."

Vickie scanned the room to get a feel for how a teenage girl lived in 2019. To her surprise, a small Christmas tree stood in the corner of the room.

"What's that?" She pointed to the tree.

"Oh!" Alexis rolled off the bed and flipped a switch to light the figure up. Its branches glowed different colors.

"Those are called fiber optics. It's supposed to be a Christmas tree."

"What does that mean?"

"Every Christmas, families in America— and all over the world, actually—put up big trees in their houses. Some are real and some are fake. Then they string lights and hang ornaments on them for decoration. On Christmas Day, the official holiday, gifts are placed under the tree."

"Odd, we never had a tree when Christmas was celebrated, only a church meeting."

"Not a Christmas nut, eh?" Alexis laughed. "Then have I a lot to show you when winter comes around. I love the holiday season so much that I like to have a little bit of it around all year. Look at this."

She walked over to an outlet and plugged in a green cord. A string of white Christmas lights flashed into life near the ceiling and lit up the entire perimeter of the room.

"Christmas lights are basically my favorite thing ever. They make me happy. And my parents said I could do what I wanted in my room, as long as I kept it in here."

Vickie nodded, her brain trying hard to assimilate everything.

A full bathroom waited at the end of the hall, followed by Craig's room. The tour over, they walked back to the kitchen to go downstairs to the basement.

"This is where your vampires are buried?" Vickie joked in an attempt to get comfortable in her new home.

"Nice." Alexis smirked. "This is something of a rec room, kinda like they did to your home. But here, it's a little smaller and, well…not as fancy."

They reached the bottom of the stairs, and Alexis started walking through the basement, turning on lights. There was an impressive array of play items to occupy their time, including an air hockey table, a pool table, a full bar with a fridge. A pair of small couches faced a TV.

A small door led to the laundry room, a freezer, and extra storage.

"I'm impressed by how much you've managed to fit in here," Vickie said. "From the outside, this house looks very small, but there is probably more stuff in here than in the castle back home."

Alexis nodded. "We keep a lot of stuff. But hey, that's what happens when you live in the same house for so long.

This is the first and only house my parents bought after they were married."

They walked back up the stairs, and Alexis showed Vickie another half-bathroom to the right of the base-ment door. They moved outside to the driveway, so Alexis could take her to the back yard and the garage. She looked into the pool and laughed at the green sludge in the water.

"You already saw the pool. It'll look a lot better in a week. We left in something of a hurry, and my dad forgot to put the cover on. He'll mess with the chemicals in the water to get rid of all the algae. Then we can swim." She looked up at the sun beating down on them. "And not a moment too soon. Whew. It's hot."

A shed had been attached to the garage for easy access to tools and firewood in winter. The yard overlooked a large reservoir that had been dug into a field.

"There were never any buildings, but we used to build forts out there and stuff. It was all level until the city tore everything out and dug this reservoir. We get a lot of rain during certain times of the year, and the intersection down the road floods. They dug this so it would overflow into here, instead."

They turned and walked back to the house.

"And that's the house. This is your new home. It's small, but there's plenty of room for all three of us. I'm excited to have you here. I know my dad is, too. How do you feel?"

"I don't know," Vickie replied as she walked back into the kitchen. "This is a lot to process."

"Come have a seat and take a load off." They walked into the living room. She shot her father a smirk when she saw him sitting in his chair with his feet up already. "That didn't take long."

"Hey, lay off. I missed this."

Alexis explained the significance of the other recliner as they sat on the couch. Vickie nodded, and they shared a brief moment of silence for Alexis' mom.

"How's it feel to be home, Dad?"

Craig stretched his legs and spread his toes as far as he could. "I can't hear you over the sound of myself relaxing."

Alexis showed Vickie the TV, how it worked, and the media server that was connected to it, offering even more movies and shows than what they had in the castle.

The vampire looked out the front window and saw a cemetery. "Is that what I think it is?"

"Yeah. When my parents moved in here, that was all trees across the street. It was remote, really cool, and private. But in the last two years or so, they came in and pulled out all the trees so they could expand the cemetery. Now, instead of staring at trees and feeling like you're alone, you can look at all the dead people."

"As if we don't think about death around here enough." Craig pursed his lips. "I wonder how much the value of this house dropped when they did that. Stupid city."

"Dad, will Vickie stay in the spare room, then?"

He folded his arms. "Yeah, I would say so. It makes the most sense. I'll set my podcasting station up in the basement, anyway. Or maybe my room. I haven't decided yet. I don't really need the spare room. Plus, there's a bed in there already."

Vickie rested her head on the back of the couch. "I really appreciate you taking me in like this. It's hard to believe that I'm even here. And I'm a citizen now and everything."

"Yes, well, that's…great, isn't it?" he said. "I didn't think we would be able to pull it off, but I am very happy it all worked out. You're safe here now, and we'll get you into the high school and you can settle into a normal life."

"It'll beat running away from angry townspeople," Alexis said. "You'll like living here. Milwaukee has all the fun of a big city, but you still have the small-town feel. I love living here. I wouldn't move anywhere else."

"You're going to fit in great." Craig nodded definitively. "And with Alexis behind you, you have someone who can lead you around when you need it. You'll make friends, build your own life, and can do whatever you want."

Vickie took another deep breath. "Truthfully, I'm intimidated by all of this. It's a little overwhelming. I used to be in the safety of the castle, and now I have all this freedom."

Alexis smiled. "It's a different time now. You'll like it. Here, you have choices. And those choices can be great. You'll make mistakes, and those aren't so much fun, but we'll be here to help clean the mess up. After all, we're your family now."

"Speaking of that…" Craig lowered his feet to the floor and straightened in his chair. "I know you'll have a different last name, but I want you to think of me as your adopted father, Vickie."

"Really?" At first, she bristled at the thought. He was a nice man, but he wasn't her father.

"Yeah. And for the record, that doesn't mean I'm trying to replace your father. But I want you to see me as a dad, not the dad. I'll play that role for you. I want you to rely on me and come to me when you have problems. I'm not saying you have to put me on a pedestal or love me the same way you did your own father. All I'm asking is that you trust me like you would your father. Please."

Vickie was silent for a time. "Thank you." She wasn't sure if she could or would, but she appreciated the sentiment behind his request.

"I have a sister," Alexis shouted, then laughed.

"Basically." Craig smiled sleepily. "That's how this will work. We have to pull together as a family and move forward in this new life and watch out for each other."

"And show each other a good time. I have the perfect thing for that. We got back in time for Summerfest."

CHAPTER TWENTY-EIGHT

"Time to get a taste of the modern world, girl!" Alexis announced as the SUV pulled into the Park 'n Ride.

Craig put the car into park and turned to face them. "All right, girls. You need to be safe. I'm trusting you both to behave and not get into any trouble. Alexis, please watch out for Vickie."

"Don't worry, Dad. We'll be fine."

He chuckled and shook his head. "All right. Have a good time."

The girls clambered out into the thick evening air. In a few minutes, they would be on the Summerfest grounds.

This was the annual music festival in Milwaukee. Heralded as the "biggest music festival in the world," it attracted big-name bands and scores of smaller groups. For over a week, music played on multiple stages morning, noon, and night.

"Are we going to see a band?" Vickie asked as they walked to the bus stop.

"We're going to see a bunch of bands. When you go to

Summerfest, you walk around and go from stage to stage until you find somebody you like. It's a lot of fun. And unless you go to the main stage, it's all included in the cost of your ticket. We'll wander, get some food, people-watch, the works. It's a great initiation into life in Milwaukee."

The bus pulled up to the stop and they boarded with a crowd of tourists. After about ten minutes, they disembarked on the lakefront near of a large sign that read **HENRY MAIER FESTIVAL PARK.**

They paid for their tickets and pushed through the turnstile, then checked their bags at security. A large fountain sprayed water into the air in front of them while kids and a few young adults ran through to cool themselves off. Vickie's head seemed almost to spin with how rapidly she turned it to take everything in.

The house overwhelmed me. This might make my head explode.

In every direction, she saw people from all walks of life. They pushed and shoved their way through the crowds, shoulder to shoulder, to get from stage to stage. Long rows of eateries and food counters snaked between the stages to offer everything from sausages to pizza to sandwiches to burgers, and everything in between. The only thing more plenteous than the concessions was the beer stands.

And if the sights weren't overwhelming enough, the music was. Loud voice and power chords blared and echoed. Yet, for reasons Vickie couldn't determine, they never overlapped. Once you were out of earshot of one stage, you could hear the next one, and so on.

"What do you want to do first?" Alexis shouted.

"I don't know what's going on," Vickie replied.

Her friend nodded, then gestured for her to follow. "I need to eat."

The two girls shoved their way through the sweaty crowd until they reached a pizza counter beside a large stage with a motorcycle hanging over it.

"That's the Harley Stage." Alexis pointed to the Harley-Davidson logo above the video board showing who was on the stage. A small country rock band was jamming out, led by a large bearded man wearing a cowboy hat and jeans.

The first few dozen rows in front of the stage were all metal benches. For some unknown reason, no one sat. Instead, everyone stood on the benches to cheer the band on.

Farther away from the stage, the seating turned into metal picnic tables. Yet again, most people stood atop the structures rather than sitting down as was their intended purpose. A select few—mainly older patrons—actually sat at the tables eating.

"Where do we eat?" Vickie asked.

Alexis laughed. "Standing."

They ordered pizza and sodas, then stepped off to the side to watch the band play. Alexis tapped her foot and bobbed her head as she ate and reveled in her American life once again.

After they wolfed their food down, the girls walked through several tents of merchants selling personalized photo frames, t-shirts, and other tchotchkes. At first, Vickie was excited.

This feels almost like the market I used to walk through every day.

However, much to her disappointment, most of the items on sale were junk.

They exited the tents in an area that was surprisingly quiet, given the half-dozen bands all playing at the same time.

"Fun, hey?" Alexis said. "This is Summerfest."

Vickie smiled politely, then noticed a young man stumble past. He reeked of booze and was terribly unkempt with his eyes half open and his shirt tied around his waist.

Beer sloshed freely out of the plastic cup he held practically sideways in his hand.

"You did say you'd seen some drunks in your day," Alexis said.

"Yeah, but they didn't look like that," Vickie responded, and she continued to stare.

"Summerfest brings out the rookies. It's simply a fact. These are the people who can't get drunk anywhere else. They can sneak beers here, though, because there are so many people that it's hard to police."

Groups of shirtless guys with backward hats stumbled by, cheering and chugging their beers. Other men in tank tops wore sunglasses in the evening. It was a place where everyone tried way too hard to be cool.

"You don't drink?" Vickie asked.

Alexis laughed. "No, I can't yet. You have to be twenty-one years old to drink here in America. Or at least close to it if you want to pull it off. I'm way too young. And I wouldn't be able to hide it from my dad anyway. He'd know."

A scantily-clad couple walked past them, their hands all

over each other as if nobody else was around. "It's times like this that I'm glad I can't drink yet. Besides, I don't think I'd like to be like these people. They all look stupid."

Vickie nodded emphatically. Girls with too-short skirts and shirts that barely covered their torsos marched together, arm in arm, cheering, laughing, and drinking. Old men shuffled along in Hawaiian shirts with their gray beards hanging from their chins to cover their chests.

"There is quite a variety of people here."

"That's the fun of people-watching, my friend. It's wall to wall people, and they're all entertaining."

The vampire was still a little skeptical of how much fun they were really having. "This is what we do? Walk around, listen to music, and watch people?"

"And eat. Yeah. It's fun to get out of the house. The lake is right there, so it stays cool outside. It's a summertime tradition out here. Plus, there are usually some bigger bands that play at the free shows. Sometimes, you get a group from the 1990s to play. There are up-and-coming groups here, too. Last year, I came here with a group and we saw a husband-and-wife band that's huge now because they played the theme song on an HGTV show."

Vickie nodded. "I don't know what that means."

Alexis laughed. She'd forgotten how much she still had to teach Vickie and reminded herself not let her own pleasure at being home derail the hard work they'd already put in.

They walked past several beer tents, each of which offered five or six different brews.

"How are there so many different kinds of beer here?"

A broad smile spread across Alexis' face. "You know

how I said we were known for our dairy? Well, we're also known for our beer. We have a lot of beer here!"

"Really?"

"Oh yeah. You know that big stadium we drove past on the shuttle? That's the home field for our baseball team. They are literally called the Milwaukee Brewers. So, yeah, beer is our thing." She smiled to herself. Sometimes, explaining things out loud made one realize how ridiculous they really were.

"Do you like beer?"

Alexis shook her head. "Not really. I haven't had it much. My dad let me have a sip here and there when I was younger. I think it's gross, personally. He says you need to acquire the taste, but I don't know if that's something I even want to do." She stuck her tongue out in disgust.

Another tent showed young girls having a series of swirls drawn across their hands and arms in intricate patterns.

"What are those?" Vickie asked.

"Henna? It's a kind of tattoo but it's not permanent. When you look at people who have pictures drawn on their arms—like that guy over there—those are tattoos. They're permanent. Henna tattoos are this special kind of dye paste where you get something drawn on you and it stays for a couple of weeks. Do you want one?"

"Does it hurt?"

"Not at all. It's only paint."

"Then let's do it." Minutes later, the two girls were sitting on pillows on the ground while henna artists sat in front of them.

Vickie had a heart drawn on her ankle, and Alexis had a special woven design around her arm.

The vampire laughed. "It tickles, but it looks amazing."

"This is the kind of thing you do when you can't drink at Summerfest. There are lots of other things we can do, too, when we're done here."

After the ink dried, the girls wandered to the far end of the Summerfest grounds, where they found carnival-style games. It was an opportunity for Alexis to teach Vickie about some of the sports in America.

During a basketball-shooting game, Alexis showed her how the ball went into the hoop. After a few practice shots, Vickie showed herself to be a natural and sank a dozen shots in a row to win the game.

For her prize, she was given a small green stuffed bear.

"So, think about it," Alexis said as her friend squeezed the toy. "That is your very first American possession. You've never owned anything in America in your life. Now, you do. You'd better save that thing."

The vampire laughed, and she cradled it close as they walked up a set of iron steps into a semi-truck holding the latest in console video games. This was another area that was a little too much for her senses.

The 3D effects of the games on big immersive screens combined with the sound effects and music pumped out of massive loudspeakers almost sent her into a frenzy. Alexis was wise enough to notice the signs, took Vickie by the arm, and led her out of the vehicle before she lost control.

Her fingertips were buried in the green bear, poking holes through the fabric's exterior.

"Well, that didn't last long," Alexis joked. "That's okay. There's plenty more to do here."

They strolled ahead to take in a basketball demonstration by some stunt players. The girls marveled at the somersaults and flying dunks that the team displayed.

Vickie smiled. She was starting to enjoy her life as an American. If it was all like this, it would definitely be a fun time. Alexis smiled with her. She loved being able to share these experiences with somebody who knew how to appreciate them.

CHAPTER TWENTY-NINE

"We're in the Dairy State. Let's get some ice cream."

The girls walked to a tall stand shaped like a giant ice cream cone. Vickie didn't understand the purpose of the sign until the server handed her a cone filled with a scoop of chocolate ice cream. Alexis also had a chocolate cone, paid the server, and they strolled together along the lakefront.

"I know way too many people who like vanilla ice cream," Alexis said between licks. "For my money, it doesn't get better than chocolate. Vanilla is pointless. Even strawberry is better than vanilla."

"This is really good." Vickie slurped quickly and somehow smeared chocolate all over her face.

"Oh…" Alexis stopped her. "Wait here." She jogged to a nearby stand selling grilled corn on the cob and returned with a stack of napkins. "Wipe your face. I didn't think you might coat yourself in ice cream. She chuckled. A little tip —try to avoid getting food all over your face. People frown on that."

Vickie nodded. "Keep a clean face. Noted."

Their course took them farther along the lake. The city skyline lit up the coast. The tall apartment buildings that provided lakefront views hosted small crowds on their balconies as they waited for the evening festivities to begin.

Large white rocks provided ample seating for those too young to drink, although many snuck in small plastic bottles of liquor to pass around. Other kids smoked cigarettes, and the pungent smell of marijuana hung in the air.

"Walking down here can be a chore." Alexis coughed from the smell. "It's a beautiful view, and it'll be great for the fireworks, but man, people can't help themselves. Idiot kids have to smoke."

In the dark distance, a small spotlight illuminated a section of a small island separated from the rocks by a few hundred yards of water.

"What's going on out there?" Vickie asked and pointed at the tiny land mass.

"That's where the fireworks will fire from."

"Fireworks?" Vickie raised her brow in concern.

"Oh, don't worry. Think of it as a really cool light show with explosions. I know you get a little overwhelmed, but this is the kind of thing you want to learn to enjoy if you're going to be a teenager in America." She needed to push her friend carefully to get her used to some of these activities. They only had a couple of months until school started and she'd be on her own more often.

They set a lazy course along the shore while observing the kids on the rocks partaking in their vices.

"So, that boy who was with your friends..." Vickie finally said.

"Eric?"

"Yeah, Eric. Who is he? Does he go to the same school that we do? Or will, I guess?"

Alexis smiled. "Yeah, Eric is one of my friends. He's actually one of my first friends. I met him first period of my first day of Freshman year. He's a really good guy. Hangs out with a lot of girls because he thinks the guys at school are stupid. And they totally are."

"The four of you hang out a lot?"

"Every weekend. Jess and Jamie are friends from grade school. I met them in choir. They're great. Eric sings with us, too, but he's also a cross country runner."

Vickie squinted in confusion. "He runs across countries?"

Alexis laughed. "I'm still figuring out this communication gap we have. No. Cross country is the name of a sport. It means you run long distances. I think it's like three miles or something like that."

They found an empty area of rocks that wasn't populated by smokers and sat. A breeze blew off the lake to whip their hair into their faces. Alexis gathered her locks, pulled them back into a ponytail, and offered a ponytail holder to Vickie, who did the same.

A few light waves crashed on the lower rocks.

"Will we get wet?" Vickie watched the waves carefully.

"It would have to be a major storm for the waves to reach up here."

A fireball rocketed from the island and exploded in a dizzying green flash. The report from the firework echoed across the water.

Vickie's hands slammed into the rock she sat on. Alexis reached over to assure her that everything was fine.

"That's fireworks. They can't hurt you. They're honestly only loud noise. It's supposed to be fun. And you'll have to move now."

Vickie looked down. The rock she sat on now had a massive crack running through the middle of it. She stood and the two halves fell apart.

"Did anyone see that?"

Alexis looked around casually. "I think you're good. But try to keep it under control. This is a test for you. You have to be able to go through this kind of stuff without worrying about being under attack. You're safe here."

Vickie looked out across the lake at the island. It was far away, and they were shooting these bombs directly into the air.

Being a human will be difficult. It's like I have to fight all my instincts at once. Every urge inside me—the pieces of me that I've trusted my entire life—will have to change. I'm not only away from home. I'm away from myself.

"What would happen if I…just was a vampire?"

"What do you mean?"

"What if I was proud about it? Open? If I tapped into my powers whenever I needed to? My father used to exhaust me trying to keep my powers hidden. Maybe I can actually walk around as a vampire and nobody will be bothered by it. You say I'm safer here."

"Yeah, or maybe everyone will be bothered by it." Alexis pointed to a rock and told her to sit down. "Vickie, I know it's tiring, but nobody knows how to deal with a vampire around here. In America, there's no such thing. You would be unique, but not in a good way."

"How so?"

She folded her arms and rested them on her knees. "First of all, in your best-case scenario, you become famous. That's great. But you'll never have any privacy again for the rest of your life. And people will target you. They'll try to fight you or even kill you for being what you are.

"And let's go further than that. If you are really a species that we have never had scientific evidence of, you could become a lab rat. The government would probably want to get their hands on you so they can study you. Either way, you don't get to be yourself. You lose your life in almost every sense of the word."

Vickie twisted her mouth in frustration. "I want to be normal and comfortable."

Alexis scoffed. "Being normal doesn't mean you're comfortable. You get one or the other. Nobody in high school is comfortable. We're all in there trying to be people whom we're not, really. You can't even be comfortable around your friends, because they will take whatever weird thing you do as a reason not to hang out with you. That's how high school is."

"It doesn't sound like much fun."

"It's not. But it's not supposed to be fun, either. You can't move on in life without a high school degree. You're there to get an education, make a few friends, and also be miserable with everybody else."

Vickie wasn't really enamored with this pep talk.

"You won't be comfortable. So what? You also won't be

alone. I'll be there, backing you up, watching out for you. We're sisters now. Sisters help each other. We'll make sure you can find an outlet for all this…energy, or whatever this is."

Another rocket screamed into the air and exploded. This time, there was a quick bright flash and a boom that shook their chests.

Alexis watched Vickie's reaction. The vampire held her breath and squeezed her hands together, but she didn't hit anything, break anything, or jump. "Now you're getting it. React like that, and you won't stand out so much."

Vickie exhaled. "Do you think I can hang out with your friends? Will they like me?"

"Of course!" Alexis stood on the rock to stretch her back. "You're great. They'll love you. Jess and Jamie are sweethearts. If you're basically my sister, they'll watch out for you, too. You're already heading into high school with a few friends. Shoot, some people take years. You're off to a good start."

"What about Eric?"

Alexis watched her new sister's face closely. "You think Eric's cute, don't you?"

"Yes, I do," she replied matter-of-factly. "Should I tell him that the next time I see him? That's a compliment, right?"

Alexis put her palms up. "Um, yes, but no. Don't walk up to a boy and tell him that you think he's cute. That's a bad move."

"Why?"

"Because you have to play the game a little. If he doesn't like you, then you've ruined his friendship before you even got started. And I don't want everything to be awkward around you and my friends. Wait a while, okay? That's another urge you can fight."

Vickie frowned.

Another instinct to ignore. That doesn't make any sense. Why can't I compliment someone?

But she knew that listening to Alexis' advice would be a priority in the coming weeks and months while she found her feet as a "normal" human being.

"Sorry. I know that's confusing," Alexis said, noticing her reaction. "It's not because I want you to be miserable. I want you to be happy! But let's relax. You've only been an American for two days. Pace yourself. You have a lot to learn before we get into things like dating."

That was an understatement. Alexis wasn't even sure how vampires dated, what romance looked like to them, or anything remotely close to that. For now, she would try to keep the vampire from thinking about boys entirely. She had enough things to teach her.

The spotlight went out on the island.

"What's happening?" Vickie asked.

Alexis sat on the rock again and scooted forward. "The test fires are over. Now, the real show is about to start. She grabbed her by the sides of her head and leaned in closely until their noses nearly touched. "Remember, this is fun. This is not an attack or a threat. Fight every urge to treat it like that. Enjoy this!"

She released her head, and Vickie turned on the rock to look at the night sky.

Initially, the explosions made her anxious. Her knees knocked, her toes tapped, and she couldn't sit still. But as the show wore on, the bright colors were enchanting. Even the big booms became fun as she felt the vibrations travel through her body.

Vickie glanced at the apartment buildings on the lakefront. The balconies were packed, and the apartment dwellers had all turned their lights off.

They're all pushing forward to watch this from their homes. How threatening could this be?

Over the course of the display, her shoulders relaxed, and her breathing normalized. She even laughed at a few of the larger explosions.

Alexis spent as much time watching Vickie as she did the fireworks. She wanted to see her friend enjoy herself without being so overwhelmed all the time. Whenever the vampire smiled, Alexis laughed.

It's nice to see her finally having a good time. Maybe she'll fit in, after all.

The explosions became more intense and the smile dissipated from Vickie's face. She even flinched a few times.

"This is the grand finale," Alexis explained quickly as she leaned forward to shout in her ear. "It's the best but a little louder than the rest of it."

Boom after boom rocked the lakefront. To Vickie's surprise, the onlookers cheered and laughed. They smiled and clapped. The people watching the fireworks enjoyed every minute of it.

Follow their lead.

She focused on their pleasure and a big smile crossed her face. She still felt uneasy, but she managed a few laughs and even clapped a few times. The kaleidoscope of colors flashing in the air combined with the unique shapes and the teeth-chattering explosions to create the dazzling spectacle and distraction she needed.

Still, she had trouble fighting all her instincts.

Alexis caught a glimpse of her smile in the light of the fireworks. "Vickie, fangs."

The vampire ran her tongue along the inside of her mouth and realized that her fangs were, in fact, showing. She squeezed her lips together quickly and nodded at her sister, who patted her on the back.

After the grand finale was over, the lights of Summerfest resumed, and the bands played again. The smoke from all the explosions drifted along the surface of the water, which mesmerized Vickie almost as much as the show itself.

"Do you do these shows all the time?" she asked.

"No. Today and tomorrow, mainly. Then you have to wait until next year. It's a special occasion kind of thing."

"Now what?"

"Now we head on back to the buses and get home. You have a test tomorrow. You need to be well-rested because you'll see your high school for the first time."

CHAPTER THIRTY

The SUV pulled up in front of the Clear Lake High School. Its gothic structure reminded Vickie of her old home, and she took it as a good omen. A few kids passed through the great front doors at one of the building's main entrances as the girls got out of the car.

"Are you sure you want to stick around, Alexis?" Craig asked. "You'll be here a while."

"I've got it, Dad. I want to offer my support. Don't sweat it. I'll find stuff to do."

He admired how supportive his daughter was. She brought a positive energy wherever she went, exactly like her mother. Craig smiled. "Okay. Don't do anything your mother wouldn't." He turned to his adoptive daughter. "Hey, Vickie, go get 'em. You'll do great."

"Thanks...Dad!" Vickie said with a forced smile. It still felt strange to call the man who had been a stranger only two weeks ago such an intimate name. But in an effort to fit in and be normal, she went along with it.

Perhaps I'll get used to calling him that along the way. But he's been good to me...is good to me. He's my future, my family with Alexis.

"How did that feel?" Alexis asked as they walked up the sidewalk to the front door.

"Weird." Vickie squinted in the bright sun. "But I never called my father 'Dad.' His name was 'Father,' and that was all. This is different, at least."

Alexis patted her on the back. "Being normal is a lot of work, isn't it?"

She shook her head. "It really is. Okay, so this is the high school."

"This is the high school. You'll spend the next couple of years in this place, so get used to it."

She pulled the silver handle on the front door, and the two of them stepped into the lobby. Vickie raised her eyebrows at the sight. The structure was as large on the inside as its bleak stony architecture hinted on the outside.

Two doors to her left led to an auditorium that seated over a thousand people at a time. Dual hallways stretched and intersected in front of her on their way to and from various classrooms, lockers, and stairwells. The closest stairwell was only a few feet away from a pair of doors shaped suspiciously like the auditorium's. Closer inspection revealed a hardwood polished surface covered in painted lines with two large glass panes and a strange metal circle that hovered in the middle of it. Alexis explained that this room was known as the gymnasium. Normal kids called it the gym.

"This building is exceptionally large. How do you not get lost here?" the vampire asked.

"Oh, you totally do. I mean, you will. After a while, you

get to know this place well, but you'll definitely get lost a few times first."

"That's reassuring."

Vickie couldn't tell if her new sister was serious or testing her sarcasm. "Follow me. The test is in the cafeteria." Alexis walked ahead and lead Vickie to one of the many stairwells. They skipped down the steps, which opened into a lower lobby. Four more hallways and a large classroom branched off from the location. But that wasn't what they had come to find.

The cafeteria was a wide, open, square space filled with long rectangular tables and benches not unlike what the two had seen at the Summer Fest. However, instead of drunk minors and stoners, a group of adults in prim suits and dresses looked over the tables with precision as hopeful youths squirmed under their gaze.

"Go on," Alexis said encouragingly and pushed the girl toward the windowed swinging doors. "Walk in there, and you'll see a table in the front. You only have to tell them your name. And what is your name?"

"Vickie Hewitt." It still halted on her tongue, but she could easily attribute that to nerves. After all, she was at least somewhat nervous.

"There you go. Don't worry about the rest of the building. Don't think about the lockers and the hallways and the classrooms. You're only here to take a test."

"Right." Vickie tried to calm herself down. "Why am I nervous? I know all the necessary information forward and back."

Alexis shrugged. "Because it's a big deal and you don't

want to screw it up. It's okay. Everybody goes through that. Do you have your pencils?"

"Yes."

"Then you're set. Get in there and make us proud."

Vickie nodded, and Alexis gave her a quick hug of encouragement.

She smiled as she watched the doors swing shut behind her adopted sister.

Vickie will do great. There's a bagel place up the road from here. Maybe I'll get myself a bite to eat while I'm waiting around.

After a few more minutes to make sure Vickie was in, she jogged up the stairs to return to the front door.

Meanwhile, inside the cafeteria, Vickie approached the table with caution. Despite her confidence in herself, her heart still beat rapidly.

This is the first time you have ever been alone in public in this country. The last time you were alone, an angry mob chased you down the street.

She gave her assumed name to the proctor checking prospective students in. She was promptly handed a sheet of paper filled with hollow circles and a test booklet.

"Please don't open the booklet until the instructor tells you to," the woman said. "He will walk you through each section. If you're caught working ahead, you will be disqualified and automatically failed."

The woman smiled despite the intimidating message she gave so glibly. The butterflies in Vickie's stomach flapped more frantically, and she could feel the beginnings of her senses heightening. Thanks to the training she'd had with Alexis, however, it wasn't nearly as bad as it could have been, and she quickly regained control.

"Where should I sit?" she asked meekly.

The woman waved her hand. "Anywhere you'd like." Again, she smiled warmly. This time, there was no threat to her words. "Be sure to leave space between yourself and any other testers, so we can avoid any chances of copying."

Vickie found an empty table and sat, then peered around the cafeteria. A wall of windows allowed sunshine in on one side. On the opposite side, a retractable wall opened to reveal a small pocket of tables that were kept separate for reasons she wasn't sure of.

Behind her, two doors opened into what appeared to be a line that offered food—or would have, if it were lunchtime.

Garbage cans bumped up against massive pillars in the middle of the room, and vending machines were jammed into a small square space away from the main area.

Get used to it, Vickie. You'll be in here a lot if you pass this test.

The instructor stood from one of the tables on the end, shouted directions to the test-takers, then asked if there were any questions.

One young man raised his hand. "What if we get hungry? Can we hit up the vending machines?"

"You may not get any food from the vending machines during the testing period," the man announced as he adjusted his thick black-framed glasses. "However, there will be a break after every period, and you then will be allowed to stand and stretch, visit the restroom, and get a drink of water. During that break, you may get something to eat."

Vickie liked the idea of grabbing a snack, but from

where she could see, the vending machines required money and she had none.

For the next several hours, Vickie took test after test, answering questions on mathematics, American history, world history, and science. Much to her surprise, the test felt fairly simple. She understood the questions, and the answers came to her quickly. Her vampire brain had done its job.

Over six testing periods, she finished with about twenty minutes to spare each time. She struggled with boredom, and her speed concerned her. This might not be deemed normal.

Should I take more time? Am I working too fast? What does that even mean? Do other people notice that I'm sitting here now? I'm supposed to fit in.

When the entire testing session was completed, she stood and walked out into the lower lobby, where Alexis waited for her.

"It took you long enough," she joked.

Vickie sighed. "I'm exhausted." The test might have been easy, but the strain of keeping her nerves together and avoiding an anxiety attack had wrung a lot out of her.

Alexis chuckled. "Yeah, wait until you have to do that every day. Welcome to school."

One week later, Alexis charged into the house with an armful of mail. A large manila envelope with the school's insignia sat on the top.

"We have results!" she crowed triumphantly. Vickie and their father came running. Alexis handed the envelope to the other girl and grinned. "They're your results. You do the honors."

Craig walked behind Alexis and put his hands on her shoulders as they waited eagerly for the news.

Vickie tore the envelope open and scanned the first page of the packet, then read it out loud.

"Congratulations on your successful completion of the Aptitude Test for Clear Lake High School. It is our pleasure to welcome you to the student population."

Alexis cheered and Craig joined in. Then she rushed in for a congratulatory hug. Vickie blushed while Craig applauded.

"That was the last hurdle," he said. "Now we only have to...you know, survive high school."

"I'm in," Vickie said with disbelief. "I've only been awake for a few weeks and I'm going to high school."

Alexis smiled. "The fun is only beginning."

Back in Austria, a group of shrouded figures huddled around a small altar in the basement of a cathedral.

Candlelight danced around the perimeter of the room. No one's face was visible.

"There is one that remains," one of them announced. "She has survived the Sang Crusade. Our greatest fear has been realized, and we must move to act."

The adventures and challenges don't end here. Follow Vicki, Alexis and Craig as she continues her journey as a teenage vampire in The Girl in the Back Row.

FREE BOOKS!

WARNING:

The Troll is now in charge.

And he's giving away free books
if you sign-up!

Join the only newsletter hosted by a Troll!

Get sneak peeks, exclusive giveaways, behind the scenes
content, and more.
PLUS you'll be notified of special **one day only fan
pricing** on new releases.

CLICK HERE

or visit: https://marthacarr.com/read-free-stories/

The adventures and challenges don't end here. Follow Vicki, Alexis and Craig as she continues her journey as a teenage vampire in The Girl in the Back Row

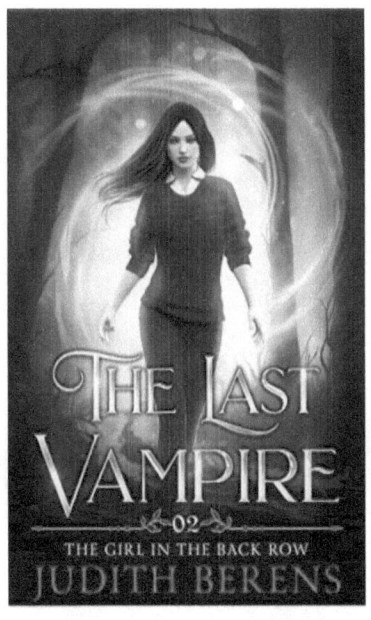

AVAILABLE FOR PURCHASE HERE

**Find the compass, save the world or
save herself?**

Dating is harder for Maggie Parker than running down a
felon. Now add in magic.

Did she just see a compass fly?

Can she learn how to use the magic of bubbles to chart
a new course in time? It's a lot harder than it sounds.

Join her on her quest to rescue passengers on an
ancient ship – a big blue marble called Earth – and save
herself.

AVAILABLE ON AMAZON AND IN KINDLE UNLIMITED!

AUTHOR NOTES - MARTHA CARR

APRIL 29, 2019

It's the start of a new series! And there's even more to get done in the day – okay, yea to that too! But, like the rest of you I have other things to get done. That's kind of under control – I can plan for it, budget time, work it out.

Fortunately, so that I don't get too far into time management – I have these two furry girls. The good dog, Lois Lane and the sweet Leela. Lois is a 90-pound Pointer mix who was born deaf. Her profile would have to read – loves food of any kind and some things you wouldn't call food, tearing apart stuffed toys, leaning against people till they give in and rub her back, and running as fast as she can.

Leela is a nine-year-old Pit Bull mix with the most beautiful brown eyes. She's a more recent addition – she was formerly the Offspring's dog. You're really a parent of grown children when one of your pets started out in their house. Leela's profile would say loves to sleep, back scratches, belly rubs, being completely covered with blankets and long walks.

That's all great – even with the occasional clean up in the house – don't ask – or Lois eating a box of chocolate turtles – including the cardboard box. The emergency number operator laughed and said she would have had to eat a lot more. Note to self – all food must be behind closed doors. She's like a bear when it comes to food.

Or things that weren't toys getting chewed, or Leela getting up every night from where she's sleeping and making her way to me, snuggling up behind me. Picture big bed and me hanging on to the edge.

But what got me searching with intent on the internet for doggie day care was the howling and the barking. I'd be lost in thought, creating some twist in a story, thrilled I was making a breakthrough and Lois would suddenly let out a deep, loud bark. If Google could translate it, it would sound like "Drop the drugs!" It restarts my heart every time. She does it when she spots anything going by the window or sometimes just because it's been too long since she barked. If she's really digging it she runs just ahead of me where she technically can claim she can't hear or see me, so didn't know I was a little teed off at it.

People know my house by the loud dog, spinning in a circle and barking every time they go by.

I've tried training, treats, time out (she howls and barks), standing in front of her. Nothing. Leela hesitates when this happens, looking at me with those big brown eyes but when she sees I can't get it to stop she gives in and starts howling along with her sister. Big fun.

And I had a feeling what those two really wanted was a few more furry friends to play with. Every time the dogs behind us were out by their fence those two took off like a shot to whine and paw at the ground. Leela had never been to daycare but like I said, I had a hunch.

And I was right! Leela who loves to sleep in pops up in the morning now, watching me expectantly waiting for the word. "Let's go!" She bounds down (and remember she's an older pittie with a bum knee), hopping around and howling. Both of them run circles around me as we go down the hall. It's a weird parade.

They've even made Pets of the Week already, certificates and everything, which Leela promptly ran over trying to go say hello to one of her new friends. That's life and I wouldn't have it any other way. Glad I found a little peace and quiet in the middle of the day. Glad I get to go pick up the riot every afternoon. Enjoy the new series – it's a good one. Back to work for me.

More adventures to follow.

AUTHOR NOTES - MICHAEL ANDERLE

MAY 13, 2019

THANK YOU for not only reading this story but these *Author Notes* **as well.**

(I think I've been good with always opening with "thank you." If not, I need to edit the other *Author Notes!*)

RANDOM (*sometimes*) THOUGHTS?

Hello!

Since this is a new series in a (somewhat) new genre (YA Vampire) I'm going to introduce myself and give you a little background.

My name is Michael Anderle, and I'm an author of over 30 books and a collaborator on hundreds of others in my universes and series collaborations.

I've been publishing since November of 2015 with stories in Paranormal, Science Fiction, Urban Fantasy, Gamelit / LitRPG, Romance, Action Adventure, Vigilante and a few others I probably have forgotten.

This story was born when Martha and I decided we wanted to stay in YA (a place Judith Berens, our pen-name has a lot of success) yet didn't want to do another Oriceran book at this time.

You know, spread our proverbial wings and all?

So, we were shooting around ideas and the concept came to mind to create a character with a similar background as Martha - all about being a reporter but move the time to today.

Martha has many friends who have left the reporting profession not because they want to, but because the Internet has killed many of the newspapers which employed them. We have something a little similar in our story and our Father is trying to scratch that itch with the new found power of Podcasting.

Then, they find an honest to God vampire and what would he do? Would he tell the truth, or would he have to hide her?

Further, what is the mystery of why she is alone? Have her parents been killed? If they haven't, why aren't they back for her?

What happened to her people, and is she truly the last of her kind?

Finally, what is she going to do about those test(s) she needs to take in high-school when she is technically hundreds of years old?

We hope you enjoy The Last Vampire series as we go more deeply into our characters, their lives, and their stories.

AROUND THE WORLD IN 80 DAYS

One of the interesting (at least to me) aspects of my life is the ability to work from anywhere and at any time. In the future, I hope to re-read my own *Author Notes* and remember my life as a diary entry.

Cave in the Sky (™) Las Vegas, Nv USA

I'm sitting on the couch writing these author notes because my office is a mess.

It's full of boxes of stuff to help organize my closets, and the gentleman setting it up is almost finished. THEN comes the unenviable time when I have to put all my stuff back into the closet, decide what I'm giving away (No, I don't think I'll ever get into a medium men's sweater ever again in my life…) and what needs to go into storage.

Our condo is nice, but it isn't large. The winter clothes really do need to go to the storage unit down the street and stop taking up space in the one general closet we have.

I hear a vacuum, so WOOT!

We have book 02 about 50% complete in this series (just the writing part, not the editing or anything like that.)

Tomorrow we travel to the Science-Fiction and Fantasy Nebulas con near Los Angeles tomorrow. We will be there until Sunday meeting with other authors, fans, and hanging out chatting with those in the industry.

I hope to get more work done and less socializing. However, I'm not above a few late nights at the bar, talking stories.

Chat with you in the next book!

FAN PRICING

$0.99 Saturdays (new LMBPN stuff) and $0.99 Wednesday (both LMBPN books and friends of LMBPN books.) Get great stuff from us and others at tantalizing prices.

Go ahead, I bet you can't read just one.

Sign up here: http://lmbpn.com/email/.

HOW TO MARKET FOR BOOKS YOU LOVE
Review them so others have your thoughts, tell friends and the dogs of your enemies (because who wants to talk with enemies?)... *Enough said ;-)*

Ad Aeternitatem,

Michael Anderle

JOIN THE ORICERAN UNIVERSE FAN GROUP ON FACEBOOK!

CONNECT WITH THE AUTHORS

Martha Carr Social

Website: http://www.marthacarr.com

Facebook: https://www.facebook.com/
groups/MarthaCarrFans/

Michael Anderle Social

Michael Anderle Social
Website:
http://www.lmbpn.com

Email List:
http://lmbpn.com/email/

Facebook Here: https://www.
facebook.com/TheKurtherianGambitBooks/